Beyond the Veil

Jeannie Wycherley

Sign up for Jeannie's newsletter http://eepurl.com/cN3Q6L

Cover design by Francessca at **Francessca's PR & Designs**.

DEDICATION

For Richard B. A. Sharp
With love and admiration from your big sister

and
to all the men and women on the thin blue line.
Thank you!

PROLOGUE: WHEN DEATH COMES CALLING …

If death were a dance, it would have a catchy rhythm. Two beats per second. One two, one two.

On the other hand, it would be more difficult to dance to the rhythm of births per second. The number of births is equal to four beats every second, and increasing. That's a little too fast for comfort for most dancers.

But the rhythm of death—one two, one two—that's a nice, even rhythm. Think about it: one two, one two and another two people have shuffled off this mortal coil. Two people who have drawn their last breath, perhaps after a long illness, lying in bed surrounded by the people who loved them. Dying in comfort, in clean surroundings, with health professionals on hand to ease their passing.

Of course there are those who lie dying in a place in the world where death is brutal. Where medicine is in short supply and clean water is a luxury. Those for whom death is a welcome release.

Wait. That term? Shuffling? You can almost imagine the departed forming a long and orderly queue, can't you? They're patient. They've had their turn in this world, and now they step beyond the veil, intent on what comes next. They creep forwards, scarcely casting a backward glance at those who weep behind them. What will be, will be. The next stage is a welcome adventure.

As time goes by, the speed at which the queue forms increases. Once upon a time, when the world was relatively young, whole seconds would pass before someone took their place and the queue was easily managed. So what of those who supervise the queue? Fear not, practice makes perfect, and in spite of the quickening pace of population mortality, everyone continues to proceed at a considered rate, precise and sure. Life may be a waiting game, but death is even more so.

To be sure, there are blips. There are occasions when massive surges in the numbers joining the queue slows things down, but rest assured, the veil is always drawn back calmly and quietly, allowing each individual to step through at their own pace. No-one is rushed. However, a deluge of death—a terrorist attack here, a tsunami there, a landslide maybe, or a drone strike—this can cause a backlog, sometimes even a crush. Mistakes happen.

And then there are sudden deaths to factor in. Lonely unexpected deaths. An explosion in the brain, a catastrophic heart attack. A brutal demise at the hands of others. Violent deaths through your own intervention. Mechanical failure. Crushing accidents. Simple misadventure. Human carelessness or negligence. People not looking where they were going.

One two. One two.

So much can happen in one single second.

All of life and death is here.

***

The time is 08.42.07 on the 22nd of May. Heidi Huddlestone is stepping onto a zebra crossing near the Bullring in Birmingham. Her blonde ponytail swings jauntily. She's due into work by 9, so she has time to grab a coffee. She's thinking multiple thoughts: slightly concerned about an issue she was having with her graphic design software before she left work on Friday, pondering whether that will impact on her impending deadline this afternoon, while simultaneously marvelling that on this Monday morning in late May, the sky is a brilliant blue and the sun is warm. She's happy.

As she trots out onto the busy crossing, dodging the oncoming pedestrians, she slips her hand into her cross-body shoulder bag and feels for her purse, hunting for some loose change so she can buy her coffee. She knows there's a £2 coin hiding somewhere.

At exactly the same moment, 161 miles away, Laura Goodwin is lying in a hospital bed. Her husband Tom is with her. He's thirsty and wants to grab a cup of tea from the restaurant but doesn't want to leave his wife. Laura and Tom have been married for forty-one years. She's fifty-nine years old, and until a suspected mini-stroke the previous evening, they had never spent an evening apart. She has a headache and feels a little spaced out, but that's to be expected. She's connected to a variety of machines. They beep endlessly. She's tired. She looks at her husband and tries to smile. He's obsessed with tea.

At 8.42.08 Heidi is startled by tyres screaming on tarmac as a vehicle close by accelerates hard. She partially turns. A large black shape flies into her peripheral vision. Someone is shrieking. There is a flash of sickening bright white pain, and she is flying through the air.

Heidi's head collides with the kerb.

Meanwhile something in Laura's brain fizzes. Her vision fades to grey, and Tom disappears from her sight. Her husband stands alone, staring at his wife, not comprehending her absence. The machines are beeping, shrill and insistent. A nurse calls for help, and Tom steps back perplexed. Laura has gone.

One two. One two.

***

Out of the blackness flares a tiny speck of light, as though someone has struck a match. The light seems far away. No. Getting closer. Or perhaps it is not so much the light that is closing in as Heidi moving towards it. She is confused about where she is and thinks to stop, but she has the sensation of being drawn by a thread, a gentle but firm tugging, so she has no option but to carry on.

There are others around her. They bustle gently but don't make contact. Are these people crossing the road with her? Why is it dark? Fear squeezes her insides, and she draws herself rigid, but for some reason she can't hold on to the feeling. It melts away.

Grey shadows. The dark is less. Heidi ambles forward. With every step she feels lighter, the woes of her life falling away. She sheds her worries the way a snake sheds its skin. She continues on, heading for the light, keeping step with her companions. She has no sense of inhabiting a physical space at first, no walls or a floor, but her steps are even and sure-footed, her balance perfect, her eyesight sharp.

A change. She comes upon a room, actually not much more than a wall. The room is open on three sides, and that emptiness is a void. Black. It stretches to infinity, and yet there is a sense of intimacy. Heidi waits. She will enter the room when it is her turn. She can see that there's a tall standard lamp to her left; it looks like something her grandmother once owned. It throws a yellow glow, soft and oddly muted, in a six-metre radius. The wall behind it is stained like old parchment, or skin stretched tightly over an African drum. There is a door in the middle of the wall. It is panelled but unpainted, the grain of the wood plainly visible.

Heidi stops. There are many people ahead of her. She is composed. She feels that she has all the time in the world to observe what is unfolding. She stares in fascination at a small woman in a navy dress with a peacock feather design around the hem, plump calves crossed neatly one over the other. She is wearing a deep blue pill box hat that sits jauntily over grey curly hair. Her face is cheery, and her gaze is bright and intelligent. She perches on a plain wooden bench next to the door and taps her knee. Heidi hears the faint scratching of long fingernails against the dark polyester of her skirt with every tap. She appears to be counting out a rhythm. One two. One two.

The people in front of Heidi move steadily forward, and Heidi wonders whether there is not one door but many. The closer she gets to the head of the queue, if she glances sideways, the more doors there appear to be. It's an optical illusion. The doors open, someone steps through, the doors close. When she concentrates, she can see there is just one door.

Just one middle-aged woman and a much older man are

ahead of Heidi now. The man steps forward as the door opens. Heidi spies a curtain, heavy lace, aged the colour of buttermilk. It is lifted from the other side and a wizened hand beckons him through. The curtain is dropped and the door closes.

The woman ahead of Heidi strides forward. The door opens, exposing the curtain, but the rhythm is interrupted. The peacock woman sitting on the bench pauses her tapping and turns her head, her eyes glitter in the soft light. The curtain billows inwards. Until now, all movement has headed sedately one way, forwards to the door, and the atmosphere has been serene.

Now something seems off-kilter.

The middle-aged woman in front of Heidi pauses, uncertain of how to proceed. A dark shadow, perhaps a person without earthly form, flies into the waiting area and collides with her. The woman is pushed back into Heidi, then falls to the floor. For the first time since joining the queue, Heidi has a sense of her physical self as she is joggled. She helps the woman stand. They stare at each other, a brief moment where they each acknowledge the existence of the other, and then the woman pushes past Heidi and dashes away, back along the route they had previously traversed to get to the door.

Heidi is now at the head of the queue. The door opens once more, and there is a flurry of activity. The being that steps through now does so with purpose. Heidi is unsure what she is seeing. A person with a human form, after a fashion, but tall and clad head to toe in the same buttermilk lace that falls into place behind the door. Judging by the shape of the headdress, it has horns, but the lace covers those protuberances and fully obscures its face. Dozens of large black birds fly through the door after her. There is a loud ruckus as they caw and beat at the air and then give chase, following the middle-aged woman as she rapidly departs the way she arrived. The veiled creature's head rotates, an unearthly movement, stone grinding against stone. It observes the retreating figure as it sprints away and then turns to regard Heidi. Heidi feels the icy grip of terror as its gaze falls on her.

Heidi cannot see a face but senses eyes burning into her own. For the first time since she became aware of her new existence, something akin to fear stirs in the pit of her stomach. She desperately wants to move forward, to step beyond the veiled curtain, into the light beyond, into peace, but this creature – another woman if the long dress is anything to judge her by – is an obstacle that she cannot bypass.

The veiled woman steps towards her and slowly lifts a pale hand. The nails are as black as tar, the tips of her fingers charcoal. Dead flesh. Heidi is repulsed but unable to step backwards, away from the horror, only forwards towards the door. She reluctantly inches towards the woman, who places her hand gently but firmly on Heidi's chest.

Heidi's body jolts violently, and she is thrown up into the air, before tumbling back onto the hard ground. Warm air rushes into her lungs in a sudden fury. Until that moment Heidi had been unaware that she was no longer breathing.

Someone, somewhere is counting…

One two…

***

08:45:16

"One and two and three and four and one and two—"

"Wait. I've got a pulse. I think I've got a pulse. Yes."

"Is she breathing? Put your ear to her mouth."

The lycra-clad cyclist is kneeling next to Heidi, holding her wrist, trying to keep track of her pulse. He is desperate to be helpful but shaken by the scene of total devastation all around him. Bodies. A black van. Terrorism. That's all he can think this is. It's the current weapon of choice to drive a vehicle into a bunch of pedestrians, isn't it? There's blood everywhere. He's kneeling in it; it's soaking into his leggings; he can smell it. This poor woman in front of him, crumpled into the kerb, is responsible for some of it. Quite a lot of it.

He does as he's told. "I think she's breathing. Yes."

An off-duty nurse has been administering chest compressions. She sits back on her haunches, exhales, then leans forward to double check Heidi's breathing again. The cyclist is right. She is breathing. It's shallow, but she's alive.

Her black country accent is broad and familiar. "Stay with me, bab," she says to Heidi. "The ambulances are on their way. You're going to make it. You're going to be fine." She looks up and smiles reassuringly at the cyclist. He's deathly pale, and she's frightened he's going into shock.

"You'll make it too, champ," she says, "you're doing really well." And suddenly he wants to weep.

***

09.26.22

Tom stares down at the lifeless body of his wife, his mouth and eyes dry. He can't take it in. A massive stroke they said, and even here, right in the middle of the hospital, where you might expect them to be able to perform their medical miracles, they hadn't been able to save her. They had tried – of course they had tried—to resuscitate her for twenty minutes, but the doctor in charge, Tom had forgotten his name already, had called it. Time of death 09.18.00.

He is unsure what to do. They had called him into the room after delivering the bad news. They told him to take all the time he needed.

He puts his hand out hesitantly. He's a plumber by trade, and he likes to keep fit. For his age, his hands are strong and his skin is healthy. By contrast, Laura is already looking pale, the rosy hue he associates with her, his long-time love, is fading quickly.

He strokes her forehead and thinks about her brain beneath the skull and wishes his hand could extract the badness, the way an apple peeler can extract a rotten apple core. She is perfect in his eyes and always has been. He can't bear to think of her any other way.

Her eyelids flutter and he jumps, startled. Fear and incredulity pulse through his body, and he turns for the door, squawking for a nurse. He desperately wants Laura to be alive, but he's frightened the fluttering is a natural post-death occurrence, like the voiding of bladder and bowels. He opens the door and calls a nurse in. There's one standing at the nurse's station making notes. She frowns and idles towards him, clipping the biro to the clipboard she's marking.

He attempts to explain as she joins him, but his words are confused. Instead he gestures into the room where Laura is lying. When the nurse stops dead in her tracks, Tom careers into the back of her.

Laura is sitting up in bed, her eyes wide open. She observes the nurse and Tom staring at her and appears to find them funny. She giggles. The nurse edges away. "I'd better call the doctor," she tries to say, but her words are drowned out by the sound of Laura's increasingly hysterical laughter.

CHAPTER ONE

Polly Forster pulled the handbrake on and stared at the house in front of her. She had been called to attend the address following a call about a disturbance involving two women and a child. The neighbour, an elderly gentleman, had chosen not to investigate himself and simply called the police. He claimed that the house belonged to a normally quiet family. The old-fashioned lace curtain in his front bay window had twitched as Polly pulled up in her marked car, and the light in that room had been extinguished almost immediately. No doubt he hovered behind it, scrutinising her every move.

Back-up was on the way, but it was en route from out of town. Durscombe, being a small town, had limited resources, so Polly elected to proceed by herself. She could never be certain whether time was of the essence in situations such as this so she had to make an informed decision based on her previous experience.

"4286 to control. Attending at 42 Neville Gardens."

"4286 received. Standing by."

No 42 was a large 1930s semi-detached redbrick in a good area on the outskirts of Durscombe. The house had a more recent attached garage and a short, winding drive. The front door was closed, and there were lights on in the living room and the front bedroom. Polly climbed out of the Corsa and cocked her head to listen. Everything seemed quiet. Her heart beat a little faster. She had attended dozens of domestic disturbances over the previous ten years or so, and she had yet to arrive at a quiet address. Normally she had to wade in to prevent the perpetrators kicking seven bells of shit out of each other. It was never pretty. But this silence? This was a new one. The hairs prickled to attention on the back of her neck. A quiet house after reports of a disturbance was not a good sign. She smoothed some loose strands of hair away from her face and took a moment to slowly scan the street.

Nothing to see.

As she made her way up the drive, gravel crunched beneath her feet. She skirted a relatively new red Toyota Yaris, in need of a wash, but used in the past few hours, judging by the clean windscreen. She edged close to the bay window and peered into the living room beyond. Unlike the neighbours, there were no net curtains here. The furnishings were crisp, fresh, and modern in soft shades of grey, and the paint on the walls a non-committed cream. There were some children's toys on a rug in front of a huge TV, tuned to Coronation Street, but there was no-one in the room.

Polly sidestepped to the front door and pressed the doorbell. It didn't appear to be working. She tapped. There was no reply. So she tapped again and then tried the handle. It was unlocked.

Cautiously, she pushed the door open and peered into the hall beyond. The lights were on in here too, displaying a coat rack with a variety of coats, jackets, hats, and scarves, including a pink mackintosh that might fit a five – or six-year-old, and three pairs of dirty Wellingtons: small, pink, and flowery; large, blue, and flowery; and larger still in plain black.

"Hello?" she called, then listened. There was no reply. She waited, holding her breath. The faint sounds of dialogue from the television filtered through from the living room, but apart from that, nothing moved or made a noise.

Polly didn't like it. A sixth sense told her that she wasn't alone. Once more she considered waiting for her colleagues to arrive, but there was no telling where they were. She slipped carefully into the hall. It was feasible that the owner of the house had stepped out momentarily, perhaps to visit the local shop or takeaway, and had taken their young child with them, but to Polly that seemed an unlikely scenario. The car was still in the drive after all.

"Hello," she called again. "Police."

When there was no response this time, Polly thumbed her radio. "Control. 4286 attending at 42 Neville Gardens with no obvious sign of the occupants. Do you have an ETA for the Abbotts Cromleigh car? Over."

The radio fizzed. "Delta Charlie to 4286. Be advised, ETA of four minutes."

"Received." Not far away then, tractors and cows on the road allowing. Polly stepped farther into the hall, glancing up the stairs as she did so. There was no movement up there.

She eased her way past the open living room door on her right, then glanced back in. Coronation Street had given way to some commercials—a supermarket advertising its spooky wares with a suitably fitting song. Monster Mash. One of Polly's favourites. Halloween was coming.

She continued on to the rear of the house, through a door straight ahead, moving sideways into the room. It was huge, a kitchen diner, recently extended Polly guessed, judging by the smell of fresh paint and wood. State of the art folding glass doors opened out onto a decking area and the garden beyond. The doors were closed and there was no sign of anyone out there. The appliances and worktops in the ultra-modern kitchen were shiny and modern, the oven was on, the washing up bowl full of bubbly water.

But there was nobody around.

Polly dipped a finger in the sink. The water was warm.

Swivelling around, her heart thumping more quickly, Polly spotted another door, slightly ajar, next to a large American-style fridge. It sported several locks, so it seemed safe to assume this was the door into the garage.

Polly crept to the centre of the kitchen, the skin on her scalp tingling. At last she recognised sounds of life, faint sounds beyond the door. A dog perhaps? She cast a quick eye around the room she was in. No obvious sign of dog bowls or toys, but that didn't mean it wasn't kept in the garage.

"Hello?" she called again and moved close to the door, one hand reaching for her baton to check it was in place. She could hear someone crying beyond, snuffly breathing.

"Hello? Police!" Polly called and pulled open the door.

Oh shit.

She wasn't quite ready for what she found. Her stomach twisted, but her professionalism and experience came to the fore. Decent lighting in the garage allowed her to take in all the details. A woman, in her late thirties, early forties possibly, lying on the stone floor, limbs splayed, blood pooling beneath her and spattered on the walls. This woman lay still, creating no sound.

A second woman however, stood shaking at the other end of the garage. Blood streaked her face, covered her hands and stained her clothes. Bone thin, she wore a long striped jumper, denim jeans, and a bright red woollen beanie hat. She raised shaking hands to her face, staring aghast at the woman on the floor, gulping air, huge sobs racking her slight frame.

"Stay where you are," Polly instructed, adrenaline pumping, her voice loud in the garage, breaking through the other woman's panic. She thumbed her radio again, "Delta Charlie, this is 4286, single crewed, requiring urgent assistance at 42 Neville Gardens. Unconscious casualty in the garage. Female. Aged .... approximately forty or so. Stab wounds. Suspect on scene. Does not appear to be breathing. Require an ambulance to this address. Now!"

"Delta Charlie received. 4286, assistance is on the way. ETA two minutes. Ambulance dispatched to your destination."

Polly turned her attention to the shaking woman again, warily stepping slowly towards her. "I'm here to help you. Are you hurt?" She circled the blood on the floor, keeping her tone light. The woman didn't look at her, that wasn't a good thing, her focus remained fixed on the body on the floor. "Hey my love," Polly said more sharply, and the woman darted an alarmed glance her way, face the colour of spoiled milk. Her mouth moved, but she seemed incapable of speech.

"Are you okay?" Polly repeated, and the woman stepped towards her, walking into the blood on the floor. Polly looked down and spotted the knife, much closer to the shaking woman than to her.

"Stay right where you are!" Polly shouted, holding one hand out, palm up, the other on her baton. Her heart pounded. She needed to get a hold of this situation, right now.

The woman stared back at her in confusion, shaking her head. "It wasn't me, it wasn't me." She held her empty hands up as though to show Polly that she held no weapons, and stopped moving. Her eyes were huge in her face, terror etched in her features. Polly looked again at the blood covering her and wondered what the story was.

She darted forwards, grabbing one of the woman's thin wrists and yanked her back, away from the body and the blood. She twisted the woman's arm behind her back easily enough and reached for the other one, pulling her hands together to the rear then snapping handcuffs on her. "Kneel," she instructed the woman, and manoeuvred her, so that she was angled away from the woman on the floor.

"Stay there," she ordered, and the woman shrank miserably away from her.

Keeping half an eye on her, and still within touching distance, Polly squatted next to the victim, reaching for her neck, searching for a pulse. Nothing. Shit.

"Did you see what happened?" Polly asked, standing again, and once more beginning to edge around the growing pool of blood.

"Yes." A simple word, but the woman stumbled over it, quivering violently and struggling to breathe.

With the woman in her control, Polly relaxed a little. She heard the sound of cars outside. Doors slamming, heavy footsteps on the gravel. The cavalry had arrived. About time. "What's your name, love?"

"Heidi," the woman replied, stuttering over the H. "Heidi Huddlestone."

CHAPTER TWO

DI Paul 'Petty' Pettigrew chewed his left thumb nail as the interview with Heidi recommenced. He had elected to watch from his laptop after briefly meeting with his DCs, Sarah Yardley and Eddie Gibbs, outside the interview room to ascertain the best way to proceed. They needed more information from Heidi but really weren't getting anywhere. Petty's gut told him Heidi wasn't a killer, but until he had all the facts at his disposal, he wasn't taking any chances.

Heidi's frailty was of immediate concern for Petty. While holding her in custody the police had a duty of care for her, and he didn't want to risk fallout if Heidi was unfit to be held. A medical professional called in to check her state of health discovered Heidi had been a victim of the Birmingham terror attack five months previously, suffering head injuries. Petty didn't know whether this was pertinent to the current case, but he needed to ensure she was fit to be questioned. The doctor had given the go-ahead for initial questioning, but the interview was taking longer than they had anticipated and Heidi had rejected the offer of a solicitor.

"Let's take it from the top," Gibbs said.

Directly opposite Gibbs, Heidi nursed tea in a plastic cup, palms wrapped around the drink as though it provided her only source of warmth. She wore the thin grey track suit offered on arrival in custody. During processing, her hands and nails, and the blood on her arms and face, had been swabbed, and the samples, along with her clothes, had been bagged up and sent for forensic analysis. Her head, now devoid of the woollen beanie she had been wearing at the scene of the murder, sported a short, fine layer of blonde fuzz. Vivid red scars above her left ear told their own traumatic story.

"Tell me about your arrival at 42 Neville Gardens, Heidi," Gibbs asked.

Heidi shrugged. "I got there, I don't know, maybe some time after seven." Her voice was soft and tired.

"How long after seven? Do you recall?" Gibbs asked.

Heidi shook her head. "I'd been walking for a while. I don't have a watch."

"Do you have a mobile?" asked Gibbs. "Most people tell the time using their phones these days?"

"I do have one, yes, but I didn't have it on me. I left in a bit of a rush."

"You didn't have your mobile or a handbag with you?" pressed Gibbs, and Heidi shook her head again, then remembered she needed to speak up for the recording. "No."

"Tell me what else you were carrying on your person," Gibbs asked, and Heidi shook her head again.

"Nothing."

"What about keys? Your house keys?" Gibbs asked.

"Yes. They were in my jeans pocket," Heidi replied and waved at the door. The police had taken her clothes and all her belongings, so surely they knew where her keys were?

"Tell me where you walked from, Heidi?"

"I walked from the town centre. I'm staying in a house in Budleigh Place. But I walked to Neville Gardens on Durscombe Rise from the town."

"You told us you've only been out of hospital a few weeks. Explain why you would walk all that way?"

Heidi dropped her head. They had been over this several times. Observing on the monitor, Petty's instincts told him Heidi was holding something back, but his officers hadn't managed to get to the bottom of it yet.

"Heidi?" asked Gibbs.

"I thought I saw someone I knew. I followed them."

"Them?"

Hesitation. "Her."

"And did you know her?" asked Gibbs.

Heidi stared hollowly at Gibbs. "No."

"Explain to us why you followed this person that you thought you knew."

"I wanted to talk to her."

"You followed her all the way to Neville Gardens from town?"

A nod. "Yes."

"Did you call out to this woman? Stop her so you could talk to her? Did you let her know you were following her?"

"No. I just kept following her. I don't think she wanted to talk."

"How could you know that?"

"I think she knew I was following her. I think she wanted me to follow her."

"But you have said that you didn't know her anyway," said Gibbs, and Heidi shook her head. Gibbs pursed his lips. "So you followed her to Neville Gardens. Had you been there before?"

"No," said Heidi, crinkling the edges of the plastic cup. "I haven't been to Durscombe since I was a kid, well a teenager. I was fourteen the last time I came here. I was with my parents and we stayed at my aunt's house. The house I'm staying in now. Back then we spent all our time on the beach. I didn't get to know the town really."

Gibbs nodded. "Tell us what happened when you arrived at Neville Gardens."

"The woman went inside. She used the front door. Just walked in. Like she knew the house. I waited. Not long. There was shouting, and a child crying. Really angry shouting."

"So explain what you did then."

"I went in. I used the front door, and I went in." Heidi drew in a shuddering breath. "There was a little girl in the hall, in her pyjamas, and she was crying. She was frightened. I bent down and I told her everything would be all right. I told her to go upstairs."

"And she went? By herself?" asked Gibbs.

"Yes, she did."

"What happened then?"

"There was more shouting and then a scream." Heidi swallowed. "It was downstairs. Sounded like it was coming from out the back. I went through to the kitchen, and the door was open ... out into the garage ... and I heard ... a cry ... a weak kind of cry, so I went through, and there was a woman lying on the floor. She'd been cut, right here," Heidi ran a finger under the left side of her chin. "It was deep. She was bleeding heavily. And there were other ... wounds." Heidi rubbed her forehead with shaking fingers. Her skin so pale and translucent it could have been the thinly veiled covering of a cadaver.

"How was the victim known to you, prior to this?"

"Known to me? I didn't know her. I don't think I'd ever seen her before."

"Perhaps you didn't recognise her?"

"No. I didn't." Heidi scrunched her forehead up. "I didn't recognise her, because I'd never seen her before."

"But this was the woman you followed back to her home, from town?"

"No, it wasn't."

"Can you explain why you went into the house if you didn't know the occupants, Heidi?"

Heidi sat back in her seat, her face a mask of terror, as though she realised for the first time exactly what the police were insinuating.

Heidi shook her head. "No. I can't explain that. I didn't know whose house it was. I didn't think about what I was doing. I just followed the woman from town. I wanted to talk to her, but she never turned around, she ... led me to this house. I followed her in. Because of the screaming. That's all I can think of."

"And when our officer appeared on the scene, there was just you and the victim in the garage. Where was the other woman? The one you followed into the house? The one who had presumably been arguing with the victim? Can you explain to me where she went?"

"No. I don't know."

"She wasn't in the garage?"

"No."

"Had she ever been in the garage?"

"No. Yes. I mean, I don't know. I didn't see her there. I went in, and it was just the other woman on the floor."

"And you didn't see the woman you followed from town in the kitchen?"

"No."

"You didn't see her leave the house at all?"

"I told you. No."

"Can you explain how she managed to get out of the house, without being seen by either yourself or our officers on the scene?"

Heidi shook her head, her mouth a soft O of misery, tears in her bloodshot eyes.

Gibbs swung back on his chair and glanced across at Sarah. There was no alternative exit in the garage beside the up and over door, and that had been locked. The glass doors into the garden were locked from the inside. Any intruder would need to have left the house through the front door, or the window in the lounge, or they could have remained hidden in the house when the first officer had arrived on the scene. It was possible that the murderer had left the house, unheard and unnoticed, while Polly was apprehending Heidi. Of course it was, but it appeared unlikely.

It was also possible that Heidi was lying through her teeth about what had happened.

CHAPTER THREE

Adam Chapple snapped the lid of his laptop down and blinked with relief from the resulting lack of glare. He stretched, cramped and weary, hearing his shoulders and neck crack. After a long day, he still hadn't accomplished everything on his to-do list. He'd spent the past few hours browsing various social media sites while perched precariously on the edge of his sofa, searching for clues as to the whereabouts of his nineteen-year-old son, Dan, but the search had proved elusive, a constant theme of the past few months.

With no idea where Dan had vanished to, Adam was at a loss. His son had suddenly disappeared from his halls of residence during the last week of summer term. A backpack went with him, along with his bicycle, his iPad, and a few personal items. Adam's gut instinct told him his unhappy son had taken off travelling, something he had always wanted to do, although it was a little strange that his bank account had remained untouched. Adam was at a loss, but to be fair, their relationship had become a little strained in the months leading up to his disappearance, nonetheless Adam missed his son and wanted to know everything was okay.

For some part of every evening, Adam found himself scouring Facebook, Twitter, and Instagram, but could never find any fresh evidence of what his son was up to. Dan had disappeared without trace. Kids were known to do stuff like this, especially those who had problems, as Dan did. Adam of all people understood this very well, but when it was your own child who had disappeared into the world, it caused unrelenting anxiety.

Adam contemplated a beer. There were a few bottles of ale in the fridge, but it was after midnight and he was working an early shift. Far better to have a glass of water and get some shut-eye. He wandered through the hall and into the dark kitchen, yawning, and filled a glass. The kitchen window looked out onto the turning circle of his Close. In the dim light from a street lamp, he saw a marked Vauxhall Corsa pull up in front of his drive, blocking his car in.

Adam's hand twitched, water sloshing from the glass on to the worktop. He set the glass down carefully and rubbed his eyes. This couldn't be good news.

He watched from his window. Two figures exited the car. The woman in uniform was instantly recognisable. Polly Forster, six feet tall, imposing, and one of his closest friends. She was joined by a plainclothes officer, also instantly familiar as he moved closer to the front door. The security light blinked on and Adam recognised his DI, Paul Pettigrew, generally based in Exeter. So what was he doing visiting Adam's home in the middle of the night?

He took a deep breath and headed for the front door, yanking it open before they had time to ring the bell and disturb the neighbours. Polly was wearing her hat. Adam liked this less and less.

"Polly," Adam nodded. "Sir?"

"DS Chapple, Adam? May we come in?" asked Petty. Adam's stomach rolled. He stepped back to allow his colleagues to enter the house. If they needed to hold an official conversation, it was better not to have it on the front step.

He closed the door after them and indicated the way through to the lounge. He brushed past them to move the coffee table and his laptop, then swept his notebooks into a neat pile so that Polly and Petty could sit down. "Please."

They settled themselves on the sofa, and Adam took an armchair, perching once more. This seemed to be his habitual way to sit these days. "Do you have news for me?" he asked. "About Dan?"

Petty looked momentarily confused, but Polly jumped in quickly. "No, it's not about Dan."

"Ah," Adam breathed out and relaxed. Whatever he was about to hear, at least his worst fears were without grounds.

Petty straightened up. "DS Chapple, can I ask where you've

been this evening?"

Adam frowned at the formality of the question. "Where I've been? Do you suspect me of something?" Adam knew how this worked, he was required to answer the question. "I was at the station till seven-ish. I'm sure Tooley can vouch for that," he addressed this to Polly who nodded. Tooley was the front desk clerk at Durscombe police station. "I came home via Waitrose, where I bought a sad little curry-for-one and some razors—I probably have the receipt for those—and since then I've been online pretty much the entire time searching for clues as to the whereabouts of my missing son." Adam paused to let that sink in. "Sir."

"I'm sure that will all check out. I'm not worried." Petty's tone was softer, friendlier. "Look, I'll cut straight to the chase. Adam, I'm sorry to have to inform you that we were called to an incident this evening at 42 Neville Gardens."

Petty paused. Adam looked blank. The address meant nothing to him.

"We found the body of a woman there, and unfortunately there was nothing our officers could do. An ambulance was called but she was pronounced dead at the scene." Adam stared at Petty and waited, his mind running through a catalogue of women he knew who lived in Durscombe. "We believe the woman was Nicola Fallon. We're awaiting formal identification."

The cogs in Adam's brain whirred. How many women did he know called Nicola? There weren't many. Frowning he turned to Polly. "Nicola?" he asked, and Polly nodded, and it was a look on her face that gave it away. "As in my ex-wife, Nicola?" Adam asked aghast. Polly nodded again.

Adam slumped back into his seat, genuinely shocked by the news. Nicola was dead? He could picture Nicola on their wedding day, looking elegant and timeless. They'd been ridiculously young back then. Totally naïve. Too much water had flowed under the bridge since that day. They had been separated for fifteen years and divorced for thirteen of those.

"When was the last time you saw her?" Petty's voice called

him back to the present.

Adam sat forwards again and sighed. "Fallon, you said?"

"Yes, that's the information we have," answered Petty.

"She moved away a long time ago. To London I think. She must have remarried." Adam rubbed the finger below the knuckle where his wedding band had once resided. He was quiet, thinking back through the years, his emotions fighting each other for precedence. She had walked out. There had been threatening letters from solicitors. An acrimonious divorce. A broken-hearted Dan. But still, at the back of Adam's mind, he could see Nicola's soft brown hair, gently curled and looped up into a sophisticated bun, her eyes shining, that day they were married.

"I haven't seen her in fifteen years. After she left we only communicated through lawyer's letters. It was expensive." She'd enjoyed bleeding him dry. Hadn't cared that he was the sole provider for their son.

"You didn't see her in relation to your son at all?"

Adam harrumphed. "She didn't just leave me, she left our son too. The cruellest thing she ever did—and believe me she was a cold woman—was walk away from her four-year-old."

"You had custody?"

"I had full custody. Uncontested. She never expressed any interest in Dan, never wanted to see him. So I was spared the whole dropping-him-off-at-weekends-then-picking-him-up-again jamboree."

"You weren't aware that she was living in Durscombe?"

"I had no idea. She left me for some guy she met at a night club, but I don't think it lasted. At least I don't think she was with him when the divorce came through. I didn't know she'd moved back. I hadn't seen her around town."

"Did your son have much contact with her?"

Adam started to retort bitterly, but he was a police officer and a good one, and it paid to think as rationally as possible. He had, for the sake of his own sanity, brushed off his divorce and any feelings he had about Nicola a long time ago. However, he couldn't say the same for Dan with a similar amount of certainty.

"It was much more complicated for Dan," Adam replied, his voice soft with compassion for his son. "He wanted his mum so badly. In the early years he …" Adam's voice faltered, he remembered his son wetting the bed, and the nightmares he'd suffered, night after night, frightened of losing Adam as well. A lump formed in Adam's throat. That was private business, between him and Dan. He held those details back out of love for his son. Instead he said, "He struggled not having his mum around. And then suddenly, when he was eleven or so, he stopped talking about her."

"He never spoke about her at all?"

"No. Not really. I think we had one conversation about it on his eighteenth birthday. He said he was legally entitled to track her down, but I don't know if he ever did that. He never mentioned it to me. And then he went off to University so I hadn't seen him a huge amount. I expected him home for the summer, but he never came."

"And he's registered as a missing person?"

"Yes, since May. He left his residence at the University in May, and he hasn't been seen since."

Petty was silent, considering the information. Polly met Adam's eyes and gave him a sympathetic smile. They were good friends and colleagues in a small police station. She knew most of this stuff already.

"I guess you have no idea why someone would want to hurt your ex-wife?" Petty asked.

Adam shook his head with a wry smile. "She was a cold fish. I have no idea who she upset this time. Any more ex-husbands in the mix?"

Petty shook his head solemnly. He stood, and Polly followed his lead. "Do you have the receipt for your shopping?" Petty asked as he reached the front door. It was good evidence of Adam's whereabouts. It would let him off the hook.

"Yes, one second," replied Adam and disappeared into the kitchen. The bag he had used was on the floor by the fridge.

He reclaimed the receipt, smoothed it out on the kitchen table, and returned to the officers by the door. He handed the receipt to Polly.

"See you tomorrow," he said.

CHAPTER FOUR

Adam found a space and parked up in the short-stay car park, then quickly slunk down the alley that ran between the fishermen's cottages, to the rear entrance of The Blue Bell Inn. He stuck to the shadows and kept his head down, picking his way through the smokers in the backyard. It wasn't that he was up to anything overly nefarious, but he was hoping to escape the notice of any of his colleagues who might be out and about this evening. He ordered a pint of Otter, the local brew, from the bar and then found his way to one of the smaller rooms to the side of the old thatched pub.

Once upon a time, smugglers would have gathered here of an evening, rubbing shoulders with the local ne-er-do-wells, but nowadays, the pub offered good food and a friendly vibe in a recently renovated 'olde-England' style. What had once been a warren of small rooms had mostly been knocked through into one large one, but two or three of the private rooms still survived, whitewashed and with no doors but a large wood-burning fire kept each of them cheerful. Polly was waiting for him there, occupying a padded church pew and nursing a pint of Guinness. This room was dimly lit and smelt of wood smoke, but it was cosy enough. She smiled as he arrived. Dressed in civvies, her hair fluffed out around her shoulders, she looked tired. No doubt she'd been putting in the overtime on this latest case.

"Do you want another?" Adam offered, gesturing at her glass with his own, but Polly shook her head.

"Driving."

Adam settled down on a rickety wooden seat opposite her. "Yeah, me too." He took a gulp of his ale. It tasted good. "I need this after yesterday."

"It's a bad business all right," Polly said. She was astute enough to know why Adam had asked her to meet him here

27

this evening. They went way back, and occasionally engaged in a little light flirtation, but had never taken it any further than that.

"What can you tell me?" Adam asked, his voice low.

Polly pursed her lips. "Not much, you know that."

"I hear they've got someone though? A woman?"

Polly shook her head. She squinted through the entrance of the room, checking no-one was walking towards them or hanging around, then leant in closer to Adam. "They're holding the suspect at Exeter. I don't fancy her for it though, Adam, and neither does Petty, I'm sure."

"Why? The suspect was caught red-handed wasn't she?"

"Yeah, I found the suspect on scene, covered in blood, but apart from that, we've got nothing. Her prints weren't on the knife we found with the body, and she didn't have any other weapon on her. No connection to the victim that we can figure out at the moment. We've drawn a huge blank."

Adam frowned. "So what was she doing there?"

"Apparently she just stumbled upon it. Her story is that she followed somebody she thought she knew, all the way from the town centre to Neville Gardens. She witnessed this other person entering number 42 and heard screaming, so went in and found Mrs Fallon."

It felt odd to Adam to hear Nicola addressed as Mrs Fallon. He wondered about her new husband.

"When did Nicola move back into town?"

"Six months ago. She and her husband had been renovating the property so they've been coming and going over the summer. They have another house in Lewisham, that's their main base, but fancied a seaside bolt hole apparently."

That would explain why Adam hadn't run into her then. He wondered whether Nicola had considered looking him up. And why had she come back anyway? He supposed she had every right, this was her home town after all. However, after fifteen years of never seeing Dan, why had his mother chosen to virtually move next door to her son and ex-husband? Without letting them know, nonetheless?

And whom had Nicola upset in the few months she had been back in the area?

Durscombe was a sleepy seaside town, its small population swollen by tourists during the summer season. The cliché that everyone knew everyone else wasn't true here by a long shot, thanks to all the second homes and retirees, and people were moving in and out all the time, but still, serious crime was virtually unheard of in the area.

"The husband?"

"Dominic. Out of the country on business. He arrived back this morning and identified Nicola's body a few hours ago. There's a little girl. The in-laws came to take her. I guess Dominic will have reunited with her."

A half-sister for Dan? "Was she in the house?"

"Upstairs. Didn't see the actual murder, thank God."

"Cause of death?"

"Adam you know we don't have those results in yet!"

"Give me your best guess. You were at the scene."

"Honestly!" Polly glared at him, but Adam knew she was only playing with him. She pretended to glower at him. "How about 'exsanguination due to multiple stab wounds'?"

Adam grimaced. "Good enough, I guess." He pondered over what Polly had told him so far. "So this woman you found in the house? The suspect. Local?"

"From Birmingham. Recuperating by the seaside after the terrorist attack."

Adam whistled. "Really?" he searched Polly's face and she grimaced.

"Yeah. Not pretty. Fractured her left leg in two places, broken ribs, and head injuries."

"Head injuries?"

"Yep, and I know what you're thinking, so yes, we're doing a psych evaluation, but so far her doctors in Birmingham seem to think it's unlikely that she had a psychotic episode of some kind as she's shown no sign of psychological trauma at all."

"That can't be ruled out though?"

"No," Polly agreed and swigged some of her Guinness.

"It's one of the avenues that Petty's pursuing … among many. Including you."

"Naturally. I wouldn't expect anything else."

"And your son." Polly shot Adam a meaningful look.

This news gave Adam pause. "He's looking at Dan for this?" Polly shrugged, her eyes wide. "Well damn. I hope he finds him for me."

They lapsed into silence, each of them thinking of Dan. Polly knew how much Adam was hurting. The weeks, and now the months had gone on and there was still no word from him. Polly couldn't imagine what it was like to be a single parent, waiting for a phone call about a missing child that never came. Adam maintained his stiff upper lip, especially at work, but she knew he had to be worried stupid.

Adam drank deeply, then set his glass down on the table harder than he intended, making Polly jump. He smiled at her ruefully. She reached out and patted his hand, then withdrew it before the gesture became uncomfortable. She was a good friend.

The mood was broken when Polly's phone, on the table between them, beeped and vibrated. Polly flipped it over and lifted it into the light, thumbing through her messages. "Gibbs," she announced. "Heidi's been released without charge pending further investigation."

"Heidi?" Adam smiled, and Polly glared at him. It was a slip.

"Where's Heidi-from-Birmingham staying while she's in Durscombe?" Adam asked conspiratorially and winked at her.

"Adam—"

"Come on Polly, you know I can find out easily enough, if I want to."

"Oh, you're incorrigible."

"You love me," Adam grinned.

"I most certainly do not. 18 Budleigh Place, overlooking the park, but I didn't tell you, okay?"

Adam winked and raised his glass to Polly. "Okay."

CHAPTER FIVE

Adam spent a large proportion of his life in the car. The seaside town of Durscombe might only have a small catchment, but Devon and Cornwall was a huge area to police, with resources across the region spread much too thinly to be effective. Adam's main duties kept him south of Exeter, but his area of responsibility was wide and included many far-reaching rural communities. Today, after a busy shift running around the lanes looking into machinery theft from a large farm, Adam had waved goodbye to Tovey on the desk and was intending to head home to finally complete some outstanding paperwork, in the company of a microwave meal and a bottle of craft beer.

The sun was dipping below the horizon as he headed for his car, the sky fire-bright in deep orange and vibrant pink. It would be a still evening. He paused as he unlocked the car and breathed deeply—countryside and fresh sea air, it couldn't be beaten. If he could summon the energy, maybe he could walk along the prom with a bag of chips and watch the sea as it lapped against the shingle and let the paperwork wait until later. He often did this. It helped him relax and gather his thoughts. This was one of the things he most loved about being based in Durscombe. He might not have the most exciting career, in terms of investigating crime, or the largest array of criminals to chase and apprehend, but the beauty of the surrounding countryside and the proximity to the coast made everything about his life better.

It was typical that the one big case that Durscombe had seen for years happened to involve his ex-wife. He was barred from working on it, of course. Rumours around the station were that the evidence was circumstantial, but the mysterious Heidi was still in the frame.

Adam drove out of the parking area and turned right,

heading home, but without really thinking about it he almost immediately indicated right and turned again. A left at the bottom of the road and he was in a narrow residential road, where tall Victorian terraced houses lined one side of the street, overlooking Durscombe's park.

This was Budleigh Place.

Residential parking was limited to the road, and neighbours were rabid about guarding 'their' spaces, but Adam was fortunate to find an empty slot. He pulled up outside number twelve, parallel parked, and examined the row of houses. He counted away from himself until he identified number eighteen. It looked very much like every other. Five or six steps up to the front door, a tiny front garden with iron railings and a latch gate, a tiled entrance to a recessed front door, and a large bay window. A light burned in the window. The rest of the three-storeyed house was in darkness.

He shouldn't have, he knew that, but within seconds he had exited his car and meandered nonchalantly along Budleigh Place. He glanced into the park. Locals used it as a cut through to get to town, and he could see a few kids on bikes and a man walking his dog. The river cut the park in two, a hundred yards from where he stood. It was calm and peaceful, an idyllic place to live.

Turning his back on the park, he crossed the road. Number 18's gate was propped open, rusty and down on its hinges. With a few steps he was at the front door and his finger was on the buzzer. A harsh rasp vibrated through the house beyond.

At first Adam thought no-one would answer. But eventually a figure shuffled into view beyond the frosted glass, and the door opened.

Polly's description of Heidi's injuries had been thorough, but Adam was still taken aback by his first view of her. She was a slight woman, perhaps five-foot-five or six, but heartbreakingly thin and therefore appearing smaller. Her skin was deathly pale, apart from the angry red scarring above her left ear, stretching along her cheekbone and under her eye. There was evidence of a dint in her skull, and her hair was cropped closely all over her head. She wore loose jogging bottoms and a long red jumper, but from the way she hugged herself, she gave the impression of being freezing cold. Adam figured she could be aged anywhere between her early thirties and early forties. She appeared haggard and ill.

As Adam stared at her, the woman shyly lifted her left hand to cover the scarring on her face and head, uncomfortable in the light of his scrutiny. Adam caught himself and apologised.

"I'm sorry. Heidi, isn't it?" He held his hand out. "DS Adam Chapple from Durscombe police station, just around the corner. I thought I'd pop around and introduce myself." Adam didn't show her his warrant card and had no intention of telling her he was not involved in her case. He didn't like to be evasive, but he felt compelled to find out more about the case and Heidi's involvement in Nicola's murder. Observing this frail woman standing in front of him, he couldn't see how she would have had the strength to have felled his feisty ex-wife.

"Oh," said Heidi. Her grey eyes grew huge as she looked up at him. "Would you like to come in?"

She stepped away from the door, and Adam bit back a feeling of guilt as he walked in after her. The front door opened straight onto a large open plan lounge diner with a polished parquet floor and plain white walls. The room was sparsely furnished and the available light came from two side lights on stands, for while there was an ornate fireplace, only candles graced the grate and they remained unlit. There was no television, just a few books on the table. Stairs led up to the next floor.

Heidi had obviously been lying on the sofa prior to Adam's arrival. A blanket was thrown to one side, and her slippers lay crookedly under the coffee table. The house was very warm, radiators blasting out heat in spite of the mild October weather, but perhaps Heidi felt the cold. She reached over the sofa and grabbed a beanie hat from the arm, yanking it over her head, covering her skull and scars.

"Could I offer you some tea or coffee?" Heidi asked

politely, heading for the glass door. She walked with a slight limp, Adam noticed.

"That would be lovely, but please, I've already disturbed you. Allow me?" Adam followed her into the small, neat kitchen. It was slightly dated but good quality and built to last. The worktops were clear of clutter. "We coppers get used to making tea for folk."

"It's fine. I needed to stand and stretch my leg a little," Heidi said. "It gets cramped up sometimes." She lifted her knee and stretched her leg behind her.

"Does it hurt?" Adam asked, and Heidi nodded.

"Sometimes. Well, to tell you the truth, most of the time. But it could be worse, right?" Adam was surprised how little bitterness he sensed in her tone, given what had happened to her. "There's a teapot in one of the cupboards behind you. Not sure which. I don't get many visitors. Would you mind?"

Adam pulled open the cupboards one after the other. They were sparsely equipped with crockery, glassware, and pots and pans. Everything was clean and almost precisely placed. He found the teapot, decorated with seagulls, nestling alongside some old-fashioned Tupperware.

"Are you renting this place?" asked Adam.

"No. It belonged to my aunt and she passed away last year, so it kind of belongs to my dad now. I don't think he knows quite what to do with it. I think he would have sold it before, but with what happened to me, he hasn't really had the time. He may still sell it, I suppose. In the meantime, I thought the sea air would do me good." She laughed suddenly, not entirely without humour, but Adam heard a note of desperation there too.

Heidi loaded up the tray with mugs, milk, a bowl of sugar, and the teapot. "I have custard creams. Do you like those?" Adam nodded, and she smiled. Her smile lit up her face, and for a moment she looked less worn and world weary. "Oh good," she said softly. "They're my favourites. Would you carry the tray for me?" And she limped away from him and into the living room once more.

Adam followed her dutifully and, once Heidi had made room, deposited the tray on the table. "Would you mind if I took my jacket off?" he asked.

"Oh goodness, of course not. Sorry. I seem to feel the cold terribly, so the heating is up way too high." She waited for him to get settled on an armchair, and then huddled onto the sofa once more, pulling the blanket over her legs. Her fingers smoothed the blanket down, and Adam saw her face cloud as she waited for him to ask questions.

He regarded her objectively. So slight and pale, so obviously riddled with pain, how had she walked from town to Neville Gardens and overpowered his ex-wife? She wouldn't have possessed the strength.

"Do you like Durscombe?" he began gently.

She looked across at him and smiled uncertainly. "I thought I did." Adam nodded. He could understand that. "I thought I was getting away from my troubles. My dad thought it would be better for me to stay down here for a while, to try and get my strength back. I hadn't imagined I'd run into more … trouble."

Adam noticed the repeated reference to her father. "You mentioned your dad. You're obviously very close. You're not in a relationship with anyone?"

Heidi smiled and shook her head. "No. Not at the moment. To be honest, I've never met the right man. Isn't that what we say? I don't know what the right man might look like. I've had boyfriends. Not lately. I've been happy enough on my own. Yes, you're right. I am close to my dad. He lives near me. We see each other a few times a week."

"In Birmingham."

"He lives in Harborne. Posh area of Birmingham, yes. I have a flat just outside of there, handy for the train. I miss hearing the sound of the trains. It's very quiet here." Heidi looked towards the window and the park beyond. She gestured at the tea. "Would you mind?"

"No, of course." Adam busied himself pouring the tea. Milk and two sugars for himself, just milk for Heidi. He handed her the mug and noticed her hands were shaking.

"Are you all right to chat about all this, or would you rather I left?" asked Adam. He was concerned about Heidi's pallor, and if she collapsed or was taken ill while he was talking to her, that would leave him with a few questions of his own to answer.

"No, this'll put me right, don't worry. They told me there would be more interviews, so I might as well get on with it."

She was so trusting, Adam thought. "Well, you can stop me at any time. Okay?"

She nodded her understanding, so he continued. "Heidi, tell me what happened the other day. In your own words."

Heidi grimaced and looked down into her mug of tea. "It's like I told the other officers. I saw—"

An ominous rumble emanated from somewhere above. Heidi started in fright and glanced nervously at the ceiling. Adam looked up too, half expecting cracks to appear in the ceiling, but his attention was diverted when a sudden gust of wind blew the wrong way down the chimney, knocking the candles in the grate flying. His mind grappled for a rational explanation, his first thought that he was witnessing a residue of old soot billowing into the room. However, as he watched, the cloud of soot formed a shape, and this seemed to suck energy into itself, shrinking in size to form a dark silhouette, little more than a shadow. It flew straight at Adam. He yelped in surprise and ducked. It flapped around his head, and he could distinctly hear the sound of wings beating near his right ear. He tried to shoo it away, thrashing at the air with mounting alarm, but his fists found only thin air.

Then it shifted its attention, and Adam watched as it whirled around the room, flying high at first, circling the ceiling lights, then swooping down at Heidi. She shrieked in fear and tried to stand in order to run away, but her feet tangled in the blanket, and she collapsed to her knees on the floor, the contents of her mug spilling across the blanket and rug, while the mug shattered into pieces on the hard floor.

Adam stood to go to her rescue, but then ducked once

more and fell to one knee to avoid the shape as it flew towards him, buffeting at his head and shoulders. Tiring of his own inaction, he finally leapt to his feet, shouting at the bird, watching it as it flew in circles around the room. It moved quickly and he wasn't certain that its form had much substance beyond a shadow, but when it headed for the window and the gathering gloom of the early evening beyond, it sounded solid enough.

The bird smacked against the glass with a loud clattering, colliding so hard that the window vibrated—in a form firm enough that Adam thought it would smash the glass for certain. Heidi cried in alarm once more and Adam rushed towards the window, intending to open it, expecting the bird to have another go at getting out, wanting to prevent it from beating itself to a bloody pulp or breaking its neck, wanting to help it if he could¬—but by the time he reached the window, the bird had disappeared.

In confusion, Adam pulled back the curtains, searching for the whereabouts of the thing. It had completely vanished. There was no obvious sign of it anywhere. He walked around the room, assuming the bird was stunned and frightened. He cocked his head, listening for the slightest sound but there was nothing except Heidi's ragged breathing. Eventually he dropped to his hands and knees and scanned underneath the furniture. Nothing was moving. There was no sign of a bird, or indeed any other creature.

Standing once more, Adam returned to the window. It was closed securely and the glass remained intact. There was no means by which the bird could have found a route out of the house this way.

Peering outside, Adam could see across the road, beyond the parked cars, into the park. A slight movement drew his attention, and as he watched, a mysterious figure in the near distance paused on the path that ran alongside the river. Unless it was a trick of the light, the person appeared to be staring straight back at him. Illuminated only by one of the muted street lamps, Adam quickly surmised it was a woman, although her garb was peculiar, old-fashioned in the extreme. She wore a long dress, reaching down to the ground, light in colour, and she was heavily veiled, an eerie bride, standing alone in the dusk.

Except she wasn't entirely alone. A number of black birds flew in circles around her head. She didn't acknowledge their presence or seem alarmed by them in any way.

Adam frowned, his heart beating quickly in his chest.

He didn't like this situation, or this odd bystander, and his natural instinct was to investigate. He dashed to the front door and flung it open, chasing into the street, intending to apprehend her in the park and ask her what she had seen or what she had expected to see, but in the four or five seconds it had taken him to reach the iron gate, she had vanished into the shadows, and the birds had disappeared with her.

Puzzled, Adam walked slowly into the park and looked around. As he would expect at this time in the evening, there were several people walking their dogs, but the kids on bikes had gone home for their dinners, and the veiled woman had evaporated. Concerned for Heidi, Adam turned about and made his way back to Number 18. He glanced across at the bay window as he climbed the front steps, examining the outside for cracks in the central window pane. There didn't appear to be any damage, but he could see an outline of something on the glass. From outside he couldn't make out what it was.

Re-entering the house, he found Heidi struggling to stand, her face set tightly with pain. Adam helped her to her feet and settled her back on the sofa. Her blanket was sopping wet, but when she exclaimed about the mess and tried to stand again, Adam gently stopped her.

"Let me, Heidi. You stay there," Adam instructed, his voice firm. "What the hell was that?"

Heidi kept her head down and didn't directly answer. "There's kitchen roll next to the sink," she said instead.

Perplexed by the whole episode, Adam found the light switch in the kitchen and quickly grabbed the kitchen roll. He spotted the envelope he'd seen earlier too and took the opportunity to give it a cursory glance. It had been forwarded to Durscombe. The original address for Heidi Huddlestone was Litchfield Way, Selly Oak, Birmingham. Useful information, he was sure.

He swiftly mopped up the spillage in the living room swiftly, poured Heidi more tea in a new mug, and replaced the candles in the grate. The floor around the hearth was spotless. He felt along the inside of the chimney for soot, but it had been swept clean and probably not used for a good few years. If what he had witnessed had been caused by a rogue gust of wind, whatever the dark shape had been, it had not been a cloud of soot.

That left a bird or some other animal, but Adam couldn't see how it had escaped the room. It had hit the window and simply disappeared. He took the kitchen roll over to the window and examined the floor beneath the bay. There was no dead bird. There were no feathers.

Remembering the mark he'd seen from outside, he glanced up. He could clearly see the outline of a bird with a large wingspan, stretching almost the entire width of the pane of glass, nearly a metre across. He peered more closely at the silhouette. He had seen something like this in a newspaper once. When a bird collided with glass it left an impression caused by 'powder down', or feather dust. Adam rubbed gently and the dust adhered to his finger. A bird had collided with the window from the inside, and then completely disappeared.

That just wasn't possible.

"Did you see her too?" Heidi's voice, flat and miserable behind him, interrupted Adam's fevered contemplation.

Turning, Adam frowned at Heidi. "Her? What do you mean?"

"It's a bird, isn't it? That you can see in the window?" When Adam nodded, Heidi went on, "A raven probably. It's not the first time that's happened. I moved down here, from home, to get away from it. I thought it would help."

"This has happened to you before?"

"I first saw the bird when I left hospital and moved into my dad's house. The first few times I thought I would have a heart attack. It's not something I've become used to, and I can't explain it, but ..."

"There was no bird though. There's no trace of one."

"Not a physical one, no. There never is." Heidi's tone was bleak.

Adam ran a hand through his hair. He felt absurdly out of his depth suddenly, without any real control of the situation. Here he was, a police officer of twenty-two years good standing. He used rational analysis, logic, patience, and a lot of hard graft to solve his cases. Birds that were not physically here were not part of his life experience. There had to be another explanation.

There must have been a bird. End of. It had escaped some other way, and he had missed it.

"What did you mean when you asked me if I'd seen her too? Seen who?" he asked.

Heidi's brows knitted together as she thought about what to tell him, her grey eyes sombre. She weighed up her response before she answered. "You saw a woman, dressed in lace, with a heavy lace headdress, yes?" Adam thought about the figure he had witnessed so briefly. A heavy lace headdress did fit the bill, but there was something else he vaguely recalled, the odd shape of her head. He nodded.

"She's the woman I followed to the house the other day."

"The day of the murder? The woman you followed from town?" Adam turned back to the window and peered out beyond the darkness once more, searching among the circles of light on the ground along the path, for the woman or any sign of her. A lone man walked slowly into view with a small white dog. The dog halted, sniffed at some length, cocked a leg against the lamppost, and then he and his owner moved on. Adam knew he should go back out there and have another look for the woman. She might not have gone far. He could ask other park users if they had witnessed anything unusual too, or seen a woman fitting her description.

"It's a waste of time going after her. You won't find her

unless she wants to be found," Heidi said quietly, the desperation etched across her face. "Believe me. I've tried."

"Who is she?" asked Adam, still intent on heading back outside.

"I don't know her name," Heidi replied. "I met her when I died."

***

Heidi leaned back against the sofa once more and sighed wearily.

Adam had made a fresh pot of tea, and when they were both settled once more, he had asked her to tell him everything, right from the beginning, but one look at her face and Adam knew, with sudden clarity, she would tell him a story—and it would be what Heidi thought he as a police officer wanted to hear. Perhaps something she thought he could handle. He stopped her before she could get going. "Heidi, I want you to tell me everything, even the stuff you didn't share with the other officers. There are no cameras or tape machines here."

Heidi brought her mug of tea to her lips and stared down at it, the fingers of her free hand tapping against the side, as she considered what he'd said. She wouldn't look at him.

"If I'm going to help you, I need to know the whole truth. Half-truths never help anyone."

"You're going to help me?" she asked, her nose wrinkling slightly, her tone laced with doubt.

"If I can, yes."

"It's all such a mess. No-one will believe what I say. Not you, not anybody. Even my dad thinks I'm crazy. He thinks it's the knock on the head I've had. That's what he calls it, 'a knock on the head'." Heidi shot Adam a defiant look. "You won't believe me either. So, why would you want to help me?"

Adam understood that building trust in this situation was vital. He took a deep breath, then exhaled calmly. Time to lay his cards on the table. "Okay. Look Heidi, I haven't been entirely honest with you …"

"What do you mean?" Heidi bolted upright in alarm. "Aren't you a policeman?"

Adam put his hand out to placate her. "Yes, yes, I am." He fumbled around in his jacket, hanging off the edge of the chair, trying to find his wallet and his warrant card. He flipped it open to show her. "DS Adam Chapple. That much is true. I'm based in Exeter, but occasionally work out of the local station around the corner from here. However, I'm not working this case. Not officially."

"Then what are you doing here? I'm not a damn freak show!" For the first time Adam heard some energy in Heidi's voice. He placed his wallet on the coffee table and held his hands out, palms up, in surrender.

"Honestly? The woman who was killed? In Neville Gardens? That was my ex-wife, Nicola." Adam watched as Heidi's face creased in horror. "We separated and divorced a long time ago," Adam placated her. "I have no feelings for her anymore, beyond an obvious sympathy for her family. But I'm not emotionally involved with her in any way. I'm not after vengeance. I'm just trying to find out the truth of what happened to her."

Heidi regarded him distrustfully, searching his face. "There's something else, isn't here?" she asked. "That's not all of it."

It was Adam's turn to look uncomfortable. "No, you're right. There is more. It's my son. Mine and Nicola's son. He's missing. He's been missing for a little while, and I guess I just want to make sure there is no link between the death of Nicola and my absent son. I want to know that no-one is going after my son or has hurt him."

"Ah," Heidi sat back abruptly. "I see." Adam watched her. She studied her nails for some time, thinking. Finally, she nodded.

"All right," she said. "I'll tell you everything."

Shifting her weight and making herself comfortable, Heidi gazed towards the large bay window at the front of the room.

"I'd been having a nap here on the sofa, something I'm prone to do more often these days. I think it's the painkillers. I'd pulled the curtains. It was an overcast afternoon; do you remember? I slept a little later than I intended and when I woke up, I was groggy. I went to the window to open the curtains a little, thinking maybe I'd walk in the park for a while if it wasn't raining. But the woman in the veil was out there."

"This wasn't the first time you'd seen her though?" Adam dug a little, the devil was in the detail, but he was impatient to get to the crux of the matter too. "You said …"

"I know what I said." Heidi put her head in her hands. "Oh this is so difficult." She groaned, her voice muffled.

"Look, how about I promise not to pass judgement?" offered Adam. "I still feel like you're starting in the middle of the story."

Heidi straightened up and glared at him. "I don't like to talk about it. What do you want to know? About my 'accident'? Monday 22nd May. The Birmingham terrorist attack, when the stolen van was driven into a crowd of people during the morning rush. Do you remember it?" Adam nodded. Of course. It had been all over the news, all over social media, the only thing people could talk about for days. The whole country had felt aggrieved and angry.

"I don't remember it. I don't even remember the days immediately before it. My last memory before those men drove into me on a pelican crossing at The Bullring, is of my taking a Zumba class on the Thursday previously. I lost over seventy-two hours of memories before the incident, and then all of the time I was in a coma afterwards." Heidi ran her finger around the rim of the mug in agitation. Round and round, round and round.

"According to an estimate by the woman who worked to save my life—her name was Nora Ludlow by the way—I was clinically dead for just over three minutes. Nora, and a cyclist whose name I have never found out, resuscitated me on the road and kept me alive until the paramedics arrived.

"I was taken to hospital, with skull fractures, leg fractures, and broken ribs, and placed into an induced coma. A few days later they performed surgery to relieve clotting on my brain. I don't remember any of that either. The first thing I do remember is waking up to see my dad by my bedside. That was the second week of June." Heidi scowled and placed her mug on the table, almost angrily, but when she sat back and looked at Adam, he could clearly see she was struggling not to cry.

"So that was it. Except," her voice softened, "there is one other episode I remember. I thought it was a dream. For weeks I thought it was just something I'd imagined. But now I know."

"What?"

"Immediately after the incident, I joined a queue. A shuffling queue of people. Many, many people. I couldn't see them really. Not faces. But I had a sense they were from all over the place, all over the globe. Many nationalities. And we were all headed the same way, towards a door. There was a woman there, just sitting on a bench near the door, counting people in. No-one came out. And every time the door opened I could see a curtain. A thick curtain, made of lace. Heavy and as old as time. This curtain would be pulled back and the person at the front of the queue would go through the door, step through the veil and … inside. To whatever was beyond."

Adam listened, entranced. "And you think this happened while you were … dead?"

"Yes. While I was lying on the road. I wasn't breathing. My heart had stopped. I had lost a lot of blood."

"And this woman?" Adam prompted again.

"Something went wrong, I think. The woman in front of me stepped forward. It was her turn to enter, but the door opened and there seemed to be a tussle or a struggle on the other side."

"What makes you say that?"

"Have you ever seen little kids fighting behind a curtain? That's what it reminded me of. And until then, no-one had come from behind the door, all of the traffic had been forwards. Then all of a sudden, there was a flurry, a kind of skirmish, and someone came dashing out and collided with the woman in front of me. Knocked her over.

"I bent over to pick her up, and as I started to help her to her feet, she disappeared from my grasp. It was like clutching at smoke. One moment she seemed to have substance and then she … dissipated …" Adam began to speak, and Heidi gestured at him to say she hadn't finished.

"There was an explosion of birds, big black birds, like crows maybe, they flew out of the door. Fast. Like they were fired through the door. They were everywhere. After the peace I'd felt, this was suddenly violent and intrusive. Then another person came out from beyond that door. The curtain billowed towards me, and she stepped out. It was a woman, dressed from head to toe in lace, the same lace as the curtain behind the door, but her head was misshapen … and when I looked at her properly, she was wearing a headdress and beneath the veil she had horns."

"Horns?" Adam tried to quell his disbelief. He briefly pondered what a psychologist might read into Heidi's account. His only explanation, given that Heidi obviously believed what she was saying, was that on the whole, it was a fairly rational account of what she thought had happened. It sounded to Adam as though Heidi's subconscious was trying to make sense of the incident on the pelican crossing. He could neatly package what the woman in front of him was suggesting in this way, and yet … And yet, the horns gave him pause. Startled him even. He thought back to the woman he had seen in the park. Her strange head shape could have been put down to an odd headdress, or yes, horns beneath her veil.

But that was absurd.

"Yes. I can't explain it. I'm just telling you what I saw."

Adam nodded. "Sorry, yes, go on."

"I couldn't see her face, and to be honest, I didn't want to, but she looked at me … looked through me … almost as though she could read my every thought. And then she came towards me, and as much as I wanted to back away, I couldn't. In fact, I was compelled to walk forwards, and I walked into her outstretched arm. She pushed into my chest. I felt that push. It was hard. But then it was darkness for a long time."

Heidi leaned forward. "So yeah. Initially I thought I'd had a dream, but it was so vivid and so real. And then I came out of hospital, and all of a sudden I started to see her. The woman in the veil. Not constantly, not even that often, but here and there. She scared me. And then there were the visits from those damn birds."

"Do you think what happened in here tonight was some kind of, I don't know… a spirit bird?" asked Adam.

"Do you have a better explanation, detective?" Heidi replied with a sardonic smile.

Adam squinted at the ghost silhouette of the bird on the window. The truth was, he didn't have any logical explanation. It wasn't a cheery thought.

"And the woman in the veil was the one you followed to Nicola's house?"

Heidi laughed. It was a hollow sound. "Hell no, that would be far too easy. She comes and she goes, like some nightmare vision. She appears out there in the park, watching me. I don't know what she wants. But she isn't the woman I followed to your ex-wife's house. No, the woman I followed was the only other person I could identify from that vision, my dream, or whatever you want to conveniently label it as—my after life experience. The woman I followed was the one I helped up when she was pushed to the ground. And for some reason, this woman whom I'd never seen before in my life, is now here, inhabiting the same time and the same place, and it just so happens that she's the woman who murdered your ex-wife, not me."

***

The young man at the Bird's Nest counter called his order number several times before Adam heard him. He wasn't buying Heidi's story at all. Was he? He had to admit the incident with the gust of wind down the chimney had him spooked a little, but there was no reason why the imprint of the bird had not been there before that. Theoretically he supposed Heidi could have sprayed dust or something through a stencil to get the same effect.

Really? a voice in his mind asked. You really think she's that devious and would go to all that trouble?

But damn it, anything was possible. Especially where murderers were concerned. He wouldn't trust them as far as he could throw them. Any of them. He recalled an interview with a suspect many years ago. The guy had claimed that a red haze had settled on him, and he couldn't remember what he'd done. What he had actually done was stab his long term partner in excess of fifty times. The 'red haze' he had rattled on about had probably been her blood. Adam could still remember the photographs of the scene. The blood had sprayed across the walls, and run down them, leaving lines like watery royal icing down the side of a cake. The suspect's defence team had worked hard at proving he had a brain lesion or some such nonsense. It hadn't convinced the jury though. The guy had gone down for life. Or what equated to life in the British justice system.

Adam sighed at the turn his thoughts had taken. He hated to think he was becoming jaded. He couldn't afford to let that happen. He had plenty of years of service left before he could claim his pension, but he knew it was always wise to approach suspects from a variety of angles.

The veiled woman Heidi had described had matched the one he had seen outside in the park for sure, but for all he knew she could be an eccentric neighbour.

There was something eminently believable about Heidi and her story, but ghosts and near death experiences? That wasn't what Adam was about. He was an experienced detective. There was a rational explanation for everything.

He finally heard his number. He collected his order of sweet-and-sour pork and chicken Chow Mein from the counter and returned to his car. It was beginning to rain. He drove home, pondering where Dan was spending the night, and hoping his son was warm and dry.

***

Heidi rose stiffly from the sofa, feeling unbalanced. Adam had kindly cleared away the tea tray before he left, so she didn't have to juggle the tray while she was feeling wobbly. Her blood sugar was low. She hadn't eaten since a tin of soup at lunchtime, but even so, she still didn't have an appetite. She elected to skip supper, take some painkillers, and head directly upstairs. She intended to read for a while if she could, maybe listen to the radio, but she wasn't entirely sure she would sleep. She felt anxious. What would become of the case against her? It must all appear open and closed to the police, surely?

She wondered whether Adam had believed her or not. Probably not. He'd left her his card and told her to feel free to contact him, although he hadn't specified under what circumstances. He had reiterated that he was nothing to do with the murder case. She guessed he might get into trouble for contacting her. If she had been feeling vindictive, she could have made a phone call and sent a heap of bother his way.

She limped across to the window to close the curtains, reminding herself to attend to the exercises given to her by her physiotherapist back in Birmingham in the morning. He had told her there was no reason why she shouldn't have full use of her leg again, as long as she did as he suggested. No gain without pain, he had told her.

She paused to look at the dust outline of the bird. Adam had taken a photo of it before he left. She could see the greasy smudge of his fingers where he had rubbed at the mark. She would need to clean the glass again tomorrow. Her neighbours would think she was OCD about her windows.

As she drew the curtains, the halo of light in the park beyond naturally drew her eye. The veiled woman stared back at the house, watching Heidi, some sort of sinister sentinel, stalking her, disturbing her peace.

Heidi shivered, wondering if she would ever feel warm again.

CHAPTER SIX

A slow walk along the prom returned some colour to Heidi's cheeks. She tasted the salt spray on her lips, and for the first time in days felt as though she could eat something. Durscombe contained an endless supply of cafes and restaurants to buy lunch, although quality and prices varied as you might expect. At this time of year, with the season over, nowhere was too crowded.

On her way home, Heidi took Curzon Street, the main route through Durscombe, heading north through the centre of town. She knew of a deli-come-café that sold amazing mini-quiches, complete with a healthy pile of freshly prepared salad. She intended to stop there and rest. A plate of food and an elderflower cordial would provide all the energy she needed for the trek home, then she could consider a ritual afternoon nap.

She paused at the haberdasher's shop window. She was as always drawn to the colours and the textures. Right through school and at University, she had been creative and crafty, until she'd taken her first job and work had consumed her. Before the incident, she had rarely had time to read or do anything creative outside work because her free time was eaten up by shopping, cleaning, socialising, and exercising. Now she had more free time on her hands than she knew what to do with, her friends lived many miles away, and exercise was limited to walking and stretching. As she gazed at the shiny boxed crafts on display in front of her, Heidi considered trying out a few new projects, perhaps some cross stitch or crochet. Crafts she had enjoyed as a girl.

If she wandered into the shop, she would come out loaded up with purchases. The thought made her smile. She wasn't averse to a little shopping, but when her stomach gurgled, she recognised her priorities. She needed to eat. Still, sorely tempted to go in and explore, Heidi squinted through the window at the display beyond. Gazing past the colourful skeins of wool, pipe cleaner twists, and squares of felt, she spied bolts of colourful fabric piled neatly on top of each other at the rear of the shop. Above them, drops of fine nets had been displayed for best effect. Heidi's eye was drawn to them and she dwelt on the appearance of the lace. Her stomach tipped over at the sight of the thick yellow filigree of one particular hanging. She could easily imagine the veiled woman glaring back at her.

Heidi shook away the wave of nausea that swept through her and pulled away from the shop. In her haste, she almost collided with someone walking behind her and quickly turned to apologise, then mindlessly turned about once more, the deli all but forgotten. Away, her mind screeched. She needed to hurry home to where she could feel safe.

A bell jangled and a customer exited the craft shop, walking close by. Heidi, now searching for the veiled woman everywhere, bit back a scream, momentarily convinced the woman's cream raincoat was a long veil. Heidi swallowed against a river of bile that rose in her throat, panic setting in, a familiar but unwanted companion.

Heidi's vision blurred and darkened. The shadows crowded her. Heidi batted against them, imagining she was surrounded by birds. The more she pushed them away, the more populous they became. They beat at her face and shrieked and cawed. Heidi was suffocating among the dust and feathers. She turned about, then round again, attempting to scurry clear of the birds, knowing they were only a figment of her imagination. She cried out weakly, banging against the window, disoriented and scared. People turned to watch her. Heidi placed her hands flat against the glass, focusing on the coolness beneath her palms. Breathing. Breathing. Slowing her breath.

Her heart rate slowed down and strength returned to her knees. Someone asked if she was alright and she shook them off. Finally, she could try to walk again. She reminded herself she was heading north and turned, straightening her beanie hat with hands that shook a little. All that was required of her was to move now, walk slowly. One foot in front of the other.

She hadn't progressed more than a few metres when much to her consternation a woman walking towards her drew her attention. It was the woman she had followed to Neville Gardens. The woman she had helped to her feet in her vision. She was walking towards her, large as life, not a care in the world. Heidi backed away, unsure what to do.

The woman strode forwards, calm and confident. Her head swivelled, and she clocked Heidi staring at her, but her gaze seemed strangely vacant. As she drew level, Heidi stretched her hand out. "Hey? Hey!"

The women locked eyes. "Remember me?" Heidi asked, but the woman only stared through her, her face hard. She continued walking, her head pivoting to observe Heidi even as she moved past, and then her head snapped forwards and she marched onwards, never breaking stride.

Heidi watched the older woman go, open-mouthed and sick to her stomach. This was proof that she hadn't been hallucinating the night of the murder. The police would have to believe her now. She fumbled in her bag, searching for her mobile among the odds and sods that had accumulated there. She grabbed it, all fingers and thumbs, trying desperately to activate the screen, and then find the call button. By the time her call was connected, she was frantic and out of breath.

***

Polly was on patrol in Durscombe. She had been engaging some teenagers in conversation, having received a complaint about them drinking, smoking, and swearing behind St Michael's Church. Being a police officer was certainly not a glamorous life. She knew the lads were enjoying the banter, but at times she found it tedious in the extreme. It was with relief then that she took the call from control and told the kids she would check back in ten minutes to make sure they had moved along. She practically skipped out of the church grounds, making her way out onto the High Street and cutting through to Curzon Street.

She spotted Heidi, slouching against a wall outside Frills and trotted towards her. Even from a distance she could see Heidi looked stricken. As Polly reached her, Heidi's face lit up with relief.

"Thank you for coming so quickly," Heidi blurted, her breathing coming in excited gasps.

Polly was about to respond when she noticed movement in her peripheral vision. Someone running towards them. Adam.

"What are you doing here?" Polly asked, her tone sharp.

"I was having a word with the landlord at The Black Swan, so I figured I'd join you. Back up and all that."

Polly scowled, but she turned her attention to Heidi.

"How are you doing, Ms Huddlestone? You called us about—"

"I saw her. I saw that woman again. The one I followed the other evening!"

"The other evening? You mean to Neville Gardens?" asked Polly.

"Yes. She was walking down the street here. Heading that way." Heidi pointed towards the seafront. "You need to go after her."

"I'll go," said Adam quickly. "Remind me who it is I'm looking for."

"Adam," Polly started.

"Time is of the essence, PC Forster," Adam said briskly and looked pointedly at Heidi.

"What does she look like you mean?" When Adam nodded, she continued, "An older woman, late fifties, early sixties maybe? Her hair is sort of white blonde."

"What was she wearing?"

"A green check shirt, a sleeveless black bomber jacket and jeans."

"I'll be right back," said Adam and took off. Polly stared down the road after him helplessly as Heidi wrung her hands.

***

Two hours later, after much tussling with the council and various shops in the vicinity, Adam and Polly were poring over the CCTV footage they had managed to obtain for Curzon Street.

"How difficult can this be?" Polly asked as she downloaded a file onto the laptop. "We're hardly dealing with Oxford Street, are we?"

Adam snorted. His cynicism was quickly proven correct. The first section of footage, obtained from the Council, was entirely blank, and the images from the second, taken from outside a clothing chain store, were too grainy to see. That left two more to try. The first was the Admiral Nelson, a pub opposite Frills. Polly rolled the footage straight to the time that Heidi had dialled 999 and then they worked their way backwards. Sure enough they could see Heidi reacting to a woman who walked towards her and then past her, heading along the road to the seafront as Heidi had described.

"I guess this is the woman she means," Polly pointed with her pen at the screen as the woman kept walking.

"Slow it down," said Adam, back-seat driving much to Polly's annoyance. "Replay it."

They watched it over in silence.

And then again.

It was evident that Heidi was saying something to the woman, and that the woman looked at her and didn't reply. They had a good view of Heidi, but only a rear view of the woman they were interested in.

"Let's try the last one. From the bank," said Polly and reached for the keyboard to pull up the final piece of footage.

"Wait," said Adam. "Can you just replay this further back? Go back to where Heidi is looking in the window."

Polly did so. Adam leaned in more closely. Polly could feel his breath on her cheek. He watched it over and frowned.

"Again," he said.

"What are you looking at?" asked Polly, who couldn't see anything worth noting.

"Humour me," ordered Adam. Polly played the video once more. "Stop." Polly stopped the footage. On the screen Heidi was staring into Frills. "What do you see?" asked Adam.

"I can see Heidi, and a couple of other pedestrians, and not much else," said Polly patiently. "What am I missing? What do you see?"

Adam ran his finger over the screen. "These dark shapes?"

Polly peered more closely. "Smudges on the camera?" she suggested.

"Not birds then?"

"Birds? No." Polly wound the film back a few seconds and let it run. Then back again, and this time she moved it on frame by frame."

"Enhance it. Can we zoom in or anything?" asked Adam.

"Sure," said Polly, doubt in her voice.

As she clicked with her mouse, zooming in on Heidi and the black shapes, a dark shadow filled the screen, blocking the view momentarily, then fell away. With each click of Polly's mouse, a little more detail was revealed, frame by frame, something black filled the screen. Something feathered. Polly kept right on clicking, until at last one beady eye stared out of the screen, shiny and intelligent, and then the whole of a bird's head.

"Jesus Christ, you were right!" said Polly. "It's a bloody raven or something!"

***

The final CCTV file from a camera operating outside the NatWest bank farther up Curzon Street, gave Adam and Heidi the break they were searching for. Full colour and as clear as a bell, the picture showed the woman wearing her green checked shirt and a black leather bomber jacket.

"Print that," said Adam, as though Polly hadn't thought of doing so herself. She printed out several copies and Adam grabbed the top one.

"You know I'll have to pass all this on to Gibbs, don't

you?" Polly said firmly, and Adam's face fell. Of course she would. Adam wasn't working this case. It was out of the question. Polly needed to behave professionally. Adam blew his cheeks out.

Polly smiled at his reaction, then winked. "But how about a beer later? You owe me anyway."

CHAPTER SEVEN

Coleridge Way, a looping road that ran around the outskirts of old Durscombe, had a desirable post code. The majority of the houses were set well back from the road. Polly and Gibbs were looking for 126, and at the second passing they found it, grouped together with a dozen or so semi-detached Victorian houses, built into a hill. It had no garage but a sizeable drive and a well-established, cottage-style garden.

At Gibbs's nod, Polly tried the doorbell. When it didn't appear to be working, she tapped on the door and waited. After a slight delay, she heard the sound of the chain being pulled back and the door opened. A small round man, perhaps five-foot-five, with a ruddy complexion and soft brown eyes, stood in front of them. He was wearing a cook's apron, and the sleeves of his shirt were rolled up. He shook flour from his hands, then wiped them on his apron, smiling uncertainly at the pair, noting Polly in her uniform.

Polly let her superior take the lead. "Good afternoon, sir," said Gibbs pleasantly. "Are you Mr Goodwin?"

"I am, yes. Tom Goodwin."

"I'm DC Gibbs, Devon and Cornwall Police, and this is PC Forster. Is Mrs Goodwin at home, sir? We'd like to have a word."

"Er … yes she is," Tom hovered for a moment, switching his weight from one foot to another, perhaps weighing up whether he had to allow the police access, but then he stepped away from the door and gestured inside. Gibbs allowed Polly to enter first.

The inside of the house had a definite aroma. It reminded Polly of her grandparents' house. Clean from the scent of furniture polish, but also an undercurrent of several decades' worth of dinners. Everything was spick and span, but the furniture sat heavy and static, as though it had occupied the same position for a very long time.

Polly followed Tom as he showed them into the living room. This was a bright room, tastefully decorated in cream paint with pastel flowers on the three-piece sofa and matching curtains. Through a smart conservatory, Polly saw a wheelbarrow parked in the middle of the patio, nearly full of weeds. Evidence of recent tidying up.

Mrs Goodwin was reclining on the sofa, her feet on a pouffe, a solidly built woman with white blonde hair, probably in her early sixties. She looked up as Polly and Gibbs entered the room but didn't smile.

Some solid police work had gone into identifying Mrs Goodwin, although in the end it had been relatively unproblematic. CCTV had shown her using her cash card at the bank, and a quick conversation with the bank manager, and a completed data protection form, had given them Laura Goodwin's name.

Tom bobbed out from behind Gibbs's elbow and moved to stand with his wife. "What's this about, officer?" he asked. His eyes flicked between Polly and Gibbs.

"It's probably something and nothing, Mr Goodwin. May I call you Tom?" Gibbs asked smoothly.

Tom nodded, and he glanced across at his wife. She met his gaze, her eyes oddly opaque. "This is my wife, Laura."

Gibbs made his introductions again, while Polly studied Laura. Her face sagged a little, especially around the jowls, but she wasn't unattractive, just a little uncared for. There were a selection of books and magazines on the sofa and the coffee table in the centre of the rug in front of her. She had been engaged in reading a Jo Nesbo book, which she had casually tossed aside as Polly and Gibbs entered.

"Do you mind if we sit down, Tom?" Gibbs prompted, and Tom flushed slightly, then scurried around moving books and magazines so that everyone could find a place. He settled close to Laura and patted her knee. Polly watched the gesture; it was a familiar comforting touch.

"Laura, we'd like to ask you where you were on the evening

of 18th October. This month?" began Gibbs.

Laura stared back at the officers, no recognition in her eyes.

"Do you recall?" Gibbs asked.

"I'm sorry, DS Gibbs. My wife has been poorly recently." Tom fidgeted with his apron and placed his hand on Laura's knee again.

"The 18th was just last week."

There was silence in the room, until Tom said. "My wife had a stroke a few months ago. We almost lost her."

"I'm sorry to hear that. How are you doing now, Laura?" Gibbs asked, allowing the sympathy to ooze through his voice.

"I'm well," Laura hesitated. "Much better." Her voice was low, but there was no evidence of a drawl or other speech impediment resulting from her stroke.

"You're well enough to get out and about, aren't you?" Gibbs continued cheerfully. "Only the reason I ask is that we have CCTV footage of you in town yesterday."

Polly drew a plastic folder from the file she was carrying and slid it across the coffee table towards Tom and Laura. It plainly showed Laura from a variety of angles, making her way down Curzon Street. None of the pictures featured Heidi in them, they had been carefully cropped where needed.

Tom looked at it, his expression one of bemusement. "Did you go out yesterday, love?" he asked.

"I did, as it happens," said Laura. "I needed a few things, and I popped into the Heart shop to find some new books. I like to read," she added, gesturing at the teetering pile of second-hand books on the coffee table, as though this fact wasn't immediately obvious to all and sundry.

"So can you remember where you were last Tuesday evening?" Gibbs asked.

Laura shrugged non-commitally. "You'd have to be more specific," she said, and Polly noted the bite to her tone now.

Gibbs checked her out for a moment. "Let's say, between 6.30 and 8.30." That gave Laura time to reach Neville Gardens from town and return here after the murder.

"She was here with me," Tom interjected. "This is where

she is every evening." He turned to his wife. "Don't play games with the officers, Laura. They're busy people." He met Gibbs's eye. "She was here."

"And what were you doing? Do you recall?" Gibbs asked.

"We would have been watching TV, I imagine. The BBC News, The One Show, that's our usual routine. We have our dinner at six-ish and watch our programmes, and then sometimes we have a film on at eight." Tom twisted his hands in his apron. "It's what we've always done."

"Can anyone else vouch for you both being here?" asked Gibbs. He kept his tone pleasant, but he was beginning to feel frustrated with Tom Goodwin's interference.

"What? No. We didn't have guests. It was just us."

Gibbs nodded. Polly recorded what Tom had said in her notebook.

"Laura, do you know who Nicola Fallon is?" Gibbs asked.

Laura brushed her hair from her face as though she was annoyed by it. "She's the woman who was murdered on Durscombe Rise estate last week, wasn't she? It's been all over the papers, and on the local news. My husband just told you we watch the news."

"Had you ever come across her before?"

Laura didn't even think before she answered. "I shouldn't have thought so. Not unless I'd bumped into her in Waitrose or something, or she worked at the library. And I don't think she did. Whatever it is you want, I don't think I can help you." She looked away, her face haughty.

A sudden beeping from the kitchen broke through the tense atmosphere. Laura glared at Tom. The beeping went on and on. They all sat in silence and listened to it.

"What is that?" asked Polly eventually.

"Sorry. It's the oven," Tom said. "I've been baking."

"Would you like me to turn it off?" Polly asked, and Tom stood hurriedly. "No, no, its fine. I'll go. Give me one second," and he left the room. Polly followed him, then hovered by the door.

Gibbs watched her, then turned his attention back to Laura.

"Were there any long-lasting effects of the stroke, Laura?"

Laura's eyes swivelled Gibbs's way, her pupils huge, her look acid. "Let's hope not," she said.

Gibbs nodded and pursed his lips. He wasn't going to get much more out of her here. "It would be helpful if you could come down to the police station tomorrow so that we can take a statement from you. Is that something you could do?" Gibbs asked.

"Do I have a choice?" Laura directed this at Polly.

Polly shook her head. "Not really, no."

"Should I bring a lawyer?"

"Will you need one?" retorted Gibbs and stood to take his leave.

**

Tom ushered them to the front door. He was a man who appeared to have the weight of the world on his shoulders, and Polly almost felt sorry for him. "Your cake smells heavenly," she said, in an attempt to make him feel better.

"Raspberry muffins. We've had a glut of raspberries in the garden this year," Tom nodded. "I've got a freezer full."

"Lovely. You have a gorgeous house and garden. How long have you and Laura been married?"

"Coming up forty-one years. We're making plans for our wedding anniversary."

Polly smiled. "Marvellous. You must be incredibly relieved she's recovered from her stroke so well." Tom nodded again, but his eyes had clouded over. "Thank heavens it wasn't more serious."

"Oh it was serious all right," Tom replied. "She died. They were trying to resuscitate her at the hospital, but she was dead. They called her time of death and everything."

"In that case she's made a miraculous recovery!" Polly said, wondering how far to believe what Tom was telling her. Sometimes the people she interviewed liked to embellish their stories for dramatic effect.

"She has, she has," agreed Tom, his face lighting up. "It's hard to believe. It was only four months ago after all. May 22nd it was. Yes, I'll never forget that day. May 22nd."

CHAPTER EIGHT

"May 22nd?" Adam almost choked on his pint. "Are you sure?"

"That's what he said," Polly answered, moving out of the way as a burly bloke wearing muddy Wellington boots pushed past them. The Blue Bell Inn was busy with a function this evening, a young farmers' get-together or some such, so Adam hadn't been able to commandeer the small room at the side for Polly and himself to hide away in. Fortunately, the general hubbub covered their conversation, and they didn't have to worry too much about being obviously discrete. They were standing in the corridor that linked the front bar with the rear bar and the side rooms, hoping for a table to become vacant in their general vicinity. The drawback was they were in the way of anyone heading for the toilets.

"Why's the date so important?" asked Polly, raising her voice above some raucous laughter from the bar.

Adam narrowed his eyes. "What date was the Birmingham terror incident?"

"Er … yeah … was it the 22nd? I don't remember the specifics. For god's sake Adam, I've slept since then."

"Lucky you," said Adam. "I don't think I have." He pulled his mobile from his pocket and waited until it caught a signal. Damn Durscombe with its dodgy mobile network. "Google is my friend," he announced and started tapping into the search bar. Polly huddled close and gazed over his shoulder. "There we are," Adam said, showing her. He'd found the relevant Wikipedia entry. "May 22nd."

Polly rolled her eyes. "I don't get it. So what?"

Adam started to reply when another wave of noise rushed through from the front bar, and then a chorus of the song Delilah. Adam had no idea what had triggered the singing, but it was about as tuneful as any other drunken version of the

Tom Jones' song he'd heard in his lifetime.

Polly laughed, and Adam smiled ruefully. Polly took his arm, "Let's walk along the prom and round to The Black Swan?" she suggested. Adam nodded and followed Polly as she pushed her way through the rabble and out of the front entrance.

The silence, once the heavy wooden door had swung shut behind them, was almost total. It was a fresh evening, Autumn on its way, but the temperatures were still relatively mild for the time of year. The sea was quiet too. They crossed the cobbles, walked across the road, and climbed the low barrier that gave onto the prom.

Ahead of them, the old harbour was quiet. A few boats and yachts were moored, but there was little activity here this evening. A light shone in the old harbourmaster's cottage, but the tax and excise building was closed up and dark.

Leaving the harbour behind them, they walked west and gazed out at the beach—first the sand and the shingle, and then if you walked far enough towards the red cliffs at the very end of the beach, you could see the jagged rocks below and the buoys that marked danger areas and the remains of several unfortunate wrecks.

The moon shone into Lyme Bay and caught the tops of the waves. Polly sighed. "Isn't this romantic?" she said, and Adam snorted. Polly's peal of laughter startled several seagulls scavenging by the wall, and they rose into the air crying.

"So tell me," Polly demanded. "I'm guessing you don't think it's a coincidence that Heidi was injured in the Birmingham terrorist incident and that Laura had a stroke on that day too."

Adam shook his head with mock sadness, as though Polly was a poor pupil. "They weren't just injured on the 22nd of May, Polly. Both Heidi and Laura died on that day. And they were both lucky enough to be brought back."

Polly drew up and leant against the railing. Beyond the railing, below them, was a six-foot drop to the beach. She rummaged in her handbag, drawing out her cigarettes and lighter. "I guess that really is an interesting coincidence," she said and sparked up.

"What are the chances of it, I wonder?" asked Adam. "Realistically? That you have two women who died on the same day but were both resuscitated."

"Mmm." Polly took a lungful of nicotine and closed her eyes in happiness.

"One woman in Birmingham, one woman, I assume, in East Devon. Ostensibly they've never met. Until the moment that Heidi places them at a murder scene at the same time."

Polly exhaled. The smoke wafted out into the void beyond them, twisting like mist rolling across the moon. "We checked it out, Adam. Laura was at the Royal Devon and Exeter. She had suffered a mini stroke the previous day and was in for observations. The stroke she had was catastrophic. She shouldn't have survived. She was, according to both the records and Tom Goodwin's recollection, dead for over forty-five minutes."

"Are you certain?" Adam was astounded. "I'm no medical expert, but surely, if you've been dead for that amount of time, your brain would be mush?"

Polly nodded and smoked some more.

A couple ambled towards them, and Adam squinted at them as they closed in. "Evening," he said, and they returned the greeting, strolling on by. Adam dropped his voice. "Do you believe in an afterlife of some kind?"

"You mean like heaven? No not really. It would be nice if there was, I suppose."

Adam mulled things over. They stood together quietly, watching the waves. Polly listened to the soft sounds of the night and relished her cigarette. Adam sighed. "Let's say for the sake of argument, that there is an afterlife. If there is … how would we get there?"

"How do we arrive at the Pearly Gates? I don't know," Polly laughed. "When I was a kid I used to think you just floated in the air and then you arrived in the clouds. And there was God waiting to greet you."

"A white God with a big bushy beard and eyebrows by any chance?"

"You've got it." Polly flicked her ashes over the railing.

"Isn't it supposed to be St Peter at the Pearly Gates though?"

"Well, it shows you how much attention I paid, doesn't it? You know, there's a thing for dogs. Rainbow Bridge? The dogs wait at the bridge for their owners to join them and then they cross the bridge together, so that's how they enter. That sounds pretty good to me." Polly had recently lost a Whippet she had adored.

"It does. It would be nice to think of all the people we've loved and lost waiting for us when we … what … cross over? Pass over?"

"Isn't that just a sanitised way of saying 'died' though?" asked Polly. "Are you getting soft in your old age? You've seen plenty of dead people, even here in Durscombe. And that tractor accident you were at a few years ago? That was fairly horrific." Adam grimaced. "Loads of folk don't look peaceful, do they? They don't look like they've fallen asleep. They just look like they stopped existing. Do we go on anywhere else? I don't know. Perhaps it depends which religion we practice."

Adam hadn't thought of that. "Do different religions have different places to go after death then?"

"Did you even pay attention in your RE lessons?" Polly asked, and Adam shook his head. Polly giggled. "Yeah, same here actually. But I'm pretty sure you'll find that some religions believe in reincarnation and such like, and some don't."

"Have you heard the expression 'stepping through the veil' before? Or 'going beyond the veil'?"

Polly nodded. "Yeah. I have, come to think of it. Gloria, the spiritual healer in the arcade, she uses that to describe people dying."

"Oh I vaguely know Gloria."

"Maybe that's like a Wiccan thing. I think she's Wiccan. I have a chat with her when I'm patrolling round there occasionally, and she says some weird shit."

"Wiccan? Like witchcraft."

"Yeah. Maybe." Polly flicked the end of her cigarette onto the beach below. "Isn't it? Oh I don't know. Why are you asking me? Go and ask Gloria. I'm sure she'd be glad of the business. Or Google it. Google is your friend after all."

"All right snarky knickers."

"I'm dying of thirst here, sunshine. Google may be your friend, but I won't be if we don't get another beer in soon!"

"I hear you!" said Adam, taking her arm and leading her across the road, to drop back into town.

CHAPTER NINE

It had been a slow day, and therefore news of a missing person piqued Adam's interest straight away.

Returning to the Durscombe police station after a meeting with the principal of the local college about anti-social behaviour on the nearby rugby fields, the call came over the radio just as he was parking up. The name sounded familiar— Tom Goodwin at 126 Coleridge Way had rung through to report his wife missing. Polly had let on that a Laura Goodwin was a person of interest in relation to Nicola's murder when he'd spoken to her earlier. The police station was located merely minutes away from Tom's address, so Adam cheekily showed himself as attending and whisked around the side streets.

Adam had never met Tom Goodwin before, but as he reached his destination, he could only assume that the gentleman pacing around the front lawn, with the makings of a black eye, was the caller. The man's left eye was swollen, closed to a slit, the skin puffy and red.

Adam jumped out of his car. He was the first to arrive. "Tom Goodwin? DS Adam Chapple. I believe you called us about a missing person?"

"Yes." Tom rubbed his hands through his hair and glanced both ways, searching fruitlessly.

Adam looked around too. Nothing of any interest to see out here. He needed to hear the full story, and Tom appeared distracted outside. "Shall we go indoors, sir? You can tell me everything in there." Adam shepherded a reluctant Tom through the open front door and into the kitchen, where they were greeted by a number of items of broken crockery littering the tiled floor. It had been strewn in all directions, flung with some force. Tom followed Adam's gaze forlornly.

"You reported a missing person?"

"Yes. My wife. Laura."

"Laura Goodwin," Adam noted. Bingo. All roads seemed to lead to Rome at the moment.

Adam checked out Tom's black eye. "And have you had an argument with Laura, Tom?" he asked with concern. Tom's eyes moistened, and he made a choking sound. Adam gently led Tom to the kitchen table and sat him down. "Is Laura hurt?" he asked softly.

Tom shook his head, unable to meet Adam's gaze. "No, no. I would never hurt Laura. I've never touched a hair on her head. She did this to me." He gestured at his eye.

"Was that a punch? Or did she hit you with something?" There was the sound of another car pulling up outside. Tom looked alarmed and started to get to his feet, but Adam held his hand out. He peered out of the window. A patrol car.

"It was a punch. A proper punch," Tom was saying, his voice shaking with emotion. "She lashed out at me."

"Why did she do that? Were you arguing?" Adam asked again.

"Laura was supposed to attend the police station this morning for an interview but she wouldn't go. I was trying to make her see sense, that she had to go, and it would look bad if she didn't, and she went ballistic. Started throwing things around. The tea pot, mugs, anything she could get her hands on."

"What was the interview was in relation to?"

"The murder of the woman in Neville Gardens last week. One of your colleagues asked us to come down."

"Hello?" came a familiar voice from the open front door. "Mr Goodwin?"

"In here," called Adam, and Polly appeared. She nodded at Adam and then noticed Tom's injury. She frowned.

"Good afternoon, Mr Goodwin."

"Polly, Tom's wife Laura was supposed to have an interview at the station this morning, but she didn't make the appointment and she has left home after assaulting Tom here. Can we confirm her as a person of interest right away?" Polly nodded, understanding implicitly Adam's concern about Laura's violent inclinations, and got to work on her radio.

"What time did she leave home?" Adam asked.

"An hour or so ago. Jeremy Vine's programme had just started. On Radio Two. Just after twelve I guess."

"I see," said Adam. "I assumed she'd just left, given that you were outside looking for her."

"I wasn't looking for her, officer. I was making sure she wasn't going to sneak back in and finish me off."

The level of vitriol in Tom's voice surprised Adam. There was real fear on the man's face too. Polly, listening to the exchange, looked perturbed.

"Tom? Yesterday you told me how happy you and Laura were, and how relieved you were about her recovery from her stroke—" Polly said.

"I know what I told you yesterday, but what else could I say?" asked Tom desperately. "She's not been the same woman since the stroke. She's not the Laura I love. She's changed completely. She used to be so sweet and gentle. You know we were never able to have children, so she used to devote her time to me and our cats. But both of our cats have run off since she came home from the hospital, and I don't blame them. She's overtly hostile to everyone. She's selfish and cruel and violent, and I really can't bear it anymore!"

Polly stepped forward to soothe him. "It sounds like you've been through a great deal over the past few months, Tom. Yesterday you told DI Gibbs and myself that Laura was with you the night of the murders. Was that the truth?"

Tom shook his head and looked at Polly beseechingly. "She's become so weird. She either holes herself up in our spare room playing endless games of solitaire on the laptop, or she goes out and walks the streets for hours. I never know where she is or what she's doing. She comes home late at night and she sits watching the TV for hours. She refuses to come to bed. Not to our bed, anyway."

"Tom. Was Laura with you on the night of the 18th of October?" repeated Polly.

Tom shook his head categorically. "No, no, she wasn't." He held his hands palm up to Polly, beseeching her. "Please—by all means find her and keep her out of harm's way. But dear god, I don't know that I want you to let her come back here again. She's not my wife anymore. She hasn't been since the day of her stroke. She isn't the woman I loved. It's like the real Laura died and someone else came back in her place."

He lay his head down on the kitchen table and his tears flowed thick and fast. "And I miss her. I miss her so much," he sobbed.

CHAPTER TEN

The Victoria Gardens Cemetery, built during the mid-1860s on the site of the old Victoria Gardens in order to catch the overspill from St Michael's Church in Durscombe, was a sprawling homage to the celebration of death. In the oldest part of the cemetery, tombstones of all shapes and sizes, once neatly laid out with typical Victorian precision, had partially sunk into the sandy earth. They huddled together under the shelter of trees, or nestled higgledy-piggledy and forgotten among tangled undergrowth. Moss and lichen clung to stone surfaces, obliterating names, dates, and histories.

Heidi limped around the newer area of the cemetery, with half a mind to search for her aunt's gravestone. Here, well away from the cliffs, the grass was neatly manicured, and bunches of flowers and wreathes, many of them bright and fresh, paid colourful respect to those more recently departed.

As a teenager, Heidi's first love had been photography, and she was lured to the more sombre and antiquated part of the gardens, with its elaborate tombs and mausoleums. She hadn't expected to find such a wonderful treasure trove of Victoriana here in East Devon, but here it was, and sadly Heidi didn't have a decent camera on her.

She took a few shots here and there with her mobile, determined to upload them to her laptop once she returned home later. She didn't imagine the images would require much fiddling to achieve atmosphere and mystery.

The morning started out sunny and mild, but by lunchtime the weather had changed. A sea mist rolled in and the drizzle became incessant. Now the trees, many still clinging onto their leaves, were heavy with moisture. This far south, the summer was lingering, loath to let go completely. While in Birmingham, Heidi imagined winter would have already extended its death grip.

She snapped away, taking shots of spiders' webs glistening with tiny beads of water among the bushes and brambles, looking for all the world like nature's most spectacular diamonds. Heidi crouched, her leg painful, trying to create interesting angles.

A soft sound behind her made her jump up, startled. She hadn't seen a soul since arriving at the cemetery, not even a groundskeeper, even though she'd been here for an hour at least. With difficulty, she righted herself and turned about. A young woman stood approximately six metres away, regarding her with open curiosity.

A little younger than Heidi, the other woman appeared to be mid-twenties at most. She wore her straight hair loose, and it was so black, that Heidi reasoned it could only have been dyed that colour. This contrasted starkly with her pale face, painted white for maximum ghostly effect. She was dressed head to toe in black too: a long black maxi dress, with a lace ruffle at the hem, and a three quarter length black coat in velveteen. Tough lace-up boots with thick soles and a two-inch heel finished off her wardrobe. Her eye make-up was smoky and exquisitely finished, and even her nails were painted black. She was adorned with silver jewellery, around her neck and wrists, on her fingers, and plenty in her ears and nose.

"I'm sorry," the young woman said, her voice light and musical. "I didn't mean to startle you."

Heidi laughed in a self-deprecating way. "My fault. I was miles away."

The two women stared at each other. Heidi couldn't help herself, she was quite taken with the woman's appearance. While she wasn't garbed in Victorian dress, she could almost pass as an apparition flitting among the tottering monuments. Heidi itched to take a photo of her, but she wasn't forward enough to ask.

"Were you looking for someone in particular?" the younger woman asked.

Heidi puzzled over the question. The way the younger woman phrased it made it sound as though Heidi would find a range of people here, perhaps both dead and alive. She shook her head.

"I mean, were you looking for me?"

This was even more confusing. "No, I wasn't really looking for anyone. I mean … well my aunt is buried out in the newer part of the gardens, but I was just pottering around back here, taking some photos."

"Oh, I see." The younger woman seemed oddly disappointed. "That's funny. You know I was told I'd be receiving a visitor today, a stranger, but if it isn't you, it must be someone else." Heidi wondered who had told her that and considered asking, but the conversation was getting weirder by the second. "It's just that I've never seen you in the cemetery before. Do you live locally?"

How much time did this odd woman spend in the cemetery, Heidi wondered. "I'm staying in Durscombe for a little while," she volunteered, "so I suppose you could say that I temporarily live locally, yes."

"While you get better? You've been in an accident, right?"

Was it that obvious? Heidi guessed so. She pulled at her beanie self-consciously. "In a manner of speaking," she said unwilling to discuss the Bullring incident.

"That's why I thought it was you." The young woman sniffed. "Curious." She jumped down from the monument she was standing on. "I'm Cassia Veysie," she announced, striding towards Heidi, her hair and coat flowing. "That large memorial behind you belongs to my family. My grandmothers are interred there. Were you taking a photo of it?"

Heidi regarded the impressive monument with its ornate stone pillars. It was a family tomb, clean in comparison to the others around, free of moss, with the ground around it swept free of leaves.

"No, I was trying to catch a photo of the spider web here, on this bush. Do you see?" Heidi pointed it out, and Cassia came closer to have a look.

"Oh yes! That's a good one. You should see the ones we have first thing in the morning when the sun rises. They can be huge! Extremely impressive, but oddly eerie at times."

"Do you hang out here a lot?" asked Heidi.

"Hang out? You could say that. I live here," Cassia paused for effect, then laughed. "I'm surprised you haven't heard about me. The weird woman who lives in the cemetery."

"You live here?" asked Heidi. Heidi couldn't see a house, and nothing that would pass as a home of any kind. Who was allowed to live in a cemetery anyway?

"Pretty much."

"In the cemetery?"

"I could show you? Do you fancy a cup of tea and a warm up? You look frozen."

Heidi studied Cassia. Since the terrorist attack she had become increasingly cautious and reticent to mix, much happier fading into the background. She was suspicious of others in a way she never had been previously, now naturally wary, but Cassia was gregarious in the extreme, open and warm. What motives did Cassia have for the invitation?

"Oh, that's kind, but I'm not ..."

"I promise I'm not a wolf in sheep's clothing," Cassia said, her face serious. "I just think you'll be interested in my place, and that you are in fact supposed to be my visitor today."

Heidi glanced around. The cemetery seemed devoid of all other life forms. Cassia appeared to be in earnest. Since the day Heidi had first awoken from her coma, she had regularly asked herself, what is life if not for living? She had promised herself that once she had worked through all the pain and the trauma of that awful day in May, once her recovery was complete, she would live life with renewed vigour and hope. But every day brought new challenges. However, Cassia had planted herself here, shining with dynamism and charisma, and Heidi felt reinvigorated by her warmth. Perhaps she should take a risk and have a little adventure.

Heidi took a deep breath. "All right," she said, and Cassia beamed.

"Great! This way!" Cassia skipped across to her family memorial and slipped a key into the lock of the iron gate between the front pillars. Before Heidi could express her surprise, Cassia vanished inside. At a guess, the whole building was about eighteen feet wide and twice as deep, perhaps ten feet high. Heidi hoped to goodness that Cassia didn't sleep in a coffin. That would be more adventure than she could handle.

Feeling increasingly reluctant to pursue this, Heidi stepped gingerly forwards, climbed the two steps into the tomb, and passed through the gate.

"Could you close it as you come through, please?" called Cassia, so Heidi pushed the gate closed and secured it without locking it. She trusted she wouldn't need to make a hasty getaway, but she wanted to be prepared.

Heidi followed Cassia farther inside, passing a dozen or so coffins arranged on long shelves, some of them elaborate, old, musty, some newer. One in pine, the brass still shining. Heidi turned her eyes away, not wanting to think about what the coffins contained.

Cassia unlocked another door at the end of the tomb. A light clicked on, illuminating a steep set of stairs. Heidi's stomach twisted. There was some sort of basement? What the hell did it contain? She shouldn't be doing this. Cassia disappeared down the steps, trotting easily. Heidi followed more slowly, holding on to the wall to help with her balance, her left leg tweaking with each step.

"Watch your head," called Cassia, and Heidi ducked at the last moment.

The stairs opened into the strangest room Heidi had ever set foot in. It was exactly how she imagined a Victorian parlour might have been decorated, with gas lamps and red velvet drapes, heavy oak furniture and clutter everywhere. A closer look at all the oddities dotted around revealed dozens of bottles containing a variety of coloured liquids or dried ingredients, all hand labelled and neatly lined up on dressers and wooden bookcases. There were stuffed birds displayed in glass cabinets, and small mammals—including a red squirrel with a particularly bushy tail—in a domed case, and a pair of field mice perched on a log, eyes glittering brightly. The mammals stared at Heidi as she turned in a slow arc, surveying her surroundings.

Slate tiles had been laid on the floor, with numerous rugs thrown here and there for relief against the cold. A number of small circular recessed portholes at the far end of the room, allowed the dim light access into an otherwise dark room. There were several doors off the main room, perhaps to a bedroom and kitchen area. The room smelled pleasant—of wood smoke and something dusky and sweet, lavender or dried violets perhaps.

Cassia attended to a fire built into the rear wall between the portholes. It hissed and spat angrily at her, and she hissed back at it cheerfully, until it settled and burned a little more good-naturedly. "Take a seat anywhere. I'll just put the kettle on," Cassia sang, and Heidi moved farther into the room to a large sofa, covered with throws. She sank gratefully into its depths, glad of the warmth of the fire and relieved that Cassia actually did live here, as odd as she was, and hadn't been luring her to certain death after all.

"How did you get permission to live here? In the cemetery?" asked Heidi when they were both settled and sipping at mugs of steaming, sweet tea.

"Technically, this part of the dwelling is not actually in the cemetery. The gardens back onto private land that was once owned by my great, great, great, great grandmother Amelia Fliss. Her daughter, my great, great, great, grandmother Flora, had the memorial built as soon as the cemetery opened, and Amelia's coffin was disinterred and moved here from St Michael's Church in town. The gardens were a park prior to that, but according to popular legend there were some nasty goings on in Durscombe during the 1860s and they needed more land for all the bodies they had to inter."

"Nice," said Heidi.

"Durscombe does have a rather dark past." Cassia grinned mischievously from behind her mug. "Flora wanted to be able to visit her mother whenever she chose, so when she inherited the Fliss house, she designed the crypt so that it could be accessed directly from her grounds. This dwelling has been added to and altered over the years. It has proper plumbing, two bedrooms, and all sorts of mod cons now."

"Does your family still own the land?"

"No sadly, just this. The house and grounds had to be sold off a long time ago. I'm the last one left. The last of the line. My mother died a few years ago."

"I'm sorry," Heidi said softly. Beneath Cassia's cheery, upbeat exterior, there was a certain sadness.

"You've died too, haven't you?" Cassia asked out of the blue, and her eyes were at once knowing and sympathetic.

Heidi frowned, instantly defensive. "How could you possibly know that? Who have you spoken to?" Her first thought was of Adam Chapple. How dare he?

Cassia shook her head. "It's not that I've spoken to anyone, just that I can see it."

"You can see what?" Heidi shifted uncomfortably.

"That you died. There's a shadow about you. One that tells me your life was interrupted."

"Oh? Like an aura you mean?" Heidi had heard of people reading auras before. Perhaps there was something to it.

"Kind of. I have a number of skills. Unusual gifts," Cassia said gravely. "I come from a long line of witches." She fixed Heidi with her unwavering gaze, waiting for a reaction. Heidi felt discomfited. "That unnerves you, doesn't it?"

"I suppose it does, a little."

"You don't believe in witches?"

Heidi shook her head, frowning. "No, of course not. Witches are for children, aren't they?" But even as she said this, she understood it as a blatant lie. Of all people, Heidi knew that of course there was every possibility the supernatural existed. She remembered the veiled woman and shuddered. And then there were the birds that appeared and disappeared from nowhere.

Cassia observed Heidi carefully, the corners of her mouth turned down a little.

Heidi avoided Cassia's gaze. She looked at the fire, rubbing her hands together as though they needed warming through. Her skin was rough and dry, the movement sounded loud in the ensuing silence. Finally, she shook her head. "Sorry, that was unnecessarily dismissive of me. I don't know anything about witches and the paranormal, or ghosts, or what have you. But you're right, I did die. And when I died, I saw something."

"Tell me about it," said Cassia happily, relaxing deeply into her seat.

***

Cassia reached over and patted Heidi's knee, her black fingernails shining in the firelight, as Heidi slumped against the sofa, exhausted by her tale. "You've been through a lot these last few months. On top of your injuries. This must have taken a great deal out of you."

"You're not wrong," Heidi said. "And I don't know for certain whether the police believe me when I tell them about following this woman to the scene of the murder or not, you know? I mean, I do trust in the process. They have to find me innocent—because I am—but it still scares me that they might jump to conclusions and get it wrong."

Cassia nodded. "I guess you're right. You do have to believe they will uncover the truth." She regarded Heidi seriously. "What amazes me the most though, is that you've been to the other side. I'm seriously impressed."

"Don't be. The whole thing has been a nightmare."

"Because of this woman in the veil? Who is she? Do you know? Do you recognise her?"

Heidi shook her head but wondered why nobody had asked her that before. "I don't think so. I haven't really seen her face, but no, she doesn't remind me of anyone I know. Or have known. It's difficult to tell."

"Do you have anyone spirit-side?"

"My mother passed, seventeen years ago this Christmas. She had a brain .tumour. All of my grandparents have died, apart from my dad's dad, my grandpa. He's ninety-two years old and still going strong. Oh, there was my Durscombe aunt, my dad's older sister. She passed away two years ago. But this veiled woman? It's not any of them."

"Do you know what the veiled woman wants?" Cassia pressed, and Heidi shook her head glumly.

"No. You know, it all happened while I was out of it, and I've never been sure what was real and what was a dream. My interpretation of what happened was that the person who came out of the door was being chased by the woman in the veil, but how can I be sure?"

"The person that came out from the spirit world ahead of the woman in the veil? What did you see of them?"

Heidi wrinkled her brow, "Do you know, I've never really thought about that, or them." She thought back, dug through the memories. "I don't recall them having a solid physical shape, not the way everybody else did. It was a blur. A fast moving shadow. I can see that I had a sense that this shadow was a person, and so I've always assumed it was, but maybe it wasn't."

"All right. So, possibly, the woman in the veil chased this person, or shadow, out of the other side. And the other side, we could assume is the Summerlands or whatever we want to know it as. Perhaps the chaser is hunting the shadow?"

Heidi grimaced. "Or I made the whole thing up as the result of a bang on the head." She shuffled forwards on the sofa with some difficulty because it was like sitting in a squidgy bucket of foam. She needed to get going before she became too comfortable. The light had changed outside, and Heidi didn't fancy walking home in another downpour.

Cassia smiled and rose gracefully. She held out her hand so that Heidi could pull herself up. "Some might suggest you imagined it, but I think it's true. You know, we could try to find out? If you like? I can commune with the spirit world."

Heidi looked aghast. "I'm really not sure that's a good idea. I don't like the idea of messing with something that I don't properly understand." She half expected Cassia to take umbrage at this, but the younger woman only nodded.

"No, of course. I completely understand." She handed

Heidi her jacket and handbag and led her to the staircase.

"Thank you for the tea," Heidi said politely. "It has been lovely to meet you and chat."

"My pleasure. You're welcome to visit anytime. You know where I am now." Cassia stepped back to allow her to climb up to the exit. "And Heidi, if you change your mind and want to find out more about the woman in the veil, I'll be happy to help."

"Thank you," Heidi answered and waved as she reached the top. She closed the door and hurried to the iron gate. The fresh air of the cemetery carried the scent of damp earth and crushed leaves. Heidi inhaled deeply, relieved she hadn't been trapped underground and that Cassia hadn't transformed into a vampire with a bloodlust. She shuffled through the leaves and headed for the bus stop at the cemetery exit, feeling exhausted. At the ornate gates, she paused and turned to look back the way she had come. The glowering sky was a fitting backdrop to the eerie and antiquated cemetery.

She imagined Cassia in her little burrow house, hissing at the fire and chatting to the stuffed animals. What a bizarre place to live, and what a peculiar woman.

CHAPTER ELEVEN

Concentrating on the rhythmic slapping of his feet on the tarmac brought Adam relief from the chaos of his thoughts. This was the reason he ran. He loved the solitude of running along the lanes around Durscombe, preferably late evening or early morning. He pounded the miles away. Time alone, focusing only on his breathing and the crest of the next rise. This was his escape, and to that end he ran as often possible, covering many miles in the countryside around Durscombe every week.

Traffic could be an issue, especially during the summer, but the closest he had ever come to injury was when a cyclist had sped down a hill and almost careered into him round a blind bend. The cyclist had come away worse, with an impressive road rash and a bike that had to be written off. So at the end of the day, karma had sided with Adam.

Karma.

The thought reminded him, he wanted to go into town and chat with Gloria in the arcade. He wasn't sure if he would find much out, but he believed in approaching situations from every possible angle, and Gloria could potentially shed light on Heidi's vision as well as the veiled woman.

Slowing to a jog, he entered the close where he lived—with his small semi-detached house in need of an external lick of paint and his battered black Audi on the drive.

Adam showered and changed and took the time to grab some breakfast. Durscombe was great if you wanted an over-priced pasty or a bag of chips, but decent bacon butties were hard to come by.

Durscombe's Edwardian arcade was a rare gem of original architecture. While the original ironwork signs and gates, the stained glass windows, and the cobbles had been replaced after the Second World War with ghastly alternatives, during the boom years of the mid-90s the arcade had been restored to its former glory. Unfortunately, the recession had enough bite in the southwest to render many small businesses unviable, and several of the once popular units now remained empty, awaiting the next entrepreneur willing to take a risk, while shoppers headed out of town to retail parks or simply shopped online.

Gloria was seemingly oblivious to economic trends. Her business had occupied the same spot for nearly thirty years, and she was somewhat of a local celebrity. Everyone in Durscombe knew who Gloria was. Now that Adam came to think of it, he had some vague knowledge of her from several years ago, but otherwise their paths had never crossed in any meaningful way. Adam had never seen fit to trouble Gloria for either professional or personal reasons. He understood some police forces weren't averse to using psychics in their investigations, but in his case, the need had never arisen.

An old fashioned brass bell tinkled merrily as Adam entered the clothes side of the shop, to be assaulted by a heady wave of incense. He wondered how it was possible to spend the day here working alongside this constant barrage of fragrance. He'd be liable to sneeze his brain through his nasal cavity. One half of the retail unit was dedicated to clothes shipped in from Thailand and jewellery from Bali, and the other half was where Gloria plied her personal trade: fortune telling.

A young man of about Dan's age, dressed in a Black Sabbath T-shirt, was sitting on a stool behind the counter. He sported an impressive pair of black earplugs, stretching his lobes beyond the norm, and wore mascara with sparkly green eye shadow. He glanced up as Adam entered though and smiled politely enough. As Adam manoeuvred around the cramped shop to the counter, skewering himself several times on hangers, he could see that the lad was reading a textbook and making notes on an A4 pad. A student then.

"How are you doing?" he asked Adam in a surprisingly deep voice.

"I'm great, thanks. I'm looking for Gloria. Is she around?"

"She's always around. Do you have an appointment?" The young man cast a cursory glance at a thick well-thumbed A4 diary lying open on the counter next to the till. The page appeared to be blank for most of the day until 3 p.m.

"No, I don't," admitted Adam, wondering whether he should pull out his warrant card and announce himself formally.

"That's not a problem. She likes walk-ins. One sec." The young man hopped off his stool and headed for the rear left corner of the shop, pulled open the door there, and called up a flight of stairs.

"Mum? Mum! DC Chapple is here to see you." Adam wrinkled his brow in mock annoyance and the young man laughed good-naturedly. "I was at school with Dan. Of course I recognise you."

"You're …?" Adam struggled to remember his face, let alone his name.

"Craig. Dan and I weren't bosom buddies or anything but we were in the same class at primary school, and then he was in a few of my classes at the high school. We used to tease him about having a copper for a father." Adam nodded his understanding. "Not bullying or anything," Craig added hastily. "I mean, why would I? When you've Gloria for a mum, you don't have a leg to stand on where bullying is concerned."

Adam laughed. "It's DS now by the way."

"Oh right. Like Detective Sergeant? Congratulations on the promotion. Well-deserved I'm sure. You got me out of a tight spot a few years back. I owe you one."

Now Adam remembered. Craig had been hanging out with a group of teenagers caught with drugs on the local estate. He couldn't have been more than twelve and had been way out of his depth. The teenagers belonged to a particular nasty local family. As far as Adam was aware, both of the older lads had been in and out of young offenders' institutions for the past few years, and the eldest was doing a stretch up country. Craig had been polite and contrite, fearful of what his mother would say. Adam had quietly seen the complaint dropped and taken the boy home.

He smiled. "Of course. I'd forgotten. Hope you're staying out of trouble."

"Always. What's Dan up to now?"

The question caught Adam unawares, although it shouldn't have done. How to answer? For Adam, honesty was always the best policy. "To be honest Craig, I'm not exactly sure where he is."

"Really?"

"He took off at the end of his first year of Uni and no-one has seen him since."

"You mean like he's travelling? That's what I'm going to do when I finish my course. I'm studying botany. I intend to backpack somewhere like Asia." Craig frowned. Something in Adam's face told him all was not well. "Are you worried?"

"I know he wanted to spend time in Europe, so … I hope he's having adventures somewhere, but he never told me his plans before he left. Yeah, I'm his dad. Of course I'm worried."

Craig's face fell in sympathy. "Shit man. That's not good. Listen, if I hear anything I'll let you know, okay? I'll ask around. Some of his old friends may hear from him and I'm in touch with most people from school."

"I'd be grateful," Adam said, although he knew Dan had few friends, and most of those had already spoken to Adam. He handed his card to Craig. "Call me. About anything, any time."

At that moment Gloria clomped down the stairs and poked her head around the door. She was a woman in her mid-fifties and had long curly hair, greying at the temples but otherwise hennaed and tied up with a colourful scarf. She wasn't wearing make-up, but her face looked fresh. She beamed at Adam as though he was an old friend, the laughter lines deep around her eyes.

"DS Chapple," Craig told his mum and winked at Adam.

"How lovely," trilled Gloria, then pouted. "Or is this official business and I should be worried?"

"No, not at all! Let's call it an information gathering exercise, shall we? And it's Adam by the way."

Gloria's smile widened. "Excellent. Well come on through to my parlour," and she led him to the other half of the shop, "said the spider to the fly!" She opened the door and ushered him in.

The room had been painted a deep indigo blue, with numerous star charts stuck to one wall. Glow stars decorated the ceiling, and odd looking trinkets were displayed on simple shelves. A heavy curtain fell into place once the door was closed. There was a deep plush carpet underfoot and thick net curtains at the window that looked out into the almost deserted arcade. A round table in the centre of the room had been set with a purple cloth on which a large crystal ball took pride of place. Adam peered into it but couldn't see anything.

"Take a seat," Gloria told Adam, then flicked on a few lamps to take the edge off the shadows in the room. As Adam's eyes adjusted to the light, Gloria let a blind down and blocked the arcade entirely from view. When she turned back to him, her face was serious.

"How can I help, Adam?"

"I don't know whether you can really. I may be on a hiding to nothing. Let's say I'm 'asking for a friend', okay? This friend of mine claims to have had an afterlife experience." Adam fought for a way to articulate his dilemma. He wasn't even sure what he wanted to know. He shrugged helplessly. "And I ... I don't know what to think."

"You want to know whether it's possible there is an afterlife?" asked Gloria.

"I do, yes." That made it easy.

"In my line of business I'm hardly in a position to say that isn't the case, am I?" Gloria sat back in her chair and stared at Adam thoughtfully. "I have people through these doors all the time who want to talk to the deceased or ask me for spiritual guidance. I can do a little of that."

"You can? You speak to the dead?" Adam asked, an idea slowly forming in his mind, but Gloria shook her head.

"No, not me. I read palms, the crystal ball, the stars. I tell fortunes. I'm no psychic. I could send you to a lady I know in Torquay, but to be honest, the only people she talks to are her imaginary friends."

"So, it's not possible to talk to the dead?" Adam acknowledged his own disappointment. He thought of Heidi, of all she had been through.

"I'm not saying that. Not at all. But, and it's a big but, the dead are choosy about whom they speak to. It's not easy to cross between the realms. We, here, bound to the Earth, can't do it on a whim, and most spirits, those on the next plane, they can't do it either. Let's say for the sake of argument that your friend wanted to talk to her mother, she could use a medium and try and contact her, but if her mother has safely crossed and is happy, then she might not be available for a cosy chat. That's the way it is."

"What is the barrier that prevents that happening?" asked Adam. "Why can't we simply talk to those who have passed?" Gloria shrugged, so he tried again. "Have you heard of the expression, 'beyond the veil'?"

"Yes, it's used in certain spiritual circles—mysticism, paganism, Wiccan and the like—by some, not all, followers of those creeds. We all have our own beliefs after all. I have some friends who firmly believe that we are immortal souls on Earth but we are all on an evolutionary path to wholeness that occurs after death." Adam looked puzzled, so Gloria explained, "Our souls are born into this physical plane, and over time we develop consciousness about who we are and what our purpose is. We are all training to be divine beings here on this Earth, and then when we cross over, we go beyond the veil as the divine. There are people who believe we can learn to exist in multiple dimensions simultaneously however."

"On Earth and in the afterlife?"

"Apparently so. But I have never seen any evidence to prove that happens."

"So, going beyond the veil?"

"Would mean crossing over onto the spiritual plane.

Becoming spirit. Going beyond the veil means entering a new existence, one that we can have no knowledge of while we are bound to our physical selves."

"Is it possible to die and see the plane without crossing over?" Adam asked.

"And then come back?" Gloria smiled. "I'd say certainly. Surely you have the proof you need? Isn't this what happened to your friend? Are you choosing not to believe him or her?"

"Her." Adam grimaced. "It's hard to believe."

"It's hard to believe if you have no experience or prior knowledge of the spirit world. I think if you're open to the idea that the spiritual plane exists then you would be happy to acknowledge your friend's experience and either celebrate the fact that she came back with this higher knowledge, or commiserate that she didn't complete her journey and go beyond."

Adam considered Gloria with interest. He had often dismissed her as a local fruitcake, but she was passionate and intelligent, and obviously well-read in certain matters.

"And the dead can't come back?" he asked.

"Mostly they can't, but I'm guessing you wouldn't ask that question unless you thought someone had or could. If you have evidence that someone has, then that's the answer to your own question."

Adam chuckled at Gloria's response, but she looked solemn.

"Listen," she said, "I'm not sure what has happened to your friend, or whether you're on police business, but if you're serious about finding out more, I would cautiously suggest you speak to Cassia Veysie."

"Why cautiously?"

"Because when I said I don't know any genuine psychics, that was true. But what Cassia is … is something different entirely. I'm not sure even she knows the extent of her own gifts."

"Her name is Cassia Veysie?"

"Yes, she's descended from a long line of Durscombe

witches." Gloria read doubt on Adam's face and correctly interpreted what she saw there. "Seriously, she's the real deal."

"How can I get hold of her? Where does she live?" Adam pulled out his pocketbook.

"It won't be difficult. You'll find her in the cemetery."

CHAPTER TWELVE

Another murky morning in Durscombe and Heidi found that the subdued light from outside, and relentless drizzle from the slate sky, demotivated her to the point that she had almost decided to remain curled up in bed reading a book rather than step outside for what her physiotherapist would have laughingly described as her morning constitutional.

Her conscience however got the better of her, and eventually at just after eleven she pulled on her beanie hat and pink waterproof and stepped outside to brave the elements. The wind quickly blew the cobwebs away, but the temperature was mild enough. She stood on the top step of the house and breathed in the soft air with its slight salty tang and decided she'd made the right decision by heading out.

She crossed the road in front of her house and squeezed between the parked cars to access the entrance of the park, intending to walk along the river until she reached the town, but her progress was halted almost immediately. A short, round man wearing a flat cap to protect his head against the rain and a navy blue mackintosh that almost drowned him, leant against the gate blocking her way. Heidi smiled at him politely, assuming he would open it to let her through.

"Are you Ms Huddlestone?" the man asked rather abruptly, and Heidi stopped in her tracks, fearful of what he wanted from her. Too old to be a policeman, she figured he might be a journalist.

The man recognised the look of fear on her face and voluntarily took a few steps back. "I'm so sorry," he said. "I didn't mean to startle you, or intrude in any way." He took off his cap as though by baring his face and head completely he was opening his soul for scrutiny. "My name is Tom Goodwin. I'm Laura Goodwin's husband."

By now Heidi's alarm was increasing, and she retreated

another few steps towards the safety of her house.

"Please," Tom begged. "I just want to talk to you."

"I have nothing to say to you, Mr Goodwin," Heidi responded. "The police told me not to talk to anyone about the case."

"Has anybody told you that my wife has gone missing, Ms Huddlestone? Have they suggested that your life might be in danger?"

Heidi observed the look of fear on Tom's face and remained where she was in the middle of the road, warily watching him, the drizzle falling down on them both.

"Where is she?" Heidi asked reluctantly.

"I don't know," Tom responded, and now his voice was softer, full of pain. "Believe me, if I did, I would turn her in to the police."

"You believe your wife is guilty then?" asked Heidi, incredulous. So far nobody had intimated she could be innocent. It had reached the stage where she assumed she would always be guilty of the murder by association, for merely finding herself in the wrong place at the wrong time.

"I—" Tom glanced around. A woman pushing a buggy was heading towards them. Quickly, Heidi moved through the open gate. She could see Tom wanted to talk to her, but she didn't want to invite him into her house.

He followed as she limped her way down the path. When they were out of earshot of the woman with the buggy, he started talking again, keeping his voice low.

"I told the police sergeant."

"Which one?" asked Heidi. "Adam, the red-headed one?"

"Yes, Adam Chapple. I told him that I felt my wife hadn't been the same since her stroke."

"She was young to have a stroke," Heidi sympathised.

"Fifty-nine. It was massive. It should have finished her off. In fact, it did really. She died while she was being monitored in the hospital, but they ... she ... she wasn't dead."

Heidi felt a tingle begin in the middle of her spine. "You say she died? When was this?"

"22nd May, this year."

Heidi's breath caught in her throat, and she stopped walking.

"Are you all right?" asked Tom with concern.

"What time?" Heidi stammered. "Do you know what time she died?"

"Kind of. I was there with her, and I wasn't really looking at the clock. She was dead just after twenty to nine in the morning, and the doctors were working on resuscitating her for some time after that. The official time of death was 9.18 a.m., but she was gone before then."

Heidi leant against the nearest tree, the moss on the bark soft beneath her hand. She doubled over, struggling to catch her breath as water dripped from the branches above, splashing against her neck.

"Ms Huddleston, I'm sorry. I seem to have caused you more distress and that really wasn't my intention."

Heidi straightened up and shook her head.

"The strangest things have been happening to me, Mr Goodwin, and on several occasions I've figured I must be going insane. And maybe I am. But knowing your wife died, bizarrely, I'm sorry to say, it makes me feel so much better." And with that Heidi burst into tears.

Tom looked on in woeful silence, unsure what to say. As Heidi pulled herself together, she realised that she and Tom were two of a kind, lost in a mystery not of their making.

"Sorry," Heidi said, her turn to apologise. "I feel quite emotional. It's almost a relief to me that you've told me about Laura. Walk with me into town? I could do with a strong coffee now? Would you mind? I'll tell you my story."

***

Tom was flabbergasted.

"I've never held any truck with the supernatural at all," he whispered, "but this is a strange coincidence." They were sitting together in a coffee shop, busy with customers thanks to the weather. Nobody wanted to be out on the seafront when it was so miserable. The windows were steamed up, damp clothes drying in the warmth of the room. The clientele was made up largely of young mothers and children in buggies. Consequently, there was a lot of noise, and it was making Tom's head ache.

"It is. You were saying that you felt that Laura didn't seem herself after the stroke?"

"No, she didn't. Right from the word go." Heidi had to strain to hear Tom, who worried they would be overheard. "I mean, when she sat up laughing the way she did ... at that moment ... I ... pardon me Heidi, I wet myself. She scared me half to death. And she carried on scaring me from that moment until she left a few days ago."

"In what way did she scare you?" Heidi asked, troubled.

"She had become so aggressive. About everything. She seemed to have a deep anger. Against me, against the whole world. The doctors told me the personality change was some symptom of what had happened to Laura, an after effect of some kind, so after the initial consultations I didn't raise that concern again. But her habits changed."

"How so?"

Tom fiddled with the spoon on his saucer. "Laura used to love to knit, but after the stroke she didn't do that anymore. She always used to knit while we watched TV. It was her thing. But once she came home she suddenly wanted to spend more time alone; she didn't want to watch the same television programmes anymore; she didn't have any time for our cats. She didn't want to sleep in our bed with me. After all these years, it was incredibly hurtful."

Heidi looked around at all the young women living their relatively untroubled lives, drinking coffee and entertaining their youngsters, updating their lives on Facebook and planning dinner for their significant others. She was suddenly envious. How had she ended up here in this place at this juncture of time? Alone and virtually friendless, and full of confusion and doubt.

"Tom, I may have left half my brains on the road in Birmingham, but I can't help thinking that you're right. Maybe it wasn't Laura that came back. Maybe someone took her place. Maybe the Laura that has been living with you for these past few months is an imposter."

Tom dropped his teaspoon with a clatter. "You can't be serious," he hissed. "This isn't some movie."

Heidi held her hands up in mock surrender. "I know. But how else do we explain it away? My knock on the head and Laura's stroke. That's fair enough, but it's only part of the story."

Tom's face had taken a stubborn set. Heidi continued, "Tom, I met a woman the other day who knew things ... who claimed she could talk to the dead. Maybe we could approach her to see if Laura is alive or dead. We could ask her to contact Laura if she's ... in the spirit world. I would never have the guts to do it on my own, but if you come with me, you could see for yourself, and then maybe dismiss the whole thing as nonsense."

Tom looked aghast, but it was Heidi's turn to plead with him now. "I can see you don't buy into this at all Tom, but for the sake of my sanity if nothing else, please come with me. I need answers to what happened to me when I died. This woman might be able to help me, but I'm scared. I can't do this alone." Heidi held Tom's gaze and watched his eyes soften.

"Let me think about it," he said and reached forward to squeeze Heidi's hand.

CHAPTER THIRTEEN

The kitchen was a gory mess.

The first person on the scene had been a flatmate. Tyrone Watters had arrived home in the early hours after a night out clubbing. He hadn't bothered to switch the light on but had walked through the kitchen from the back door, grabbed himself a glass of water, and taken it through the hall and up the stairs into his bedroom. The first time he had noticed the blood had been when he switched the bedside light on and found the bloody streaks on his glass. His first thought was he'd cut himself whilst rummaging on the draining board for the glass, but closer inspection of his hands proved that the blood wasn't his.

He retraced his steps to the kitchen, still in the dark, and still wearing his trainers.

It was only when he turned the kitchen light on that he'd seen the body of his friend Matthew, sprawled against the kitchen cabinets, the walls dripping with blood. Tyrone had panicked and dashed through the puddle of blood to check whether Matt was still alive. He'd then slipped and slid his way out of the kitchen and rung 999 to report the murder, before fleeing the house into the street to await the first responders.

Tyrone was sitting on the back of an ambulance now, a thermal blanket around his shoulders, his eyes red rimmed. Adam felt for him. What he'd seen would haunt him for the rest of his life.

Adam had donned his forensic suit and entered the property where Gibbs was already in situ. Lamps that had been set up so that the scene could be properly photographed and scrutinised brought the kitchen into sharp, gory focus.

"Jesus. What a flaming muddle," said Adam.

"It's a tad compromised, sir," said Gibbs, "but forensics are on it."

"They're going to need to be. Any weapon?"

"We haven't found anything yet. Soco are in the backyard. Unfortunately, the yard opens out onto an alley with some garages facing this row of houses, and beyond that, there's an area of scrub dropping down to the railway line. It's a complete fucking nightmare, this."

Adam raised his eyebrows at Gibbs's choice of language and said wryly, "It's an interesting challenge is what it is, DC Gibbs. Call some more bodies in."

"Yes, sir."

"Did we get a name on the victim?"

"Matthew Riley. Twenty-one years old."

"Matthew Riley?" Adam's brow crinkled as he ran through a list of names in his mind. "That name rings a bell. What does he do?"

"He's been working at the Wild West Park this summer, earning some cash." The Wild West Park was a small amusement park just outside Exeter. It had a variety of rides with a wild west theme and kept an array of donkeys, ponies, and a petting zoo. "He was a student otherwise but doesn't look like he returned this year."

Adam's heart sank. "A student at Exeter?"

"No sir, Plymouth."

"Ah." Adam rubbed his forehead with one gloved hand. "Shit, shit, shit. I stand corrected. You were right Gibbs, this is a complete fucking nightmare."

***

Adam shifted his weight from one foot to another, standing across the road, staring glumly at the cordon surrounding the crime scene. He was expecting a phone call from Petty at any moment. It made no difference, he already knew he was off the case.

A mix of emotions washed over him. Firstly, he was confused. Two murders in the space of two weeks, both with a primary connection to his son. Matt Riley had shared a flat with Dan at their Hall of Residence in Plymouth. As the Hall was used for other purposes during the summer, the University had contacted Adam about removing Dan's belongings. He had therefore spoken to Matt on several occasions while he'd been packing and clearing Dan's stuff and trying to figure out where his son had gone. Matt had been a nice enough lad. A little lacking in ambition maybe. He'd taken a gap year between school and University, and it didn't surprise Adam in the slightest that he hadn't returned to University this September.

However, for the most part, Adam felt concerned. He'd almost successfully convinced himself that Dan had left Plymouth and headed off on interesting adventures elsewhere, travelling somewhere alone and meeting new people, because his son had often spoken of his desire to see the world. Dan had saved money from Christmas and birthdays as well as his student loan to finance a shoestring trip to the continent at some stage.

But Adam and Dan hadn't been close for eighteen months or so. Dan suffered his fair share of problems –including a battle with anxiety and depression. Adam attributed all of this to the sour relationship his son had with Nicola. Once Dan had upped and left for Plymouth to start his Geology course, he had rarely phoned his father, preferring to drop him a text every once in a while. They had shared Christmas together, and then a week at Easter, before Dan returned to Plymouth to work on a project. Communication became ever more sporadic, until eventually, when the University's accommodation office had contacted Adam to ask if he could remove Dan's things at the beginning of June, that was the first occasion Adam had realised Dan was missing.

The facts were stark. Dan's savings account had been emptied over the course of his studies. He had always been a bit of a hoarder where money was concerned and Adam had often found envelopes with cash stuffed inside his drawers and his wardrobe in his bedroom over the years. It was entirely possible Dan had access to a large wad of cash that his dad knew nothing about. However, there had been no activity on

Dan's current bank account since the previous May apart from direct debits, and in addition his mobile had not been used. Adam knew that cheap phones with new numbers were easy enough to come by, but what he didn't understand was his son's lack of social media activity. Dan hadn't been hugely interested in Facebook, and he had never had many friends, but he had kept an online profile on other sites.

Adam had been annoyed with the University for not cottoning on sooner that Dan had disappeared. Didn't they have a duty of care? It was left to Adam to report his son as missing to the police in Plymouth. It was a mystery, but all indications suggested Dan had simply taken off. It was something he had talked about doing often. He had been a troubled young man, but there was nothing that would have signposted Dan's intention to hurt himself. Adam sometimes found himself speculating uneasily whether Dan had come to harm somehow, but with no leads, no evidence, and no Dan, there hadn't been a proper investigation. Dan remained on the national database for missing persons, and it was left to Adam to keep up the search.

Now Adam pondered on the circumstances of the latest murder, and the manner of the victim's death. There wasn't necessarily a link between the murder of Dan's mother and Dan's ex-flatmate, but Adam would have been neglecting his duty not to consider it. It was a heck of a coincidence after all. The murders, in both cases, had involved multiple stab wounds. Both appeared, at initial viewing, frantic in their number and positioning. In Nicola's case the autopsy had shown that she had been stabbed over and over again in and around the chest so that the wounds overlapped. Adam knew enough about the nature of murderers to see that in this case there was a hell of a lot of targeted anger.

So who was it and what was that person's link to his son? And was Dan himself in any danger? Adam wasn't a religious man, but out of concern for the wellbeing of his son, he now found himself praying that the murderer wouldn't find Dan before he did.

As his mobile began to ring, and Detective Superintendent Petty's name was displayed on screen, Adam also recognised the possibility that the link between murders had nothing to do with Dan at all but perhaps involved himself. Maybe someone was trying to tell him something.

"Sir?" he responded. He had lined up some explanations, knew all the right things to say to appease his boss, but even while he was enlightening him, his eyes rested on Tyrone sitting in the back of the ambulance. While assuring Petty he was off the case, he started speculating about how easy it would be to interview the lad in front of him in the not too distant future.

CHAPTER FOURTEEN

Adam had been finding it hard to keep a lid on his angst. Come Saturday morning, he pounded the lanes around Durscombe with unusual ferocity, climbing the eastern hill at such a rate that he found it hard to catch his breath, but still he couldn't work the emotion out of his system. Once at the top, he turned in a circle and ran down back into the town at a slower pace. After fifteen minutes he arrived into town and ran along the High Street, dodging shoppers, before slowing to a jog along the prom.

It was a mild day, with pale blue skies, and a build-up of cloud to the west, nice enough for walking. There were a few people strolling along the promenade and taking in the views. Adam came to a stop at the far end of the prom below the red stone cliffs, the Victoria Gardens Cemetery thirty feet or so above his head. He stared up at the iron railings, balanced precariously close to the cliff edge, recalling his conversation with Gloria, and her suggestion to go in search of Cassia Veysie.

He didn't quite know what to make of the idea that Cassia was a witch, but given that he had met plenty of odd characters in his line of work over the years, one more really wasn't going to faze him. It was all part of life's rich tapestry, certainly.

Adam, beginning to tire, and having reached the part of the prom where the road ran out, decided to turn back.

"Detective?" a hesitant female voice halted him.

Adam looked around to see Heidi standing a few feet away in a rainbow coloured beanie hat and a pink raincoat, and just behind her, Tom Goodwin. Adam was taken aback to see them together.

"Heidi, hey. How are you doing? And Mr Goodwin?" Tom extended his hand, but Adam was sweating, so he apologised and declined.

"A welcome day off?" asked Heidi, and Adam smiled wryly.

"You could say that. I'm taking some time owing." He tried not to sound bitter. It had been the superintendent's idea, keen to keep him away from the two cases his team were struggling with at the moment. Two cases that Adam had a stake in.

He changed the subject. "It's a surprise to see you two together. I wasn't aware you knew each other," he said.

"No, we didn't," Heidi replied, "but now Tom's my new best friend. Well, my only friend in Durscombe really." She lifted her chin and smiled defiantly at Adam. A challenge, he thought.

"You have me too," said Adam heroically. "Have you had any more trouble with birds? Any more sightings …" he tailed off, unsure exactly how much Tom knew about Heidi's experiences.

"It's fine. I've told Tom everything."

"Oh you have? Good." Adam still felt surprised by the unlikely partnership.

"Yes. But everything has been quiet over the last few days. I've enjoyed the peace."

Adam was pleased to hear it. "So where were you two headed? Or are you just enjoying a walk?"

"I was taking Tom up to the cemetery. I met a woman there earlier this week and she claimed she would be able to help me."

Adam's heart sank. He had an inkling of what was coming. But he had to ask. "Who was the woman? How did she say she could help you?"

Heidi frowned at Adam. "Her name is Cassia Veysie. Do you know her?"

"I don't believe I do, but her reputation certainly precedes her." Adam wiped his brow, aware he still needed to warm down. "So, how are you hoping she'll help you?"

"To be honest," Heidi flushed, "I don't know. She's a strange creature, but she seems to know things. I know it sounds foolish. Tom and I have already had this conversation a few times."

"Yes, we have," agreed Tom, "but I must admit I'm curious, particularly as Heidi's near-death experience, or whatever you want to call it, seems to have included my wife. Don't you think that's a coincidence, officer? Heidi knew of Laura's existence before she met her. I find it oddly unsettling."

Adam understood exactly what the older man meant. It had been bothering him too.

"And," Heidi continued, "when I met Cassia the other day, she offered to help me. I'm not sure what she intends to do, but Tom said he would come along and give me some moral support. So yes, that's where we're headed now."

"You probably don't think it's a good idea, being a policeman and all that," chipped in Tom, and Adam sighed.

"No, you're right, I don't think it's a good idea, but," he held a hand up as Heidi tried to interrupt, "the thing is, I've been intending to have a little conversation with Ms Veysie myself anyway, so perhaps Heidi would be able to introduce us all at once?"

Now it was Heidi's turn to look surprised. "She's not a suspect is she?"

Adam smiled. Why did members of the public assume that everyone he wanted to speak to were persons of interest? "No, no, don't worry. There was something I wanted to follow up after my conversation with you. Potentially you and I—and indeed Tom—are all after the same answers, aren't we?"

Heidi beamed. "Well, that's great news. Can you come along with us now?"

Adam indicated his apparel, lycra shorts and sleeveless t-shirt. He was beginning to feel a lot cooler now he had stopped running. Chilly even. "I really need to shower and grab a change of clothes. It's going to take me some time to dash home and grab my car. Can you wait for me?"

"There's no need," said Tom. "My car is just down here in the car park. I'll run you home and we'll wait while you change."

"Perfect. If you don't mind?" asked Adam, and Tom shook

his head vigorously and led them all back to where his Citroen was parked up.

CHAPTER FIFTEEN

Heidi rattled the iron gate to the tomb for the umpteenth time, but it was locked and there could be no getting around that fact. Adam and Tom had followed her through the cemetery to the far right corner, and Heidi had expected Cassia to appear from among the headstones as though by prior appointment.

They stood around for five minutes but with no sign of Cassia, or anyone else for that matter. Heidi felt disappointed. The tomb, well-secured, did not appear to have been open for a long time. Heidi chewed her lip, wondering whether Adam believed her story or not.

Neither Adam's face, nor his demeanour, gave anything away. He smelled fragrant in the slight breeze, of shampoo and minty shower gel, pacing around the outside of the memorial, possibly looking for an alternative entrance. Heidi had filled him in on her first meeting with Cassia on the journey from his house, and he had been astonished that a dwelling had been cut into the earth behind the tomb, running underneath the cemetery wall, and under the land beyond.

Heidi, worried that neither Tom nor Adam would believe her story, quickly pointed out how well kept the area was. Tom nodded without much interest and plonked himself down on a raised grave, looking around warily, scrutinising the bushes and trees along the wall, as though he thought somebody might be hiding there.

"I'm sorry," Heidi said. "I feel like I've led you both on a wild goose chase."

"I suppose there's no doorbell?" Adam asked and laughed. When Heidi didn't join in, he straightened his face. "Cassia didn't tell you when to come back, so it stands to reason she's not here all the time. We'll just have to try another day. Perhaps she works or something."

"Maybe we can leave her a note?" Heidi suggested.

Adam reached into his pocket for his notebook and a pen. He handed them to Heidi and watched as she wrote a message with shaking hands. The brain injury had affected her fine motor skills, and while things were improving, it took time. She added her phone number and handed the note to Adam. He scrabbled around in the nearby undergrowth, picked up a rock or piece of old masonry, and weighted the paper underneath, leaving it in plain sight for when Cassia returned.

"Let's hope it doesn't rain." He patted Heidi's arm. "Come on. I'll treat you both to a pint."

***

They found themselves in The Black Swan just before five. Tom and Heidi opted for soft drinks and so Adam begrudgingly nursed a pint. Part of him would have enjoyed the opportunity to sink a few beers, but he felt that neither of his companions would approve. Instead, he sipped his drink and set himself the task of finding out more about the unlikely pairing sitting in his company.

"How did you locate Heidi?" he asked Tom, and the older man winked and tapped his nose.

"Oh it wasn't difficult, detective," he said, smiling, mischief lifting his features.

"Call me Adam, Tom, please. You make me feel like I'm at work, and I'm not." That was a white lie, he could never be entirely off duty. He hoisted his pint. "I'm definitely not at work, am I? I'm going to enjoy this."

"I've lived in Durscombe my whole life. I did my electrical apprenticeship here, and I worked as an electrician right up until I was sixty. I've got good contacts."

Adam was impressed. "I'll have to hire you for my team, Tom."

Tom laughed delightedly. "No, no, actually, I've got lovely neighbours. Lived next to us the whole time we've had our house, and that's thirty-six years. Just so happens they own the house next door to Heidi and mentioned to me in passing that there was a young woman recuperating next door after a horrible accident, and I knew that the witness against Laura was, beg my pardon Heidi, badly injured in Birmingham, and so I put two and two together and got lucky."

"Great detective work," said Adam and raised his glass.

At that moment a mobile phone rang. All three automatically looked at their phones.

"It's mine," said Heidi, and fished it out. An unknown number.

"Hello?" She said. "Oh yes. Hi! I'm sorry we missed you."

"Cassia," she mouthed at Adam. "Myself and Tom Goodwin, he's the husband of the woman I followed. I told you about her. Yes. Yes." She nodded into the phone as though Cassia could see her. "And DS Chapple, who saw the veiled woman. Yes. We were all coming to see you."

She listened for a moment. "Ah. Okay. One second." She held the phone to her chest so that Cassia couldn't hear her. "Cassia wants to know what our intentions are? Is there a specific avenue we would like to pursue?"

"What does that mean?" asked Adam, grimacing. He held his empty hands up. "What are the options?" He glanced across at Tom, who shook his head too, his eyes wide.

Heidi put the phone to her mouth again. "We don't know," she relayed to Cassia, but Tom interrupted her.

"I want to know what happened to Laura," he said.

Heidi repeated what Tom had said and listened some more.

"Right. Really? Okay. What time? That late? Yes. Say that again? Okay. Yes. See you then," and she disconnected the phone.

"Well? What did she say?" asked Adam.

"She wants to do a kind of séance. She wants us to come back to the cemetery at ten."

"Ten o'clock tonight?" asked Tom, a slight tremor in his voice.

"Yes."

"But the cemetery will be locked up by then, surely?" Adam

109

said.

"Cassia says not. She says there is a gap in the fence, behind the bus stop and near the war memorial and we can get in there." There was a moment's silence while they all processed the information and considered the ramifications of wandering around a cemetery in the middle of the night like a bunch of foolhardy teenagers.

"A séance?" Adam asked reluctantly, and Tom curled his lip slightly.

"Apparently so," Heidi replied, and her pale face took on a flush of excitement. This could mean being a step closer to finding out more about what happened to her when she died, as long as Cassia was genuine of course. They were running the risk of being scammed, she knew that. At the moment the risk was calculated, and she was prepared to take it, but in solidarity with Adam and Tom, she felt unnerved.

"Well, that will be a first," admitted Tom.

"For me too," Adam agreed. "I always thought séances were things kids did in movies on a kind of dare."

"I've never seen a séance in a movie that went well," replied Tom, and Adam chuckled.

"I was just thinking the same thing." He exhaled heavily. He had never become involved in anything like this in his whole career. What was he thinking? If it got back to his boss, he could imagine there would be words. Strong words and a number of expletives. And his colleagues would rip the piss out of him if they found out.

Still. Nothing ventured, nothing gained. He jumped to his feet and patted his trouser pocket to locate his wallet. Best to be prepared. "I'll get the whiskies in then, yeah?"

***

The whisky helped. A few hours later, the odd trio floated along the prom and managed the steep climb up the cliff road with a certain amount of aplomb. Even Heidi had succumbed to the idea that a dram would make the world a better place. Out of necessity, they had decided to order food in The Blue

Bell Inn, to line their stomachs against the alcohol and whatever was coming their way later in the evening.

After a dry day, the evening was damp. A sea mist hugged the cliff edge and higher ground, and the waning moon, backlighting the gates of the cemetery, gave everything a mysterious air. Drizzle had fallen while they had been in the pub, meaning the path was slippery underfoot. They paused at the war memorial, searching for a hidden entrance near the bus stop. Rummaging around the dank foliage, Adam finally found a gap in the fence they could squeeze through.

Adam went first, then helped Heidi. Tom squashed his belly into the gap, cursing quietly. Safely in the cemetery, Tom and Heidi exhaled in relief at the same time. Heidi laughed shakily. "I hadn't realised I was holding my breath!"

"I'm certainly glad we've got a copper with us," whispered Tom. "I feel like I'm doing something illegal."

"Technically we are," said Adam, and although he didn't whisper, he kept his voice quiet. "At the very least we're trespassing." He decided to have a word with the council in the morning about getting the entrance blocked up, but for now at least, he was on the wrong side of the law.

They joined the main path and skirted the outskirts of the cemetery rather than walk in the open. The ground was beautifully level here, and they could see the large water feature that dominated the middle of the old gardens. The fountain predated the cemetery, and in keeping with this, a number of Victorian style lamps were dotted about. Nowadays, they were electric rather than gas of course, but they didn't give off much light. Adam glanced around, searching for CCTV, assuming there would be some, but it wasn't immediately apparent where the cameras were hidden, so he put his worries to one side. He'd deal with being seen, if and when he had to.

When the land started to rise, they knew they were reaching the oldest part of the cemetery grounds. Here were grander memorials, larger gravestones teetering awkwardly in the ground, older trees and bushes, statues and sculptures. The mist swirled and dissipated in the coolness of the evening air, and dense cloud drifted across the moon from time to time, plunging them into darkness and making the going a little more arduous.

Progress slowed. Heidi was beginning to tire. She'd had a long day with lots of walking. Now her limp was more pronounced, and the glow that the whisky had temporarily induced was fading fast.

"Not far now," said Adam cheerily, spurring her on.

Heidi twisted her face in a wry expression of pain and stopped for a moment to catch her breath. Tom and Adam came to a halt too, Adam glancing casually around, always a keen observer of his surroundings, while Tom's eyes darted here and there, worried about what might be lurking in the bushes.

"It's so quiet," said Heidi, trying to contain her panting.

"Dead quiet," said Tom, but Adam held his hand up.

"I think I hear something," he said. He turned in a circle, looking about them. Heidi held her breath again. They all listened hard. There came the faint sound of water dripping somewhere and a twittering some way away. "Nah. Must have been an animal," said Adam. "Let's go."

To Adam, the cemetery appeared different under the cover of darkness, especially among the Victorian graves. These old stones didn't shine under the lights as the newer memorials did, meaning this end of the gardens was more sombre, heavy with shadows and darkness. The weight of death was greater here, the damp trees hanging over the paths and tombs, dripping with sorrow for those long gone. It was an eerie place, making it easy for the mind to play tricks on you, and Adam felt his blood running fast, his pulse increasing. He was glad of company and couldn't entirely shake off the feeling that they were being observed. The foliage along the edge of the cemetery hid the old stone wall from sight, but birds and small mammals perched or crouched in the gloom, obscured from human view, watching nonetheless. Perhaps they were the only spectators and Adam was imagining things.

After taking a wrong turning, Adam consulted with Heidi in

muffled tones. They doubled back, and tried again. This time they made the right choice, following the soft winding path into the oldest corner of the gardens. There at last was Cassia's family tomb.

They halted as one. The iron gates stood ajar this time, and candles lit up the vestibule. The stone glowed with a cool warmth.

"Jesus," muttered Tom, and Adam heard an audible click as the older man swallowed.

Heidi looked to Adam for guidance, but he swept his hand toward the tomb with a small bow. This was her party, he seemed to be saying. Adam nodded reassuringly as reluctantly she took a step forward. "Cassia," she hissed. "Cassia?"

There was no response.

Behind them the sound of a snapping branch. It was loud in the otherwise still night. Heidi spun about, eyes wide, her mouth an O of fear, probably fearing they had been followed by the veiled woman. Adam put one hand on her arm and crept back the way they had come, half-expecting to see some kids, who had perhaps followed them from town, or seen them come through the hidden entrance.

A few minutes later he reappeared and shook his head.

"Should we wait for Cassia, or go down?" Heidi asked him.

"Let's go down," Adam decided, making a move for the tomb. Heidi breathed deeply and followed him, but when he stepped aside to let her go first, she was forced to take the lead once more. Tom followed her and Adam brought up the rear.

They stepped through the entrance into the inner sanctum where the coffins lay serenely on their respective shelves. Adam heard Tom mumble, "Oh my goodness." There were more candles burning here, lighting their way through. The door to the stairs stood ajar, and Heidi steadied herself with a hand on either side, the walls guiding her as she tentatively dropped one foot and then the other, over and over, until she was safely down. She ducked at the bottom and stepped into the warm living area. The fire burned contentedly in the grate, the flames casting dancing shadows around the room. The curtains were pulled to block out any outside view of the world through the port holes, and more candles burned, arranged haphazardly among the curios and oddities that Cassia kept on display.

Adam arrived at the bottom of the stairs and walked into the low ceiling with a clunk. He cursed aloud, then clutched at his forehead. Heidi had forgotten to warn him.

"Oh I'm sorry!" she cried, and when Adam took his hand away she could see he was bleeding. "I've got a tissue," she said and rummaged in her handbag until she found what she was looking for. She handed it over and was going to say more when the fire hissed loudly and spat. They all turned about and there was Cassia, standing in the middle of the room, looking magnificent.

She was wearing a long black evening dress pulled back at the hips, in a Victorian style with a bustle, teamed with thick soled black lace-up boots. In contrast, her silver jewellery was entirely modern, with multiple studs and hoops and drops in her ears and nose and eyebrow, delicate chains forming a cobweb around her neck, and numerous rings—with and without semi-precious stones—on her fingers. Her make-up was pristine, a white face, smoky eyes and black lips; a swirling black pattern traced around her left eye and along her cheek, disappearing into her hair line. Tiny crystals decorated the simple pattern, sparkling in the ever changing light of the room.

Tom's startled gasp broke the spell.

"Welcome," Cassia smiled, her eyes sparkling in amusement at Tom's reaction. "It's good to see you again, Heidi. I hoped you would make a return visit and here you are." She nodded gracefully at Tom and Adam in turn.

"This is Tom," Heidi said. "He's Laura's husband." Tom half bowed and mumbled a greeting as Cassia took his hand and shook it.

"And this is DS Chapple," Heidi continued.

"Adam," said Adam.

"Pleased to meet you, Adam. I see you didn't manage to

duck at the beam. I apologise. I should have been here to warn you. Can I get you some ice for that?" She indicated the growing bump on Adam's head.

"Only if it comes in a glass of whisky," Adam said glibly.

"I can manage that," said Cassia and moved to a large cabinet, deftly extracting a decanter and a number of glass tumblers. Heidi declined, but Cassia poured a large measure each for Tom and Adam. She popped through to the kitchen and returned clutching another tumbler full of ice cubes.

"You won't join us?" asked Adam, helping himself.

"No, I prefer to keep a clear head," said Cassia. She busied herself, closing and locking the main entrance and dropping a heavy curtain over it, then sweeping over to the round table in the centre of the room. "Please join me," she indicated the empty chairs, waiting until they were all seated before pulling a chair out for herself.

"I had no idea this amazing house was down here," said Adam, and raised his glass to Cassia. "Have you always lived here?"

"This is where I grew up here with my mum, yes. I lived in digs in Exeter for a while, but it wasn't really for me. I came back here when my mum became sick. Four years ago now. She died in this very room."

As one, Tom, Heidi, and Adam looked around as though expecting to see Cassia's mother in the shadows. Cassia giggled. "Don't worry. Her spirit does not reside here any longer."

Adam supped his whisky. "Any longer?"

"Yes, she stayed around for a while."

"Why? Why would a spirit do that?"

"She was worried about me … being alone … grieving for her. And of course I missed her terribly. I felt she'd been robbed of her life too soon. She was relatively young. She still had things she wanted to do. But in the end, I had to convince her to move on, and she did."

There was silence in the room, each thinking of those they had lost. Tom thought of Laura, how he had wished to go with her, that terrible morning in the hospital, and his relief when she had suddenly come to. Adam remembered Nicola. Heidi thought of both the world she had encountered when she stepped beyond the veil, and the newer coffin in the tomb's vestibule above them.

"Sorry for your loss," said Tom, and Cassia beamed at him.

"And I for yours."

Tom blanched. "But Laura is still with us," he said.

Cassia considered him, her face solemn, her head tipped to one side. Then she pursed her lips. "Let's get started. We need to clarify what we're setting out to do here this evening."

There was a general settling around the table as they pulled their chairs in and made themselves more comfortable. The table had been dressed in a light coloured cloth, with three pristine pillar candles arranged around a large glass bowl. Leaves, pinecones, and berries were scattered about. It all looked very pretty, but Adam assumed the items were symbolic.

Cassia brought her hands together in front of her chest as though she were praying. "On the phone Heidi mentioned something about Tom wanting to know more about what happened while Laura was dead?"

"Yes he does." Adam looked to Tom for confirmation. The older man nodded.

"I'd like to understand more of what happened to me too. And I'd like to know who the veiled woman is, and what she wants," Heidi piped up.

Cassia had expected as much. She turned to Adam. "And what about you?"

Adam resisted the temptation to say he was just here to make up numbers. Or to get some insights into the recent murders of his ex-wife and Matthew Riley. However, he couldn't bring himself to make a joke. The occasion was more solemn than he had expected it to be. He found Cassia intriguing. She was as bright as a button and sharp-witted, and he could understand why people thought she was otherworldly. She utilised instinct well and appeared to understand what he was thinking. Even now, she was reading his thoughts. "It is vitally important that we treat the spirits with respect. They won't talk to us if they think we're messing around."

"I've seen this veiled woman," said Adam. "And while at Heidi's house I saw a bird that didn't actually exist. I want to understand what's going on and what the link is with my ex-wife's death. If there is one."

Cassia leaned his way, searched his face, and Adam sensed her doubts about him. "I promise, I'm taking this very seriously," he said quietly. "I never mess around when it comes to murder."

"Very well," Cassia sat back against her chair, then, taking a deep breath, she lay her hands on the table and straightened her back. The next time she spoke, the tone of her voice had changed, become more authoritative and less familiar. "I welcome you all to my dwelling. I encouraged Heidi to seek me out because I recognise unusual spirit activity occurring around her."

Tom shot Heidi a startled look and shifted in his seat.

"Now that I see you all together," Cassia glanced at each of them in turn, "I see the shadows of those who have crossed around you all. This is highly uncommon. I've listened to your reasons for calling upon my services this evening, and I will do my best to find the answers to the questions. However," for the first time, Cassia's calm and confident façade cracked slightly, "I've never tried to do anything quite like this before. And because we don't have a specific spirit to contact, I will have to improvise. I'm going to call on my mother to see if she can help us."

Cassia stroked the cloth. "I have never communicated with my mother directly before. I only sensed her presence from time to time after she initially passed, and never since I asked her to move on. Crossing from the world beyond to this one is difficult for the spirits, and not something any of them would ever do lightly."

Cassia breathed deeply again and dropped her shoulders. "All I ask of you is that you take your lead from me, and you do not ask questions that might anger or belittle the spirit." She stretched her fingers flat and dipped them into the large bowl of water in front of them. "I've chosen to use water as my means of communicating. This is a form of scrying that is unorthodox when it comes to séances, but it means that we, who call upon the spirit, are all connected to each other. The water is a constant. We pool our energy and that helps open the channels. I think this will be particularly effective because it seems to me that you all appear to be linked together in some way."

Cassia looked at each of them and smiled, her confidence returning. "Please join me by placing your hands in the water."

Heidi obeyed at once. Tom wiped his hands nervously on his trousers, then dipped his fingers in before committing his whole hand. Adam drained his whisky and plunged his hands in the water. It was cold, so cold it made his skin tingle.

"Good," Cassia said, and now her voice was lower, soothing. "I'd like you to keep your hands as still as possible to allow the water to settle. Concentrate on the coolness of the water, the way it feels around your wrists. I want you to imagine that there are two worlds and they are markedly different. There is the world out here in the warm air, where the fire crackles with life, and there is the other world in the cool water, that is still and quiet." Her voice lulled Adam, and he did as she said, alternating his thoughts so that he could feel the warmth of the room versus the cold of the water. "When we can all do this, then we'll be ready."

The room darkened around them as though someone had twisted a dimmer switch. Adam, focusing intensely on the cool water, lost the sense of the others around him, but Cassia's voice chimed through his mind, clear as a bell.

Cassia softly intoned, "I call upon my ancestors, upon those whose blood runs in my veins, whose memories are imprinted on my soul. I call upon my foremothers, upon the women who walked here upon this earth, and in this place long before I, and who are now dust in the wind. I call on you to join me for this night. I thank you for your legacy, for the gift of sight and prophecy that you bestowed on me, for continuing to watch over me and all I do, and for your protection and guidance. I ask for your indulgence, that I might seek an audience with my mother, a communication between this world and your own. And I ask that my companions gathered here with me this night may find some truths to the matters that trouble them. Grant me this, if it be your will, and guide me with your wisdom."

As Cassia's hypnotic tone trailed away, a heavy sigh filled the room as something that had been holding its breath for a long time, relaxed into the space. The water in the bowl rippled. Adam looked at the other fingers close to his, but nobody's hands were moving. A current coursed through his body, something akin to an electric shock. It's a trick, he thought, the water is electrified somehow. He almost removed his hands but held on. Opposite him, Tom was wide eyed, looking at Adam to take the lead. Adam tried to smile reassuringly but only managed a grimace.

"Mother?" Cassia asked. "Jacinta Veysie, are you with us?"

The light in the room dipped, and the fire hissed. Cassia looked around. "Someone is here," she said. She stared hard at the shadows, doubt chasing across her beautiful face. "Mum? If that's you, can you make some sort of sign? Or talk to me?" Adam could hear a little girl's longing in her voice.

Cassia looked all around the room, then finally came to rest in a space beyond Heidi's seat. "There," she said softly. "There. Not my mum though."

Adam, with Heidi to his right and Cassia to his left, followed Cassia's gaze. He could see nothing. Was this a sleight of hand? Wasn't this how mediums fooled people? With smoke and mirrors and a lot of theatre?

"Don't go," Cassia urged, "please." She cast a sharp look Adam's way. "She senses that you are sceptical."

Adam narrowed his eyes at the shadow behind Heidi's chair. Still nothing there for him to see. Of course he was sceptical. "I apologise," he said to the air.

"Who is it?" asked Tom, his mouth agog.

"It is not my mother, it is…" Cassia listened, "Tansy. She says her name is Tansy. She was… she says she was Amelia Fliss's grandmother. That means she is one of my direct relatives. She…" Cassia listened again, "she says she lived at Myrtle Lodge."

Adam knew Myrtle Lodge. It was on the winding road out of town that led onto the moor. It was a pretty house, covered in ivy. He wondered if Tansy had ever appeared on a Census, because that might have been one way Cassia could have gathered this information.

Cassia smiled at the space behind Heidi. "Welcome Tansy," she said. "Can you help us?"

A cold draft brushed along Adam's neck, and his hair stood on end. Cassia's head rotated as she followed the movement of someone or something as it moved around the circle. "She is amused by us, by our clothes. She asks me why I'm wearing so much paint on my face."

Heidi tittered nervously. Cassia looked at a point just above Heidi, and suddenly Heidi's beanie slipped off her head and landed softly on the floor. Heidi gasped, and Tom grunted, but both kept their hands in the bowl of water.

"Did she pull my hat off? My head is cold… I mean… my god. It feels like someone is caressing my head!" cried Heidi.

"It's Tansy," said Cassia in wonder. "She is touching your scars. She knows you died. She says you are incredibly fortunate. In her time, they would not have been able to save you. She says the fact that you are alive is fortuitous, but it is only by necessity."

"What does she mean by necessity? Can she tell you?"

Cassia's brow creased. "Tansy," she spoke to the spirit, "what do you mean. Tell us what happened when Heidi sought to cross?"

Cassia's eyes followed the spirit around the table again. "She is agitated. She says it was a mess. Something happened that should not have happened. There was a mistake." She looked at Tom. "Laura was there, with Heidi. Heidi was behind Laura in the queue." Heidi nodded. Cassia frowned, "Tansy, slow down, I can't understand what you're saying.

Adam watched the exchange. Cassia knew all of this because Heidi had told her, surely?

"Ask her about Laura," Tom interjected. "I need to know what happened to Laura while she was there."

"Tansy? Can you tell us about Laura?" Cassia listened then answered, "She's becoming confused. She's confusing me. She says there are too many questions, too much to tell us and she doesn't have long. She says Laura is lost? What does that mean, Tansy?" Cassia's face was flushed with effort. She blew a few stray hairs from her face. "She is showing me... what is it... a waiting room. There's a woman there, an old, old woman. Tansy says she's a Gate Keeper; she counts people in; she had counted Laura. Laura was about to go through but when the door opened... Tansy says someone broke out of the spirit world, and they took shelter in Laura's physical body. Laura was left... nowhere... Laura was left in the middle of nowhere."

Tom wailed.

"And now she's showing me the door opening and someone else is coming through. Who is this Tansy? Who are you showing me? It is a woman. Yes. A veiled woman. She is a soldier. Tansy says she is a soldier. She doesn't like this..."

Cassia scooted forwards on her chair, frowning, agitated. "Tansy, I can't understand what you're saying. You need to slow down!" Adam watched Cassia's eyes darting here and there as she followed Tansy's progress around the room. Then his eyes fell on the fire, burning in the grate with a phosphorescent glow, oddly blue and cold.

This wasn't right. Adam had so far explained most of the performance away to Cassia's talent as an actress, but the fire and the sudden drop in temperature unnerved them all. His years in the police force had taught him to rely on instinct and gut reaction, and right now his feeling of unease was increasing. He intuitively knew something wasn't right. He felt a prickle of anxiety in his stomach. Cassia appeared to be trying to calm the spirit down, and although Adam remained to be convinced 100 per cent that the whole scene had not been fabricated, underlying his doubt he sensed something sinister was afoot. Besides the definite chill to the air, the atmosphere in the room had a dull heaviness. Sound seemed less sharp, more leaden.

Adam rotated his head slowly to study his surroundings, searching for anything amiss. Nothing immediately apparent, but his eye was drawn time and again to the large mirror situated above the dresser opposite his seat and behind Tom. The mirror reflected the gathering around the table, and the sparkling bowl of water too, but in addition there appeared to be a shadow, a dark cloud, passing in front of the reflected image.

"Tansy says we're in danger. All of us…" said Cassia, sounding breathless and a little scared.

Heidi looked to Adam as their natural leader but noticed him staring into the mirror. She turned to examine it too. "What's that in the mirror?" she asked Cassia. Cassia looked too and saw the dusky shape materialising in front of them while the water in the bowl bubbled, darkened, and thickened to the consistency of mud. She glanced back at the water in the bowl on the table, as still and clear as it had been all evening. "Is that Tansy in the mirror?" Heidi asked.

"No. Tansy is pacing next to you, Heidi. She's agitated." Cassia addressed the space behind Heidi's chair once more, "Tansy, who is this?"

The shape in the mirror took on more form. It sucked energy from the room, and the mirror warped and wavered. The shadow there, once translucent, became increasingly solid. Once a dark shadow, it took on a lighter form. The water in the bowl in the mirror bubbled away, black and viscous, oozing over the sides, splashing the table.

"What the hell is that?" asked Tom, but the shape was distinct now.

"I think I recognise her." Heidi sounded worried.

Adam knew what she was thinking. The shape was a person, tall, the head misshapen thanks to the veil covering her horns. The large horns curled back on themselves. She was a sight both awe-inspiring and terrifying.

"Abelia. Tansy says the name is Abelia, and she is a warrior from the spirit world. She says she's dangerous."

The group eyed the silhouette in the mirror, the horned head, the shape of the veil.

"Why is she dangerous?" asked Adam, his mind racing. "What will she do?"

Cassia listened and then repeated Tansy's words. "She's here to collect the person who escaped, the person inhabiting Laura's physical body, and Tansy says Abelia will be ruthless. She's saying again that we are in danger, that we're putting our own world in danger!"

The figure turned in the mirror, gazing directly at them, the nose poked against the veil, and the glass in the mirror bulged out into the room, farther and farther, the glass screeching and straining, the sound of nails on a blackboard amplified tenfold. Adam recoiled. Where the eyes and mouth would be there was blackness, as though the head consisted only of a horned skull and deep dark pockets in the eye sockets.

With one final shriek, the mirror exploded, but not outwards, it shattered inwards, in a million pieces, away from those sitting at the table as though something in the room had thrown a large heavy item through a window. The explosion preceded a powerful wave of energy that shook the room, blowing flames out and candles over while simultaneously everyone threw themselves backwards away from the table, breaking the connection they had created, the filthy water sloshing out of the bowl and all over the table. The fire dipped and dimmed. Plunged into darkness, Heidi gasped, but total darkness was short lived, the fire flared up once more, enabling them all to see.

Adam hauled himself upright, moving rapidly, staring at the space the mirror had occupied, glimpsing a void, an infinite black abyss, a vacuum that stretched away to eternity. It pulled at him, and he might have stood and walked towards it, but dozens of black birds erupted from the inky darkness and flew at high speed into the room, missiles sent from beyond. They circled the room, beating at the occupants, twittering and tweeting, their wings loud in the confines of the dark room. Heidi screamed and threw herself face down to the floor, scrambling with difficulty to hide under the table. Cassia cried out in pain. A bird had caught itself in her hair and battered against her face with its sharp beak. She pummelled it in horror, and it squawked and shrieked at her in anger.

Adam jumped to his feet and ran to the mirror. As he reached it, the blackness collapsed in on itself and with a sucking sound, like water rushing down the drain, it was gone in the blink of an eye. Panting, partly in fear and partly from exertion, Adam reached out to touch the surface of the wall and all that remained. There were shards of glass lying among the trinkets on display on the dresser, but of the bulk of the glass there was no sign. If this had been some sort of theatrical trick, it had been a damn good one.

Total silence reigned in the room. The birds had disappeared as quickly as they had appeared.

Adam turned to face the others. Cassia shakily hauled herself to her feet, her face bleeding from pecks and scratches, her make-up smudged beyond repair. Heidi peered out at Adam from under the table, her face fearful. He bent to pick up her beanie hat then gently helped her out from under the table and pulled her to her feet.

"What the hell happened there?" he began to ask Cassia, but she held her hand up, her eyes searching the shadows once more.

"Is Tansy still here?" asked Tom, righting the candles from the table.

"No," Cassia whispered. "I don't think so. But someone is."

Everyone stood rigid, casting fearful glances around the room. Cassia rotated in a slow circle until she was facing the back of the room with the entrance opening onto the stairs and back out into the cemetery. The door gaped open, a draft flowing from the tomb above. They all knew it had been closed and locked before. Adam heard Heidi catch her breath as the veiled woman slowly inched up the stairs, not so much climbing as levitating. She disappeared into the darkness beyond.

"Abelia," said Cassia in horror.

"Stay here," ordered Adam and raced after the woman. But as he reached the door, it slammed in his face and he recoiled, rubbing his nose. He yanked at the handle, the door wasn't locked, couldn't be, but it was stuck. He heaved his frame against the wood and the door flew open, flinging him backwards. He regained his balance and chased up the stairs, the veiled woman no longer in sight. The light in the tomb had been extinguished, every candle blown out, the wicks smoking in the darkness, the scent acrid. Adam fumbled his way gingerly through the vestibule, slipping down the damp step and out into the cemetery in some relief, but the veiled woman was nowhere to be seen.

He edged out among the gravestones, searching for any sight of her. His breathing seemed loud in the stillness of the night, and his heart beat in his chest, adrenaline coursing through his blood. A movement to the left caught his eye, but when he looked that way, there was nothing to see. He jogged in that direction, peering through the bushes and around the trees, scrutinizing the shadows, looking for anything out of the ordinary.

It was cold. Past midnight. The salty mist hugged the damp ground in patches. Adam figured there might be a frost in the morning. He turned this way and that, but with nothing to see, he had almost given up hope when he spotted her. She stood on the other side of the water feature under one of the Victorian lamps, her lacey finery glowing in the yellow light, the space that her eyes and mouth would inhabit dark beneath the thick material. Adam remembered the empty void he had seen in the mirror and shuddered. Perhaps she sensed his disgust. She moved her head as he skirted the fountain and then tantalisingly, just as he reached her, she dissipated into the mist.

Adam rocked back on his heels, unable to comprehend what was happening. He twisted about sharply, looking for her, for anything, creeping up behind him. Nothing to be seen.

In frustration, he retraced his steps, attempting to rationalise the events of the previous twenty minutes and process what had happened. He'd been convinced Cassia was playing games, but the mirror, the veiled woman's disappearance, these weren't things she could have easily faked. This wasn't theatrical trickery or vaudeville illusion.

He stumbled back through the tomb and slipped down the stairs. The room was bathed in light now. Cassia and Heidi huddled together in misery, both visibly shaken. Cassia's face, streaked with the black, white, and red of her make-up gave her a child-like appearance. She clutched at Heidi who was wise beyond her years, her eyes haunted. Adam wasn't entirely surprised given the beating Cassia's self-confidence must surely have taken–her bubble of innocence had been well and truly burst. Gloria had been right. Cassia had strange and powerful skills indeed, but it was apparent she wasn't in control of them quite yet.

"What have we done?" Cassia whispered as Adam approached. He shook his head. He had no idea.

"What about Laura?" Tom asked, his face ashen, and Adam found himself fearing for the older man's health. He looked at Cassia pointedly.

"I'm sorry Tom. Tansy didn't show me any sign of Laura, either alive or dead. It was like she had just disappeared into nowhere."

"So this woman? The one who came back in my wife's body? It wasn't Laura? I was right about that?"

Cassia nodded earnestly, happy to be on surer footing. "Yes, you were. The woman who has been masquerading as Laura is not your wife. She's someone else entirely, and she escaped from the spirit world. Tansy couldn't show me why. What's obvious is that it shouldn't have happened, and the spirits are angry. They've sent Abelia to clean up the mess, and she's not happy. She's not happy at all."

CHAPTER SIXTEEN

October was late in the season to be camping, but Todd Bailey had wanted to find a unique way of celebrating his eighteenth birthday. When he'd booked, he'd noted that the website forbade booking for all-men, or all-women parties, so Todd had brought along his best mates, Greavsie and Simon 'Hoppie' Hopkins, along with their good female friends, Charlotte Wilkes and Scarlett Murphy. Hoppie had been hoping for another girl to round out the numbers, but the car could only fit the five of them so they'd had to make do. It didn't really matter. Nobody was getting lucky.

But they had enjoyed themselves. They'd arrived at the campsite on Thursday evening and inspected Todd's parents' caravan. He'd spent many childhood holidays on this campsite over the years, but this caravan was brand new. To say his parents were extremely nervous of lending him their pride and joy was an understatement. Todd had sworn blind to both of them that no harm would become the caravan, and then he had found it incumbent to inform Greavsie, his clumsiest mate, that he would kill him without a shadow of a doubt if any damage was done at all.

On the whole, the group of friends had been as good as gold. They had cooked breakfast every morning but had been diligent about cleaning up after themselves. Apart from that they existed on takeaways and snacks. Charlotte, as an enthusiastic member of the Young Greens, had insisted that they recycle as much as possible. She had been assiduous about collecting all of their bottles and cardboard and sorting everything into the correct bins at the entrance to the campsite. There had been plenty of alcohol, you're not eighteen every day after all, but not to excess. They had listened to music, but not so loudly that neighbouring caravans could overhear.

Their one fatal error was a simple one.

Whereas Charlotte's green persona was rooted in the environmental realities of global warming, Scarlett wanted to connect with 'the old ways' as she called them. Scarlett fancied herself as spiritual and new age. Over the course of the few days of their stay at the campsite, they had enjoyed several walks on the coast and two in the countryside, including the forest around Abbotts Cromleigh. Charlotte identified the names of trees while Scarlett hugged them. In the evenings, they had mostly played cards, but on the final evening, the Sunday before they would leave for home, Scarlett suggested using an Ouija board she just happened to have brought from home.

She made them huddle around the small table, lit a number of tea lights to create the requisite atmosphere, then turned the lights out.

"How does it work?" Todd asked.

"Everyone just puts a finger on this planchette here, and then we invite the spirit," Scarlett answered.

"What do you say? Just come here spirit?" asked Hoppie.

"Who's going to be haunting the caravan anyway?" asked Greavsie. "It's practically brand new."

"Maybe one of the workers who made it was killed in here," suggested Todd and widened his eyes at Charlotte. She shook her head.

Hoppie snorted. "What make of caravan is it? Is it made in Asia? Is it a Japanese worker's ghost? How will we communicate with him? Do any of us speak Japanese?"

"I'm pretty sure you'll find most caravans are made in the UK," said Charlotte.

"I'm pretty sure you'll find they're not," said Hoppie, who had no clue where caravans were made but found Charlotte incredibly supercilious and therefore took every opportunity to put her down. Charlotte merely shrugged, although she could quite happily have pushed Hoppie's head down the chemical toilet and slammed the lid down. Hard.

"So we invite the spirit, and then what?" asked Todd. He had some sympathy with Charlotte. Hoppie was being a pain in the arse. They would have to have words once they arrived home.

"Then we can ask some questions. You see on the board here, there's yes and no, and letters and numbers, so we should be able to decipher some answers," Scarlett ran her finger over the wood of the board, "if the spirit chooses to answer of course."

"Why wouldn't it want to answer?" asked Hoppie, but practically everyone was ignoring him now.

They poured drinks, arranged small bowls of crisps and peanuts, and were careful to use coasters so as not to mark the caravan's dining table, then gathered around the board. One by one they each lay a finger on top of the planchette. The mood in the caravan was suddenly solemn.

"You can breathe you know," said Scarlett, and Charlotte and Todd giggled in unison. Scarlett smiled, feeling very much in control of the situation. The others looked to her to lead, which was unusual, and she was enjoying her moment in the sun.

"We call upon the spirits to talk to us. Is there anyone there?" she asked grandly. There was a silence. "We wish you no harm. Would anyone care to talk to us?"

Hoppie looked around at all the faces at the table. "Bwahahahaha!" he bellowed, making Todd jump.

"Fucks sake, Hoppie," Todd said.

"Sssh!" urged Scarlet. "We need to take it seriously or there's no point in doing it."

Hoppie rolled his eyes but was silent.

Scarlett began again. "We call upon the spirits in the vicinity who would like to speak to us. We mean you no harm. Is there anybody out there?"

Again there was silence, and Scarlett was beginning to lose hope when suddenly the planchette moved slowly. Circling the board a few times and then cruising in on the W. Charlotte gasped.

"Who's moving that?" hissed Todd.

"Not me," said Greavsie and everyone looked at Hoppie.

"Hey, it's not me!" he scowled.

"What's it spelling?" asked Charlotte.

Scarlett spelled out the letters as the planchette ran to them. "W, h, y. Why?" The planchette was still.

"Why why?" asked Hoppie.

"What do you mean, Spirit?" asked Scarlett. The planchette didn't move.

"Maybe the spirit means 'why is it dead'?" suggested Hoppie.

"Or why are we asking it to talk," Greavsie suggested. "Maybe it was enjoying a long rest."

The planchette moved to the centre of the board and paused once more. When it started to move again, it rushed around the board swiftly.

"W, h, y… why… h, a, v, e… why have… y, o, u… o, p, e, n, e, d .. why have you opened… t, h, e, d, o, o, r, f, o, r… why have you opened the door for t, h, e, s, p, i, r, i, t, s?"

"Why have you opened the door for the spirits?" asked Greavsie.

"There's more," said Todd.

"D, a, n, g, e, r. Danger?" Charlotte spelled.

"Oh come on, screw this!" said Todd. "Hoppie."

"Hey mate, it's not me, I swear!"

"It's bullshit, surely?" Greavsie asked, glaring at the others, but Scarlett shook her head. She looked worried.

"Look, if one of you is moving the planchette, admit it now," Todd said in his no-nonsense adult voice.

"Nobody is moving it," Scarlett said and took her hand off the planchette. The others followed suit. The planchette remained where it was, and Todd breathed an audible sigh of relief.

Charlotte lifted a slightly shaky hand and took a big sip of her bottle of beer, but that was the moment the planchette decided to move all by itself. Charlotte's arm jolted, spilling beer down her front and onto the sofa.

"Oh fuck," Todd exclaimed, unsure whether to panic more about the mess or the fact the Ouija board had begun working by itself. He stood, running his hands through his hair, intent on getting a cloth to clear up, but he kept one eye on the board and what was happening there.

Scarlett spelled out the words as the planchette rattled around. "Never open the door. Beware. Danger. Beware."

"What door?" asked Charlotte.

"Christ, can't you stop it?" begged Todd, and Greavsie put his hand out to grab the planchette. It twisted in his grasp, spinning faster and burrowing into his palm. He screeched in pain and yanked his hand away as though burned. Blood flowed from his palm, spilling onto the Ouija board. The planchette created tracks in the blood as it moved around the board.

"A, b, e, l, i, a, a, b, e, l, i, a. What does that spell?" cried Scarlett, agitated.

"Who the fuck cares? Pick the flaming board up!" shouted Greavsie. "Throw the whole thing outside!"

Hoppie grabbed the Ouija board as the planchette continued its manic dance. Todd, already on his feet, barged in front of him and reached to open the door. He gripped the handle and twisted it at the same time, and then screamed in pain. His hand stuck to the door momentarily, and when he wrenched it back, the skin from his fingers and palm had stuck to the door. His hand was a raw red mess.

"What the hell?" screamed Charlotte.

"It's burning! Burning hot!" Todd bellowed in pain and fear, bending double, curling over his fist.

Charlotte ran the water in the sink. "Put your hand in here, Todd!" she ordered and he hobbled over to her, almost hysterical with the pain.

Greavsie held one hand out towards the caravan door. He could feel the heat from twelve inches away. "Oh my god, what are we going to do? How are we going to get out?"

Hoppie dropped the Ouija board to the floor and jumped on with as much ferocity as he could manage. The caravan floor shuddered along with him.

"We'll need to go out the window," Charlotte said.

"Kick the big window through," Todd said, tears running down his face. His hand was agony and he needed to get to hospital. He no longer gave a rat's arse what his parents thought. He watched as Greavsie pulled back the curtains to stare out into the darkness beyond, ready to open the window and then use force to smash it outwards. He hesitated. "Do it!" screamed Todd.

A figure in white waited outside for him. As Greavsie kicked at the window, it turned its veiled head to look his way. He paused and stared back at it. A her. It wore a long lace dress. He couldn't make out any features in the oddly shaped head, but beneath the veil, its eyes were black shadows. It stepped closer, and he could see horns. He felt a cold fear grip his insides, and then a rush of adrenaline. He didn't know what the figure wanted, but his best mate was howling with pain behind him, and he felt certain that he and his friends would be better off in the open.

Gripping the cupboards above the windows, he hoisted himself up, swung back and then drove his feet at and through the glass. As he connected, the window came away from its frame with a crack, tumbling outwards. Greavsie was propelled outside too.

He landed in the grass, the veiled woman watching him, but moving neither forward nor back. Greavsie turned to help his friends out and clearly saw them silhouetted in a blinding flash of light in the instant that the caravan exploded. His friends were obliterated, and Greavsie was ripped into two pieces, his legs and torso landing thirty yards away, at the steps of the caravan's nearest neighbour, his head in the field next door.

***

"It was all remarkably unpleasant." With one simple characteristic understatement, Polly met Adam's gaze, and he saw the pain in her eyes as she recalled the scene. Nothing more needed to be said. She looked pale and tired, hunched over a sticky table in The Blue Bell Inn, which this evening, was thankfully devoid of young farmers and therefore quiet. "Honestly Adam, I don't know what's going on with Durscombe at the moment. It's always been such a sleepy place, you know? I mean I spend all my time moving people on, tutting at inconsiderate driving, warning teenagers about drinking and breaking up the odd domestic squabble. Now we have a murder and this horrendous tragedy. I'm beginning to think I'd be better off transferring to Liverpool or Glasgow or somewhere for a rest."

Adam smiled and raised his glass to her. "Don't you dare. I'd miss you."

"Would you?" Polly managed a watery smile. "Aw that's nice. I'm glad someone would." She took a big gulp of her Jack Daniels and Coke. "Thanks for meeting me tonight. I really needed to offload. That scene at Combe Hill Caravan Park is going to stay with me forever. I can still smell it. Taste it." She rubbed her red rimmed eyes. "Five teenagers."

"Yeah. It doesn't get much worse. I'd hate to be their parents," said Adam, thinking of Dan, wondering where he was.

"Me too. There's absolutely nothing left to identify of four of them. Burned beyond recognition."

"Any idea what caused the fire?"

"Not really. At this stage, just guesses. Forensics will be a while. One of the neighbours said the kids had been pretty good, not much partying or loud music. Maybe they left the cooking gas on or something?"

"You'd have thought in this day and age there were safety measures to stop the gas leaking or exploding," said Adam.

Polly nodded. "There was one odd thing though. And I'm questioning whether there was some foul play involved. Only the neighbour we spoke to said he saw some strange woman hanging around the caravan just before it happened. He'd just taken his dog up the dog-walking field and was checking the guy ropes of his awning and he saw someone."

"What sort of strange woman?"

"Well," Polly smiled, "this is going to sound really stupid, but he said it was a woman in a long wedding dress and a veil. That's just nonsense though, right? It was dark. What's he describing? I mean, who hangs around a cold campsite in October in a bloody wedding dress?"

Adam stared at Polly in horror, his eyes hollow. He shook his head, but his mind was screaming: Abelia, who else?

CHAPTER SEVENTEEN

Adam paused in the drinks aisle examining the various whiskies on offer. He obviously had preferences, but any port in a storm. He added a couple of bottles to his trolley, and then another more expensive one for good measure. The nights were drawing in and it paid to have plenty occupying the cupboard for when he was at a loose end.

He made his way down the aisle, considered adding a bottle of gin to his trolley too, but decided it might give the cashier the wrong impression. He rounded the aisle at the top, chucking in a couple of large bars of chocolate from the sump bin display, and headed for the mixers section. If Polly came over to his place, she didn't mind drinking whisky but her preference was to drown it in bubbles.

He glanced up when he was finished adding the bottles to his trolley to see a man watching him. The chap was a little older than Adam, distinguished looking, with silver-blonde hair and warm blue eyes. He was wearing smart casual clothes, from one of the high-end nautical chains in Durscombe–the ones that kidded everyone they were local and British in origin although they were headquartered inland and the clothes were made in Bangladesh. He looked tired, a little jaded, in spite of the tan, and there were bags under his eyes.

Adam, assuming he knew the man from somewhere, smiled and nodded, and was about to carry on when the man abandoned his trolley and walked over to him.

"Adam Chapple?" he asked and held out his hand.

"Yes," Adam said, nonplussed.

They shook hands. "Dominic Fallon."

Fallon? Adam thought about the name and then realised where he had heard it before. "Fallon? Are you Nicola's husband?"

Dominic nodded. "Yes. Well, yes." The 'I was before she

was murdered' was implied in the painful hesitation. "You were her first husband. I've seen a photo of you. She had it in a photo album. From your wedding."

"She kept a photo? Well. I must say I'm surprised by that. After all these years, eh?" Adam had assumed Nicola would not have kept any keepsakes. Holding onto a wedding photo seemed out of keeping with a woman who had not wanted any contact with her son. "I'm sorry for your loss," Adam said, acutely aware that he didn't consider Nicola his own loss.

"Thank you. Yes, it was odd about the album. I found it while I was clearing out some things last week. I don't want to throw everything away. Maryanne may want some of it when she's older, after all, but … I just needed to let some things go."

"Maryanne?"

"Yes, our daughter. She's six. Missing her mother terribly." Adam recognised the pain in the man's eyes, father to father.

Adam recalled what Polly had said. There was a daughter. How could he have forgotten? "I'm sorry to hear that. Yes, it will be a terrible loss for her, for you both. I hope we catch someone soon."

"I know you were a policeman when you and Nicola were married, so you're still on the force?"

"I am yes. I'm with Exeter's murder squad, but obviously I'm not involved in this case. That would be a conflict of interest. I'm a suspect too."

Dominic nodded his understanding. "No, that wouldn't be ethical, would it?" There was an uneasy silence until Dominic smiled as though he was about to take his leave. He glanced back at his trolley. Adam observed plenty of fruit and vegetables and some very sugary looking cereals. Dominic sighed and patted his pockets looking for his wallet.

"I'm making the final arrangements for the funeral. I'm not sure whether you would like to come, but perhaps Dan might."

Adam dragged his eyes away from the man's groceries and focused on Dominic's face. Had he misheard? The way he had said that Dan might want to know about the funeral made it sound very much like the two of them were acquainted.

"Dan?" asked Adam as he processed the thought. "Have you met Dan?" Dominic couldn't have met Dan because Dan hadn't seen his mother for years. Ergo ...

"Yes, several times." Dominic cleared his throat. "Over the past eighteen months or so, and not always under the best of circumstances."

"I'm sorry?" Adam said, "You'll have to forgive me sounding a bit dense here. I wasn't aware that Dan was in contact with Nicola. He never told me he was. For years we didn't know where to find her. He said he would wait until he was eighteen and then start searching properly. You're saying he did look for her? And find her and speak to her? He never told me." Adam wasn't sure whether to be impressed by his son's detecting skills, or to be hurt that Dan hadn't kept him in the loop.

"Perhaps he didn't want to upset you," said Dominic kindly. "You'd been his primary parent for so long."

Adam frowned. Now that he thought about it, it had been a long time since Dan had raised the subject of Nicola with him. He couldn't believe he hadn't noticed Dan's silence about his mother. "Did they get on?" he asked abruptly, bracing himself for Dominic to speak about the pair's relationship in glowing terms.

Except he didn't.

"No." The answer was curt.

Adam waited for more, his lips pursed with unspoken questions. Dominic flushed a little. "Dan first found Nicola about eighteen months ago while we were still living in London but had already bought the property down here. Initially he contacted her by letter, and then she gave him her mobile number and they used to text and call.

At first, everything was fine. He was reaching out. He just wanted to get to know her, but when the date to move down here became imminent, I think that Nicola felt a little more pressured. She didn't want him visiting ... and things became a tad strained."

"Oh," said Adam, and his heart filled with pain for his son. He had found his mother, and she had rejected him again. No wonder he had become increasingly reclusive and had chosen not to discuss his mum with Adam. He probably expected Adam to say, "I told you so." Adam would never have done that, he would never have knowingly belittled his son's feelings, but there was no escaping the fact that Nicola really was a cold-hearted bitch where Dan was concerned.

So Dan had been angry with his mother before her death. Dan was a suspect, but nobody had located him yet. "Did Dan ever come to your house?"

"No," said Dominic, and he didn't even have the grace to look sheepish. "Nicola actively discouraged that."

"But he knew where you lived?" Adam continued.

"Yes, I believe he did. In fact, I know he did because we had a few cards and letters."

Adam couldn't believe that Dan would know where Nicola lived and not choose to visit her. It was entirely natural for him to want to see his mother in the flesh after years of merely imagining what she was like. Perhaps he hadn't been inside the property or even knocked on the door, but Adam firmly believed that at some stage, Dan would have ridden past the address on his bicycle, hoping for a glimpse of the woman who had given birth to him.

"Had Dan spoken to Nicola in the days and weeks leading up to her death?" asked Adam.

"Not as far as I know. There'd been a couple of angry text exchanges." Dominic appeared to find the line of questions uncomfortable, but Adam didn't care. It was natural for him to ask questions. It was his job.

"I take it you've told the police about those?" asked Adam, and Dominic nodded.

"Yes, they took her phone and her laptop, so they have everything relating to communication in the days leading up to her death."

Adam nodded. He wondered if Dan had tried to contact her since. Did he know his mother was dead? And if he did, how was he taking that? It was another reason he might have gone off the rails. Adam wished he could contact his son.

Adam pulled out his wallet, extracted a business card, and handed it to Dominic. "My number's on here, if you need anything," he said. "Or perhaps if you happen to see my son or hear from him, you could let me know. He went travelling in May or June and I've yet to hear from him, so I'm a little anxious. He may not know his mother is dead. I need to speak to him about that."

Dominic located his own wallet and handed a business card to Adam in return. Dominic Fallon, CEO of Fallon Enterprises. "I'll keep you posted about the funeral," said Dominic and returned to his trolley.

"One thing," called Adam. "Why was Nicola so reluctant to have him drop by your house?"

Dominic flushed an odd purple colour. "I don't think she had told him about Maryanne. When he found out, he wasn't … happy."

Wasn't happy? No. Adam could well believe the betrayal Dan had felt when he discovered his mother had rejected him, ignored him for years, and then replaced him with a 'new and improved' version of a child. Dan would have been beside himself.

Adam could have wept in despair and frustration. Instead, face full of thunder, he trundled his trolley around the corner, back to the previous aisle, where he loaded it up another two bottles of whisky.

Expense be damned.

***

Later he lounged on Dan's bed, nursing a large tumbler of Scotch on ice, listening to the music on Dan's stereo. Dan had inherited Adam's love of the weird and wonderful and there was everything from Zappa to Beyoncé on the playlist, and all stops in between.

Adam had hauled Dan's belongings back from University in

June, and now the boxes were stored in this room. They took up a fair amount of floor space. Adam set his glass on the bedside table and pulled one of the boxes towards him. Leaning over it, he riffled through the contents half-heartedly. Text books, A4 notepads, a maroon hoodie. Novels. Graphic magazines. Not much of interest to Adam, but he guessed his son had liked this stuff well enough. He flicked through the writing pads. Lots of notes from lectures in his son's spidery scrawl, some short story fragments, snippets of poetry, some doodles and a few sketches.

Adam shoved the box away and reached for another, a larger box containing an old rucksack that Dan had used when he cycled into University. One of the final traceable purchases Dan had made was a new larger and sturdier rucksack from a camping shop in Plymouth city centre. Adam had checked Dan's bank records, found the receipt on his desk, and retraced his steps to the shop. The employees there had not remembered Dan, but they had been able to show Adam the very rucksack his son had purchased. Adam took photos of it. Its lightweight frame, durable and waterproof canvas, countless pockets, and good size, made it perfect for a cyclist to carry abroad. Presumably Dan was travelling around Europe with it now.

Adam pulled the old rucksack from the box and tipped it upside down, emptying the contents on the bed. He watched the items fall—Dan's forgotten treasure. Some coins, his old mobile, a notebook, and some pens. Some chewing gum and a few empty crisp wrappers, a bottle of water, a couple of fliers for bands at the Student Union. There was no wallet. This, combined with the new rucksack, had convinced Adam that Dan had taken off for Europe.

Adam weighed the phone in his hand looking at it. He had read the messages when he first found the phone in the rucksack, and then he had examined the call log. That done, he had made a record of and rung every name on Dan's contact list several times over the summer, but all to no avail. He had failed to access any of the deleted texts, but from those he had seen it was notable there had been no messages to Nicola, and Nicola's number was not included in the contacts or in the call history. Not obviously that Adam could see, at any rate.

But Adam knew that even the deleted history from Dan's phone could be retrieved. He just needed the right contact at the phone company, or a warrant. He was pretty sure that if he handed the phone over to Gibbs as part of the ongoing investigation into Nicola's death, Gibbs would be able to give him a list of calls made to and from his son's number, as well as the content of texts sent from Dan to others, and responses. It might not help the murder investigation any, but potentially it would provide Adam with new information about where his son had been heading when he abruptly left the University.

Sighing, Adam gathered all the detritus together to stuff back into the rucksack, but as he did so he noticed a small zipped compartment hidden away within the front pocket. He'd seen this sort of thing before of course, it was a secure place to keep your phone, wallet, or keys, but he hadn't noticed this particular pocket before. He unzipped it and rummaged inside the tight space, assuming he would discover condoms or something similar. He found a slim wodge of paper instead. Drawing it out of the bag he discovered it was a letter, addressed to Dan at his digs in Plymouth. It had been written in neat, round handwriting, confident and assured.

The envelope was pristine, but the pages within looked like they had been handled many times. Adam opened it up, feeling as though he was eavesdropping on something essentially private to his son.

It was a letter to Dan from his mother.

Dear Daniel,

I'm really glad to hear that you feel your end of year exams went well. It is important that you make the most of all the opportunities that come your way, and I'm sure that University will help you achieve your potential.

I am afraid I really don't think you coming to visit me when you come back to Durscombe this summer is a good idea. I'm terribly busy with the house renovations, and as I told you last time, Maryanne is a little sensitive. You turning up like you did, out of the blue, scared the poor girl to death. In any case, she had nightmares for a few weeks.

I'm sorry if this sounds unkind. I'm sure we can sort something out given time, but at the moment, please respect my wish to protect Maryanne and stay away.

Kind regards,

Nicola

Adam frowned at the curt tone and sparse nature of the correspondence. That was it? And she had signed it 'Nicola' and not Mum. At least the letter answered a few of Adam's questions. Dan did know about Maryanne and the way she had usurped Dan from his mother's affections. A wave of fury washed over Adam. No wonder his son had chosen to run away.

He reread the letter, and it brought tears to his eyes. He tried to imagine how he would have felt if his mother had been so callous. He couldn't imagine an occasion where she ever would have been. Until she had died a few years ago, she had been the best grandmother for Dan, spending time with her grandson, hanging out at the beach, teaching him to cook, taking him out on fun excursions.

But nothing can replace a mother's love.

The whisky played its part. Adam let the tears come. For the first time in many years, he cried. Perched on the edge of Dan's bed, he hunched over his knees and placed his head in his hands. He cried for the hurt his son had endured for so many years, and for his own inability to help the boy when he needed it most.

CHAPTER EIGHTEEN

Adam ran off his hangover and then stood under the shower for twenty minutes, sluicing the sweat from his body and the stink of Scotch from his system. His brain was finally feeling less sluggish than it had been when he had rolled off Dan's bed at 7.30, early for a Sunday morning, but even so he was going to need plenty of coffee to keep him going through the rest of the day.

He started off by sitting at the desk in Dan's bedroom with his son's laptop fired up and several notebooks arranged and open beside him. He had a list of Dan's friends, and he was intending to systematically contact every one of them again. Where possible he wanted to speak to them in person, but failing that, where they were too far away, he would email or message them via one of the social media channels.

He worked through his list, leaving voicemail if he couldn't get through, ticking each name once he had a response. By half past one he was starving and there were only a few names left. One of them was Matt Riley, the student who had been murdered in Exeter.

On a whim, Adam grabbed his car keys and drove into Exeter. It was a drive that normally took thirty minutes, but roadworks at the motorway junction meant traffic was crawling from the coast in the direction of the city. Eventually Adam was able to pull onto a back road and head into the city by a quieter route. He utilised the side streets to stay out of the way of the backed up traffic and at last arrived at his destination: Tyrone Watters's house.

Adam rang the bell. It was pulled opened quickly by a young woman of twenty or so with pale purple hair tied in two bunches and matching jazzy spectacles. She smiled when she saw him. "Hey," she said. "It's Dan's dad, isn't it? The detective?"

Adam kicked himself for not recognising her, but he couldn't quite put a name to her face. That she knew his son was a good start however. "Sorry," replied Adam, "I've forgotten your name."

"Isla Carr. I was at Uni with Dan. We shared a flat. You talked to me in June, and…" she produced her mobile, "you rang me this morning, but I haven't had a chance to get back to you yet."

"Of course, Isla." It was all flooding back now. Her hair hadn't been purple, it had been a dirty blonde, and she hadn't been wearing specs when they'd last met, but now that she had reminded him, he remembered her.

"Are you here about Matt? The police said they would have more questions," Isla asked solemnly.

"Yes." It was simpler to say what was expected rather than admit he wanted to discuss any links with Dan.

Isla stepped away from the door. Her feet were bare, and she had sky blue nail varnish on her toes, scuffed, as though left there since the warmer weather of the summer. "Please, come in. I'll put the kettle on."

"What are you doing here? I didn't expect you to be here." Adam followed her into the kitchen. The room had been deep cleaned since the murder, and the walls and floor coverings replaced. It smelled clean and fresh, but in his mind's eye, Adam could clearly see Matt's body lying slumped in the corner.

Some things you can never unsee.

"Tyrone and I have been an item for about six months. I met him through Matt. I stay here often, mostly weekends and holidays, and he comes to see me in Plymouth."

"You weren't here on the night of the murder?" Adam asked.

"No, I've been in Plymouth, because I took a room on and I'm in contract at the moment. It should run out at the end of December, and then I think Tyrone and I are going to move in together, maybe in Newton Abbott, somewhere between Plymouth and Exeter so that it's easy for me to commute to

Uni and Tyrone to work in Exeter, you know?"

"Good idea," said Adam.

"Tyrone?" Isla called through the door to the living room. "Do you want a coffee or something? The police are here." Turning to Adam she said, "Go through. He's only watching crap telly. I'll bring you through a coffee, is that okay?"

Adam nodded his thanks and headed into the living room. Tyrone was lounging on the sofa, his feet on the coffee table. He was clad in boxers and a t-shirt and was watching a popular daytime antiques programme. Middle-aged women bartered for collectible tat at a car boot sale. Tyrone switched the TV off and sat up as Adam entered.

"Tyrone Watters? Do you remember me? DS Adam Chapple," Adam said. They shook hands.

"Dan's dad."

"That's right."

Adam made himself comfortable on a chair as Isla carried in a tray of coffee with sugar in a bowl and milk in a jug. She placed the tray on the coffee table then scooted into place beside Tyrone, tangling her limbs to sit cross legged, as flexible as an undercooked pretzel. Adam, wincing, helped himself to a mug and added two teaspoons of sugar.

"I was surprised to find you here," he started, "I imagined that the landlord would have moved you out."

"Well yeah," said Tyrone. "He's been really good. Obviously he wanted the place cleaned up and habitable, so he could get his rent. As soon as the police were done, he had the cleaners in. In fact, I've never seen the place so clean. I've lived here for two years."

Isla nodded and squeezed Tyrone's knee. "We did think about looking for a place together now rather than a few months down the line, but we'd both need to give notice, and with one thing and another, like, in my case I have to pay the rent till January, Tyrone decided to stay put here for now."

"Yeah, it's not very nice, knowing what happened. Matt was a good mate. But," Tyrone trailed off, his eyes moist.

"Have you any idea who would want to hurt Matt?" Adam

took his notebook and pen out.

"None at all," said Tyrone. "I mean he could be a bit of a tosser but can't everyone?"

No, thought Adam, they can generally rein it in if they need to. "When you say he could be a bit of a tosser, in what way? What do you mean?"

Tyrone hesitated. "Well, don't get me wrong, I don't want to speak ill of the dead, cause he was a good bloke in so many ways, but he was pretty argumentative, you know? And for a kid who hadn't really done anything or experienced anything, he was damn certain that he was always right about stuff."

"He was a bit of a wind-up merchant," Isla explained.

"Who did he used to wind up?" asked Adam.

Tyrone exhaled heavily, as though he was struggling to remember, but Isla looked Adam directly in the eye and answered, "Dan, for starters."

"Dan?"

"Yeah. Cause you know there was the four of us in the flat. Me, Dan, Matt, and Abigail, and I think Dan really fancied Abigail. She didn't want to have too much to do with him, I mean, they got on all right, but I think she thought getting involved with Dan while we were all living under one roof, so to speak, would be a bit much." Isla twirled one of her ponytails around her fist and inspected the hair for split ends.

Adam nodded. He had noticed Abi's name appearing in Dan's notebooks. There was never any annotation, just her name and some doodling, and he had found a few quick sketches of a girl. She might have been Abi now he thought about it.

"Dan wasn't the only one Matt pissed off though. Matt had a way of annoying people. He had a few very short term relationships with girls at Uni last year, but they never lasted."

"Why?"

"Because he could be incredibly snide."

"He could be an arse," agreed Tyrone.

Isla continued, "On the whole Dan kept himself to himself, and at the beginning he wouldn't respond to Matt's remarks about Abi, or whatever it was Matt had latched onto and was wanting to have a go about. He was generally pretty reserved, wasn't he? Dan? Didn't put himself about much. I thought, increasingly, as the year went on, Dan became more of a loner, spent more time in his room. Well, I already told you that when I saw you in June, after he'd left, huh?" Adam nodded. He had made a note of that at the time.

"He wasn't that reserved all the time, though. Was he? I mean, what about when he was screaming the place down?" Tyrone prompted Isla.

"Who? Dan?" Adam's pen paused in mid-air over his notebook.

"Oh that's right. Maybe I should have said that before. Matt used to wind him up about many things, including Abi. And from about March time I would say, it really all began to get out of hand."

"With Dan?" Adam asked again, crinkling his brow. He hadn't expected this.

"Yes, he would fly off the handle big style."

Adam didn't think he'd ever seen Dan truly angry, so this was news to him. "You didn't mention this before," he said pointedly, and Isla blushed.

"I figured cause you were his Dad you wouldn't want to hear all the bad stuff."

"All the bad stuff?" There was more?

"He started to keep odd hours. Stay awake all night, which he had never done. I thought he was on the Internet, but I have no idea. Then he'd sleep during the day. Sometimes he would be his usual self, other times he would be so wired. Like he was having manic episodes, you know, jumping around, being friendly and happy and excited. I knew someone with manic depression and they were like that."

"Or he would cry," said Tyrone flatly, and Isla looked embarrassed.

"Yes, sometimes he would cry for hours. I thought he must have been really unhappy about something." Isla pulled her ponytail in front of her face and made a moustache while she remembered, it made her seem very young to Adam. Isla, Dan, Matt, and Abi. Four kids playing at being grown-ups in a student flat.

"And you think this all began in March?"

"Around that time, wouldn't you say Tyrone?" Isla asked, and Tyrone nodded. "By the time we did our exams in May, he was a completely different lad to the one I'd met the previous September when we started at Uni together."

"He didn't say what was bothering him?" asked Adam.

"No. Of course now I wish he had, or that I'd asked him, and then maybe I'd be able to help you sort out where he went."

Adam tapped his pen on his notepad thoughtfully. Dan's lecturers had told Adam that his exam results had not been all they had expected, and one of them, his personal tutor, had mentioned that she hadn't been able to pin Dan down for a tutorial in the run up to the exams. It was beginning to sound to Adam as though Dan had been in the process of a breakdown.

Not for the first time Adam's thoughts turned dark. What if his son wasn't missing at all? What if he had harmed himself? It was not a possibility Adam had wanted to consider before, but it was rapidly becoming something he had to contemplate.

He half-heartedly asked Tyrone some more questions about the night of the murder. Tyrone hadn't seen anything or heard anyone. Matt had been dead by the time Tyrone arrived home, and this had been corroborated by the pathologist. Matt hadn't shared any fears with Tyrone or Isla about someone wanting to do him harm. He'd smoked pot occasionally but wasn't into drugs in a big way and didn't have a regular dealer. He'd liked a beer but didn't drink excessively. He'd had the usual amount of student debt as far as his friends were aware but nothing extraordinary.

Finally, Adam stood and thanked the pair. They walked him out. Adam noticed there were new deadbolts on the door.

"So the police have no leads on who it was?" asked Isla, and Adam shook his head regretfully.

Tyrone shook Adam's hand. "You know, one thing I forgot, and I meant to say to DC Gibbs when I saw him again. I imagined that Matt had a woman home that night. He wasn't seeing anyone, but I did have a sense that a woman had been in the house. Nothing concrete. Nothing I could prove. It was just a sense…"

Isla looked taken aback. "How do you mean?" she asked her boyfriend. This was obviously news to her. Adam looked on with interest.

"It's just that when I first arrived home, I remember smelling perfume, and given that you weren't here that night and that there was only me and Matt in the house, why would it smell of perfume unless a woman had been in here recently?"

"What sort of perfume was it? Can you remember?" asked Adam.

"Oh man, that's an impossible question. I have no idea about perfumes. I'd say it was like one my mum would wear. Or maybe my Grandma. Expensive, not something that Isla would go for though."

Isla twisted her face at Tyrone and thumped his arm. "Cheers."

Adam laughed. "That's interesting," he said. "Thanks. I'll mention it to Gibbs." He didn't know how he would quite do that, given that he wasn't supposed to be anywhere near Tyrone or, indeed, Matt Riley's murder investigation, but he would find a way. It was a good lead.

Tyrone closed the door and Adam was pleased to hear the bolts hit home. Perfume that an older woman might wear? An older woman such as Laura? Or was that too much of a coincidence?

He thought not.

***

The backlog of traffic had eased somewhat, so the return drive to Durscombe was pleasant, and Adam was glad to be ahead of the evening commuter traffic departing Exeter. The sun was low in the sky when Adam decided to turn right and drive the scenic route over the moor and along the coastal road. He entered Durscombe along the cliff road, and so the Victoria Gardens Cemetery was on his right, the gates standing open as he slowly drove past.

He made a U-turn and came back. He turned into the small car park near the entrance. It was quiet at this time of the afternoon. The council would be locking the gates at dusk. There was plenty of evidence that the cemetery had been busy with visitors throughout the day, with the bins full of flower wraps and plastic and numerous empty containers piled near the taps.

Adam wandered along the edge of the part of the cemetery that was new. The gravestones were neat and tidy, the grass short and well-manicured, and there was evidence of recent mourning and remembrance with toys and mementoes on a number of graves alongside flowers and plants. The graves tended to be a similar shape and size. For the first time, Adam wondered where Dominic intended to bury Nicola. He had no idea where her parents were interred, but they had been local to Durscombe so they may well be at eternal rest somewhere close. Turning abruptly away, he walked with purpose to the far older part of the cemetery, skirting the fountain, where he could see a council worker sweeping leaves with practised strokes and a distinct rhythm, through the tumbling headstones and dank vegetation, onwards until he came upon the Fliss Memorial.

No candles burned here this late afternoon. The tomb was dark and the gate locked. Adam leaned against it, listening, but there was nothing to be heard except for animals in the bushes and the soft noise of the sea meeting the rocks and the cliffs, beyond the railings that skirted the gardens.

"Cassia?" he called once. No response. He hadn't expected there to be, hadn't thought to find her here. It seemed that Cassia could only be located when she wanted to be.

And yet, he half sensed someone watching him. "We need

to talk," he said, keeping his voice low, hoping that if Cassia was around she would hear him.

Dusk fell steadily. The chiming of a bell coming from the direction of the gate reminded him that the cemetery was closing, and so he turned to make his way back. He walked carefully, peering into the areas in the shadows, the perception that somebody's eyes were upon him magnified with each step he took.

He made it to the gate and the council worker nodded at him. "Have a good evening, sir," he said as he swung the gate closed. Adam turned to bid him similar but the words stuttered to a halt as he recognised Abelia standing under the lamp. As the key clanged in the lock, Abelia turned away from Adam and faded away among the gravestones.

The strengthening sea breeze blew through Adam, and he shivered. He hurried back to his car, intent on getting indoors and pouring himself a large Scotch. She was on the loose, and he had no idea what she wanted, or who could be hurt by her. He couldn't turn his back on what had occurred that night. He decided to drive home via Coleridge Way and Budleigh Place in order to check on Tom and Heidi. There was no point in taking any risks and leaving his friends exposed and vulnerable.

CHAPTER NINETEEN

Heidi elected to visit the cemetery before lunch. After Adam's visit the previous night, she had sensed for the first time that even the infallible and brave detective was rattled. He'd enquired whether she had seen Abelia since the evening at Cassia's, and she had shaken her head. Everything had been quiet, and she had experienced no visitations from the birds either—a huge relief. Adam had appeared a little stressed, and Heidi had a feeling he had held back some information.

Adam had mentioned that Tom was feeling on edge knowing that his wife was still out there somewhere, so Heidi rang Tom first thing in the morning to ask whether he would accompany her to the cemetery. He had declined but only because he had an appointment with the dentist. He promised he would visit her in the afternoon. That gave Heidi a strict time frame. She would walk to the cemetery to see whether Cassia was around, and then she would catch the bus home, have a spot of lunch, and await Tom's appearance.

Heidi half-expected the tomb gates to be locked, but when she arrived at the Fliss Memorial, the gates stood open. Heidi hesitated, then made her way through. This time she acknowledged the coffins instead of averting her eyes. These women and their mortal remains were important to Cassia. She nodded her head in respect and walked slowly to the door at the far end. This was closed, but she tapped and tried the handle and it opened. She carefully descended the stairs and shouted for Cassia.

"I'm in here," Cassia called back, and Heidi ducked her head at the bottom, even though she didn't really need to, and went through to the living area.

"How are you doing?" asked Cassia. She was sitting at her table, the one they had gathered around to perform the séance, shuffling a pack of cards. It might have been a tarot deck, or she might have been playing patience, but the light was too dim to see properly.

Heidi hovered awkwardly, unsure what to do. "I'm all right. I was worried about you," she said. "After the other night." Heidi looked pointedly at the empty frame, still displayed on the wall.

Cassia laughed but without much humour. "That was some crazy shit, right?" She sighed. "I'll need to get a replacement for that mirror. I miss it being there. It startles me every time I notice its absence."

Cassia raised her eyes to Heidi, and her smile faded. They shared a look that lasted longer than was comfortable. Heidi recognised the distress in Cassia's face.

"What's up?" she said and grabbed a chair, angling it so that she could sit knee to knee with Cassia.

"Oh," Cassia laughed nervously, "I wouldn't know where to start."

Heidi took one of Cassia's hands. It was cold and smooth. "After my accident, I met with a psychologist who specialised in post-traumatic stress disorder, and he told me to start wherever I liked. 'Just jump in,' he would say." Heidi rubbed Cassia's hand softly between her own to try and bring some warmth into it. "So just jump in."

Cassia sighed deeply, then leaned in over her knees and spoke in a voice so low that Heidi struggled to hear her. "Nothing like that had ever happened to me before. Nothing that… violent. I've communed with spirits, quite a few of them over the years. My mother encouraged it. She said it was part of the gift that is handed down in our family, from mother to daughter. We work with the elements—with fire, with earth, with water, and with air—and we each have an ability to speak to the spirit side. She encouraged me to use the gift only for good, and to shy away from the shadows. I thought it would be she that came to me, to share with me the knowledge that you needed. But it was Tansy. By all accounts she was a formidable witch as was her granddaughter Agatha Wick, the cousin of my foremother Amelia Fliss, whom you know a little about."

Heidi nodded, and Cassia continued. "I've heard amazing stories about Tansy. She was wild, but knowledgeable, well-known locally and throughout Devon and into Cornwall for her lotions and potions."

"These connections with your forebears are important to you?" asked Heidi. Cassia's eyes glowed in response. Heidi could feel the energy flow through the other woman as she spoke of her family.

"Yes. When I close my eyes, I see these women stretching back in a long, long line behind me, each passing on their knowledge and their strength. When I watch the fire, I can see them dancing in the flames. They are my guardians. They have never let me come to harm."

"That must be an amazing feeling," said Heidi. "I lost my mum when I was a teenager. I missed her so much. I still do. I've never had the sense that she was with me. At all." Heidi turned her gaze inwards, looked bleakly back through the years. Sixteen years since her mum had passed away. After that short but brutal illness, Heidi had formed a close and unbreakable bond with her father. He meant the world to her. She understood that she had never experienced a long-term relationship because she hadn't ever wanted to get close to anyone else. The loss of her mother had almost destroyed her.

There had been a lot of anger at the time. A sense of betrayal that her mother would just die on her like that. As though she meant to. Heidi had completed her A Levels, then put off University for a year, and tried to heal. Eventually, time had been the healer, allowing her to go on and pretend that life was normal. All these years later, Heidi still felt cheated, but the pain had naturally eased.

"I envy you in some ways," said Heidi.

Cassia blew her cheeks out and squeezed Heidi's hand. "I'm not sure you should really. Today I feel that it's more a curse than a blessing." She shuddered, as though the cold had suddenly seeped into her bones, and stole another look at the blank frame on the wall. "I didn't realise that seeing spirits was unusual until I started school. Some other kids would get freaked out by ghosts and ghoulies but I loved all the stories about them and seeing them in cartoons and on TV. Then at some stage I started to talk to some kid I would meet up with when I walked to school. I made the mistake of trying to introduce my new friend to the lady at the school crossing and all hell broke loose. It turned out this little girl had died crossing the road years before I was born. The other kids thought I was odd, and one of the teachers really ripped into me for scaring them and spreading lies.

"So I went home crying my eyes out, and that's when my mother talked about my 'gifts' and how I should always look for the light and never the shadow. After that, she would regularly ask me if I could see so-and-so, and I always could. But I also saw those my mother couldn't and could speak with spirits that I had never been introduced to. My mother said my gift was as great as some of our foremothers, and much more powerful than her own."

Heidi raised her eyebrows. All this was beyond her experience, but Cassia spoke so earnestly, and so longingly, that Heidi could only encourage her to keep talking. "What a wonderful thing to share with your mum."

"Yes. What an amazing legacy." Cassia's eyes filled with tears. "But I have never felt like I measured up to them. My mum told me how witches were persecuted in the middle ages, and beyond, even here in Durscombe. I'm pretty sure that Tansy had a hard time of it, that would have been the middle of the nineteenth century, and my mother suggested that the reason Amelia Fliss jumped off the cliff was because she couldn't handle the spirits talking to her. These are all stories handed down to me and told as true."

"You are a worthy successor to your foremothers, surely?" Heidi soothed.

"But I feel almost like a fraud. I'm twenty-eight years of age and I've done nothing. I can turn my hand to a bit of herblore, create natural medicinals, face creams and soaps, candles and cupcakes, and I can utter spells under a full moon, and I can forage in the forests and along the seashore and in the hedgerows like any good witch. I can tell fortunes at the monthly fairs and earn a few bob, and I can attend moots and look the part. But Heidi, I feel like a façade of a wise woman. The other night I realised something profoundly important–I cannot control this gift. I am too young, and I don't know enough, in fact, now I feel as though I don't know anything at all. I have no wisdom to offer you or Adam or Tom. I have no experience that will lead us to the answers." Tears ran down Cassia's cheeks. She dashed them away, smudging her make-up. "Now I think about it, I can see how arrogant I've been. Not just with you guys, with everyone. I thought I could impress you all with what little I can actually do, my party tricks. It's pathetic. I'm pathetic."

"Oh Cassia…" interrupted Heidi, but Cassia stopped her.

"Think about it Heidi. The thing that happened the other night? Whatever it was I unleashed? I wasn't expecting that. I can't send it back. It's shaken me to the very core, it really has. Tansy warned me the séance was dangerous, but I didn't see it. Didn't see how it possibly could be. None of the spirits I have ever talked to before have ever wanted to harm me or anybody else. And then when I couldn't break it off and Tansy was frantic… I should have stopped it!"

"Cassia stop," Heidi said firmly. "The mirror was broken, but apart from that, what harm was done? Abelia was already out in the world. You didn't unleash her. That wasn't your fault." Heidi thought back over the events of that night, seeking clarity herself. "I found out what I needed to. What happened to me, it was real. I no longer feel like I'm completely out of my mind. I can't blame the head injuries for the things I've seen over the four or five months. To me, that's a positive."

Cassia searched Heidi's face and smiled gently. "I can see that, Heidi, and I'm glad that's brought you some peace. That's how I should use my gift. But Tom——"

Heidi interrupted. "Tom already knew in his heart that the woman who came back from the dead was not his wife. Or if she was, she had changed beyond recognition, and no matter how much Tom loved her, he couldn't change that. He will grieve, and we can support him."

Cassia half sobbed, half laughed. "Oh bless you, Heidi. You are so good. But you're missing the heart of the matter here. By going in search of the answers of what happened to you and Laura on the day you both died, we somehow opened a gate between this world and the one beyond. I wasn't able to close it before we broke the connection. Who knows whether I would have been able to, given more time. I'm not sure I would have."

Heidi frowned. "What are you saying? You can't mean that the gate is still open?"

"I do mean that," Cassia said, and her eyes were dark with fear.

Heidi shook her head. "That can't be so." She stood and defiantly stalked the few paces to the wall and the empty frame. She touched the frame and put her hand on the backing where the mirror had once hung. "There's nothing here. It's solid. There's no force field. We can't see any birds flying through it. There's no void or portal."

Cassia rose and came to stand alongside Heidi. "If only it was that simple. If only the fact that we can't see beyond this wall meant that there was nothing else to see." They stood together, quietly uneasy, both with their own thoughts.

"Isn't there any method for sending Abelia back?" asked Heidi eventually.

"I guess she doesn't want to go back without the soul she came for."

"The person inhabiting Laura?"

"Yes."

Heidi sighed. "Then maybe that's what we have to do? We need to track Laura down." She turned to look at Cassia. "That's not something I'd relish though. I saw what she did to Adam's ex-wife. It wasn't pretty."

Cassia grimaced.

Heidi hesitated. "Could you maybe ask Tansy, or someone, where Laura is?" She saw the look on Cassia's face. "Look, I know you might not want to, but it's not as though your ability to talk to spirits is diminished by what happened. You still have the gift, and I assume it's not going to go away." Heidi warmed to her subject and brightened up. "Maybe you need to hone your skills, learn to control what you do? Hey, perhaps your foremothers can offer some instruction?"

Cassia laughed at Heidi's enthusiasm, but her face suggested she wasn't convinced. "I know you mean well," she said, "but it really isn't that straightforward."

Heidi slumped. "Yes, I suppose it's not the same as taking up knitting or crochet or something you, learn from a book or a YouTube tutorial," she said. "I don't know. I just feel that if we've started something, however inadvertently, we kind of need to find a way to finish it."

"Yes. But as you said, it really isn't that simple."

"Cassia," Heidi said firmly. "We need to try."

***

Cassia sat alone, a single candle burning on the table in front of her.

She gathered up the cards Heidi had caught her shuffling earlier this morning. Heidi had been thinking along the right lines, but this was neither a deck of cards, nor a tarot deck, although it bore more similarity to the latter. The cards had been handed down for the better part of 200 years. They were thick and well thumbed, hand decorated in a variety of ways by a succession of the women from Cassia's family. At some stage, the backs of the cards had been uniformly decorated with thick red paper, and varnish had been applied both front and back to protect the delicate images.

Among the cards were eight images of women and eight of men. There were a number of animals and a few with flowers. Earth, air, water, and fire were all represented, but Cassia had learned that there had been no rhyme or reason in the way the images had originally been chosen, apart from a strong instinctual urge to include a specific design. Every image had come to have a meaning, and Cassia's mother had taught her daughter to interpret the cards consistently, but in her own unique way.

And so she did.

When she attended fairs and offered her tarot services to the general public, she used a traditional deck. It was old, with impressive gilt edging, but it didn't have the same quality as her family deck. Just holding these cards, shuffling and thumbing through them, brought her a measure of peace, linking her ever more tightly to the women who mattered. And today she needed them more than ever.

She considered laying the cards out, one by one, to seek answers to the garbled gobbledegook within her mind, but without a direct question to ask, she feared the response. Instead, she decided to meditate on each card and ask for guidance.

She stared into the flickering flame of the candle as she absently shuffled the cards one more time, taking comfort from their thick familiarity, and then breathing deeply she plucked one from the centre of the pack, placing it gently on the cloth on the table in front of her. The card depicted a woman. Loose dark hair. An older woman.

An image of Tansy came quickly to mind. The Tansy she had seen a few nights ago. Wild haired and equally wild eyed. Cassia felt reluctant to call her back, didn't want to hear what Tansy had to say to her today. It was too soon.

She turned over another card. It was the same woman. Impossible. There was only one of each card, each one was entirely unique. She couldn't have pulled out two cards that were the same.

She drew a third one, and set it alongside the second. She knew as she turned it over what she would see. The dark haired woman, staring back at her.

Cassia flipped the deck in her hands and quickly scanned through them. All of the remaining cards were different. That was how it should be. She rotated them once more so that the red backs faced up, shuffled them quickly and this time lay the top one on the table.

A dark haired woman.

She drew again and then again, until finally she placed the deck down on the table, completely unnerved.

She looked over at the empty frame on the wall, and shivered.

There was nothing for it. "Tansy," she called, keeping her voice low, frightened who else would overhear them. "We need to have a chat."

CHAPTER TWENTY

Cassia reached Adam's house just after eleven thirty. His ordinary looking home, built in the early nineties, and situated on a quiet cul-de-sac, wasn't what she expected. Most of the houses were already locked up for the night and shrouded in darkness, but Cassia spotted a yellow glow through the glass of Adam's front door. There were only two street lamps for forty houses, and it was a dark night, so any light grabbed the attention. Cassia paused for a moment to rest. She had walked the few miles out of town and run the last part, fearing she would never make it here. Her ragged breathing puffed steam into the cool air, but she was sweating too. She wiped her face with the sleeve of her black suede tasselled jacket and rapped on the door, hoping she didn't disturb the neighbours.

The wait was interminable. She hopped impatiently, hanging on for a sign of life. Maybe he was asleep. She was reaching to tap on the glass again when a shadow fell over the door, blocking the light through the glass. "This had better be good," Adam's voice growled on the other side. There was the heavy scratching sound of a chain being pulled back and then the clicking of a lock. The door opened a crack and Adam peered through.

"Cassia?" he pulled the door open further, staring at her in confusion. "What are you doing here? Do you know what time it is?"

"I need to talk to you. And it won't wait. I'm sorry."

"Come in," he said, albeit a little grumpily, and she followed him into the hall and closed the door behind herself. He was dressed casually, wearing tracksuit bottoms and a plain grey t-shirt. His feet were bare.

She trailed after him as he walked back to his living room. It appeared as though he had been sitting at his desk: the computer was on, a Facebook page open. There were notebooks next to the laptop and he had been jotting things down–phone numbers, dates, names. A glass, almost empty, perched half on and half off a coaster, within easy reaching distance.

"Are you all right?" Adam asked.

"Yes," she said, but she looked uncertain.

"How did you find me?" Adam asked. Cassia took a seat where he indicated, perching on his sofa, her knees together, her ankles splayed, looking like a gangly rag doll with her dark hair loose and untidy, and her mascara smudged. She was wearing far less make-up than usual, and Adam could see the natural flush of her cheeks.

"I had to ask around," Cassia admitted. "I went to Gloria, and she didn't know, but as luck would have it, Craig was there and he had your card."

"That's right, I left my address with him." Cassia smiled but her features tensed up as the smile quickly fell away.

"So what's up?" Adam, still standing, picked up his glass and twirled it in his fingers as though debating whether to pour himself another drink.

"Heidi came to see me today." Cassia tangled her fingers into the tassels of her jacket.

"I expect she's still a bit shaken about the other night, isn't she?" Adam certainly was.

"She wasn't too bad," Cassia replied, her voice dull. "I was worried Adam, about the way we left things. It was all so unresolved."

Adam nodded. "Yes. I've been thinking the same thing. And in any case, I saw the weirdest thing, right before Abelia appeared. It's been bugging me."

"You saw the gateway. I know you did. I saw it too."

"And Abelia came through it?"

"Abelia was already here. But that open gate just means she can travel here and there far more easily." Cassia tugged so hard at one of the tassels that it came off in her hand. She stared at it, then shook her head. "No. That's not the main problem. You see—and Tansy was furious about this–the open gate means anyone can come through. Literally anyone. And maybe everyone."

"Oh god," Adam threw himself down in an armchair. "What does that even mean?"

"To be honest, I don't know myself. But I assume that more spirits can come through, the way that Laura did."

"As long as they're not all vile murderers, all will be fine." Cassia watched Adam, rubbing his eyes as though they felt gritty. She could almost see him struggling to regain a tenuous grip on their reality. "Jesus. This can't be happening. I should be sitting in The Blue Bell Inn with Polly discussing tractor thefts. This wasn't even my case." Yet here he was immersed in a nightmare and struggling to get to grips with ghosts and death experiences on a case that wouldn't go away. Adam shook his head, tersely, glaring at Cassia. "What did Heidi want?"

"I think she wants me to find Laura."

"You mean by communing with spirits again?" asked Adam, his sarcasm thinly veiled. "Because I have my best detectives working on finding Laura, and she appears to have vanished into thin air. I'm not sure how you could help."

"I could try to find her, you know," Cassia said defiantly, "but only if you wanted me to."

They stared at each other, Cassia annoyed, Adam nonplussed. "I'm sorry," he said eventually. "I don't know what to make of all this. One minute I have more real life than I can possibly handle, and the next I'm seeing walls evaporate and there are ghosts stalking me. If my boss gets to hear of this, I'll be taking a very long leave, that's for sure."

"It's fine," Cassia said quietly, plaiting the tassels. Now she sounded sombre. "And anyway, that's not why I'm here."

Adam poured himself another whisky. "Go on," he said, and his stomach twisted instinctively.

"Your son."

"What about him?" Adam's voice was sharp.

Cassia swallowed, and looked him in the eye, her eyes bright with unshed tears. "He's spirit side, Adam."

There was an uneasy silence, Cassia watched as all the colour drained from Adam's face. "No, he isn't," he said softly.

"After Heidi came today, I decided I should try to speak to Tansy alone. She told me."

"That's not true. He's travelling. He's in Europe somewhere." Adam gestured at the notebooks on the desk, and the laptop, the screen now timed out, black and empty. "I'm going to track him down."

Cassia shook her head, and a single tear rolled down her face.

Adam glared at her. "Did this 'Tansy' show you his spirit? Introduce you to him?"

"No."

"Well there you are then," Adam said, waving his arms with an angry flourish, the whisky slopping over his glass.

"He's gone, Adam," Cassia insisted quietly.

"There's no body. There would be a body." But Adam knew that nobody had been looking for a body. There might well be one. "You need to leave now."

"I wouldn't come all the way here to mess you about, I promise. I know Dan is spirit side."

"Don't be ridiculous. If he was gone, don't you think I'd know? I'd know! In here!" He beat his chest. "And I don't know. Now I need you to leave."

"Please..."

"Get out!" Adam spat. "And take all your hocus pocus mumbo jumbo claptrap and sell it to someone who actually believes in your bullshit."

Adam advanced on Cassia, and Cassia, alarmed by his sudden aggression, stood and darted into the hall. She turned at the front door, "I'm so sorry," she tried, but Adam made a couple of rapid steps in her direction, and she flung herself through the front door and out into the cold.

The door slammed closed behind her, and she stood and listened as the locks turned. She waited on the step, catching her breath and focusing on her breathing before walking along the drive and back into the close. She hadn't gone more than a dozen steps when she heard a wail of despair from the house behind her, like the cry of a deeply wounded animal.

As much as she wanted to go back and offer comfort, there was nothing Cassia could do for Adam, and so she walked on, tears slipping down her cheeks.

CHAPTER TWENTY-ONE

Tom lay in his king-size bed staring at the ceiling. From time to time lights crossed the room as cars drove down the lane outside. His house wasn't on a main road, but it was a handy cut through for people driving from east to west in Durscombe rather than driving into town and back out again. He found the familiarity of the lights, and the rumble and whine of the cars passing by strangely comforting.

It helped him feel less alone.

He reached across the bed. Laura's side was cold, unslept in, just as it had been since the night of her first stroke. Tom couldn't grasp how much his life had changed in less than five months. One minute she had been the same old Laura and they had been planning the trip of their lifetime to Florida for their wedding anniversary, and the next she had been completely altered. At first he had rejoiced merely in her continued existence. After the trauma of her death, when she had come back to life so miraculously, he had sworn to cherish her in whatever guise she presented, as he might have if she had been suffering with Alzheimer's or Dementia. However, she had become so wholly unrecognisable from the moment she awoke in hospital, and so totally unlikeable, in spite of her appearance remaining much the same as she always had, that Tom had seriously doubted his capacity to continue to care for her.

It had quickly become evident that Laura did not need anybody to care for her. She was compos-mentis and entirely capable of looking after herself. She suffered no noticeable side-effects from the stroke, no impediment to her mobility, cognitive abilities, sight, or speech. She was a medical miracle. All the doctors repeated this endlessly.

So why then had he grown to fear her so quickly?

After nearly forty years of marriage, Laura desired nothing

whatsoever to do with Tom, had hardly wanted to share this space with her once beloved partner. She was hostile. Refused to speak to him for hours on end. She refused to undertake any chores around the home, even when she had fully recovered. Once she became physically abusive, this had spelt the end for Tom. He had been relieved when she left.

And heartbroken. The relief didn't prevent him missing his wife of thirty-nine years, and all the love they had shared. He missed their easy intimacy, the sense that there was someone else looking out for him. Laura had provided him with the best reason to jump out of bed every morning.

He reached his hand across to her pillow and stroked it, imagining her face there.

"I love you," he whispered, and when a tear squeezed out of his left eye and rolled across his cheek, he blinked it away rapidly and rolled over.

That would never do.

***

He slept for a few hours but woke suddenly, his heart beating quickly in his chest. Disconcerted, unsure what had awoken him, he squeezed his eyes closed and opened them again to try and clear the bleariness, then pushed himself to sitting, listening carefully.

The road outside was quiet, no cars, but he could hear the sound of a voice, perhaps a radio or a TV somewhere downstairs. Fairly certain he had switched everything off before he ventured upstairs earlier, he swung his legs out of bed. He was wearing the plaid pyjamas that Laura had bought him the previous Christmas so didn't bother to grab his robe. He intended to return to bed within a minute or so anyway.

He crossed the landing and started to descend the stair. As always, the third one down from the top creaked and when it did so, the voice stopped. Tom paused, his senses tingling in alarm. He held his breath and listened. The voice began again. Tom cocked his head and frowned. He was certain it wasn't a radio. It had to be a person. The voice was low, deep, resonant. Tom was suddenly afraid of what he would find downstairs, but he couldn't remain poised halfway down the stairs all night. Taking a deep breath, he slipped down the next few steps. The voice halted again as though it could sense Tom's movement, but Tom was committed. He clung onto the banister and swung around the newel at the bottom in a rush, then padded in his bare feet along the hall and into the dark lounge.

Silhouetted against the partially open glass patio doors was a figure—a woman with a sports bag slung casually over her shoulder. Although Tom had been expecting to find someone in the room, it still took him by surprise. He cried out in alarm and flicked a switch, bathing the room in light. Laura slammed the patio doors closed, then turned to glare at him from under her fringe.

Tom was struck by her appearance. He wondered whether she had been sleeping rough since he'd last seen her. Her hair was unkempt, greasy even, entirely unlike the Laura of old. She wore ill-fitting jeans and a baggy jumper, dirty mud-spattered trainers, and a dark pink fleece. A filthy hand grasped the bag at her shoulder, and grime or something worse was engrained in her nails.

"Laura," Tom said, and his voice shook. He walked around the coffee table in the centre of the room, heading towards her. In his heart he wanted to offer comfort, but his head told him that she wouldn't accept it from him.

The woman who was both his wife but not his wife, turned to look at him, the flesh of her face oddly slack, her eyes unfocused.

"What are you doing here, darling?" he asked. "You know the police are looking for you, don't you?"

Laura rolled her head on her shoulders like a boxer limbering up for a prize fight, an odd movement for a woman of her age. She dropped the bag to the floor and shook her arms out. Tom took a cautious step backwards.

"Why are the police looking for me?" Laura asked, her voice little-girl-twee. "What could they possibly want with me?"

"They think you might be in some sort of trouble, Laura," Tom soothed, desperately trying to placate his wife. "Listen, why don't I make us a nice cup of cocoa and then you can speak to them about it. Or Adam Chapple, the nice detective, who came around before." When Laura didn't lash out at him, Tom felt emboldened. "Do you remember him? He can help us sort all of this out. Maybe it's all a mistake, my love. You can put the police straight, can't you? What do you say. Shall I warm some milk on the stove?"

Laura lifted her chin and rolled her eyes, the whites showing momentarily, and then dropped her head again. "You can do what you fucking well like, old man," she said quietly. "But if you boil any milk, I'll throw it over that fucking ugly head of yours."

Tom gasped and Laura tipped her head back and roared with laughter. "Oh Tom. You're a case! Why are you bothering me? Why are you even here, you stupid fuck!"

Tom shook his head, fearful of her aggression but still wanting her to be his Laura, his loving wife. He lifted his hands in a conciliatory fashion. "You know why I'm here. It's my home, Laura. Our home."

Laura hunched her shoulders and arched her back and swung her head around, a panther stalking its prey. She began to pace in front of the window, watching Tom's every move. She kept her voice low when she resumed speaking, but it was all the more terrifying for that.

"I'm not Laura. Can't you fucking see that you cretinous piece of shit? You're blind. Or stupid. But how stupid do you have to be? Why are you even pretending that I'm Laura when you know I'm not?"

Tom shrugged, unsure what to do or say that wouldn't make matters worse. "I just want you back the way you were," he tried. "I want you home, Laura."

"I told you I'm not Laura. For Christ's sake man, listen to me for once. You know I'm not Laura, because you were told so. Weren't you? Didn't your little friend Cassia tell you that?

In any case, it should have been obvious to you from the word go, but you wanted to go on playing happy families, didn't you?" Laura's voice was deceptively calm. Suddenly she lashed out with one arm and knocked a vase and a plant pot from the sideboard with a single clench-fisted punch. At the same time, the main light was extinguished, and the room was plunged into darkness. Only the light from upstairs offered Tom some illumination. "Didn't you?" she roared.

Tom retreated in fear, backing away until he reached the wall behind him and could go no farther, trapped between the sofa and Laura as she headed towards him. He cowered.

"Tom, you're incredibly stupid." Her voice was little more than a mutter, a drone, as though she was talking to herself and not to Tom at all. She babbled on and on. "I was happy for you to be along for the ride while I was getting my bearings. It's odd being in this body, some old chick with bad knees, and I've got to admit I wasn't overly happy about it, but it's about making the best of a very bad job. I had to get used to it. You gave me the time to do that, and I'm grateful. I'm kind of sorry you've been caught in the cross-fire, but then I guess somebody would have had to be. If it wasn't you it would have been somebody else, wouldn't it? With any luck I can find a way to switch bodies, maybe grab someone a hell of a lot younger soon. That would be useful. It will help if I have to make a quick getaway some time. But now I know who I am and what I'm doing, I don't need you anymore. I don't need your whining or your interference, and quite frankly it's been driving me up the fucking wall. So I'm sorry Tom but you're going to have to go. Yes. You're going to have to go, and I'm going to have to be the one that ejects you."

"Please," begged Tom. Laura advanced on him, hatred glittering in her eyes, her mouth curling with disgust.

"I'm going to put you out of your misery, Tom. I don't know if you'll ever see your Laura again, and really? I don't much care." Laura bent to Tom and clasped him around the neck with one impossibly strong hand. He shrieked and tried to fight her off, clawing ineffectually at her with his stubby fingers and short nails.

Laura dragged him to standing. Tom closed his eyes tightly, fearing what would happen to him next and praying it would be over quickly, but a sudden hiss interrupted them. Tom opened his eyes and looked past Laura's shoulder as she half turned, struggling to see what had interrupted her. She backed away from whatever was there, dropping Tom who fell to his knees, and then made a run for the living room door.

Coughing and rubbing at his throat, his eyes streaming, Tom pushed himself up, looking to see what had scared Laura. There was a glow in the garden beyond, just outside the doors. A figure, its deformed head covered in a thick cream veil. Tom had never seen Abelia before, but both Adam and Heidi had described her, so he knew who this was. Her presence was awe-inspiring in the worst kind of way. She was surrounded by energy, a pulsating force field of some kind, that pulsed around her as she hovered on the decking immediately outside. Then, as though she had suddenly made up her mind, she strode through the glass doors as though they weren't there. Tom's stomach hit the floor. What sort of being could do that? Nothing you ever wanted to meddle with if you had a choice. Tom's knees lost their strength, and he feared he would pass out, but Abelia didn't even glance his way. From the hallway, Tom could hear Laura grappling with the locks of the front door. The ones he had remembered to secure before heading for bed.

Tom was terrified and in two minds, but after nearly forty years, and in spite of their recent exchange, his loyalty to Laura meant he would try to protect her at all costs. He needed to halt Abelia's progress. He couldn't let her get hold of Laura. "Stop," he roared, and to his surprise Abelia paused. She turned her head, a rigid movement reminiscent of someone with a frozen neck, and regarded him in silence. Tom stood straight, facing Abelia. "Leave my wife be," he commanded, trembling in anticipation of Abelia's wrath.

"You're a fool to yourself," a disembodied voice from beneath the veil addressed him, and the sound chilled him to the bone. There was no warmth, no emotion, just the deep clipped tones of something less than human, rock dragged across concrete. "This is not your wife, just the shell of her meagre existence on this plane." She dismissed him, looking pointedly away, and took another step towards the hall.

In sudden desperation, Tom threw himself at her and wrapped his arms around her waist. She surprised him by how solid she was. He had half expected her to be made entirely of lace. She had no flesh to speak of, not an ounce of fat, nothing soft. She was hard to the touch, as though carved from wood. He was unable to grasp her and began to slip.

Tom heard the front door fly open and the sound of footsteps running away down the drive. Laura was making a successful getaway. He had one knee on the floor and was about to lift himself up and try and run himself when Abelia reached down and with one savage blow broke Tom's arm. He screamed at the sudden shooting agony and fell to the floor. Abelia's foot connected with his head, as she edged past him. Tom reached for her, desperately clinging to consciousness, his good arm falling short of the folds of her skirt, then his world faded from one of dim artificial light, to grey, before a merciful darkness swallowed his consciousness.

***

Tom opened his eyes and sat up with a loud gasp of fear, his heart beating hard against his chest. One hand clawed at the air in a desperate attempt to ward Abelia off.

"Shhh, you're okay, you're going to be fine," a familiar voice soothed him. Tom turned bloodshot eyes to his left to see Heidi sitting on a chair next to his bed in a raspberry coloured beanie. Close by, he could hear machines beeping and hushed voices. Somewhere down a nearby corridor, somebody dropped something with a loud clang and laughter followed.

"I'm in a hospital?" he asked, and Heidi nodded and smiled. Tom, his head thumping with the worst headache he had ever had, noticed his right arm in a temporary cast, but other than that he seemed relatively unscathed. He wasn't hooked up to any machines, and it appeared he was in no imminent danger of dying. Relief flooded through him.

"Laura?" he asked.

"She's not here. You're safe. Relax."

Tom nodded, but he remained agitated. Heidi shushed him again. "Just lie back. I'll tell a nurse you're awake." Before he could protest, she was on her feet, moving away, but she halted before she'd taken a few steps and returned, bending down to him to whisper, "By the way. I lied and told them I was your daughter. I hope you don't mind?"

He tried to shake his head, but it hurt too much. His skull felt as though it was trapped in a vice. "No," he answered hoarsely, "although I think the accent might give it away."

"Just pretend to be a Brummie for me then," Heidi said with a wink and limped away. Tom was able to watch her until she exited the room. He relaxed a little, thankful for Heidi's presence here, then glanced worriedly around the room. Five other men shared the ward, two with visitors, one old chap fast asleep, the other one, a younger man, reading a book. He noticed Tom looking his way and smiled. Tom nodded at him, then looked out of the window to his right. He wondered how long he had been in the hospital. He guessed it was afternoon.

Heidi returned, following a smiling nurse, who took his blood pressure, pulse, and temperature, filled in his chart, and told him the doctor would be along to see him in a while. She raised the head of the bed before rushing off again to answer a beep.

Heidi resumed her seat and patted his good arm. "How are you feeling?" she asked.

"Rough," he said, his throat scratchy. He coughed.

"Would you like some water?" Heidi asked, and when he nodded, she poured some into a glass and added a straw. Tom lifted his head and drank a little. It eased the dryness of his throat.

"What happened?" asked Heidi. "The neighbours called the police. Said there had been a disturbance."

"Laura came home," Tom said, and his eyes prickled with pain at the thought of his wife. "Except, whoever that is, it's not Laura, is it? It's not her, Heidi. Not my wife."

"I know, Tom, I know," Heidi stroked his arm sympathetically.

Tom drew a few shuddering breaths. "I really think she would have killed me, whoever it was. But at the last minute, we had another visitor. The most unwelcome visitation." Heidi knew what was coming and grimaced. "Abelia. It must have been her. The woman you told me about."

"She came into your home?"

"She stepped through the glass doors as though they weren't there. She wanted Laura."

"She's going after Laura? If you think about it, that makes sense. That's what we found out at the séance after all. It's what she wants."

Tom nodded. "Maybe I made a mistake. I tried to stop Abelia. I didn't want her to reach Laura. I tried to hold Abelia back. Should I have let her have her? I just couldn't. I tried to protect my wife. Even though that thing ... is not my wife."

"Oh Tom," said Heidi mournfully.

"I know. I know." Tom sighed, bone weary with grief. "It's not her and yet I just couldn't bear the thought of Abelia catching up with her. What if there was some tiny aspect of Laura left in her? How could I lose her again?"

Heidi nodded her understanding. "But maybe this whole nightmare would be finished if Abelia took what she wanted. Maybe she'd go back to where she came from, and we could just get on with our lives?"

Tom could see that. It made sense. "I know. I do. I just couldn't do it." He wiped his eyes with his good hand and cleared his throat. Heidi lifted his glass to him once more and helped him take a drink. He finished the glass and slumped back against the pillow. "Heidi? What if Abelia wants to take you too? Maybe she thinks you cheated death at the same time as Laura and she wants you back. Have you considered that?"

Heidi stared in horror at Tom.

***

The doctor confirmed a broken humerus. The medical team had set Tom's arm while he'd been out. He had some superficial bruising and a probable concussion, but the doctor happily informed Tom that he could expect to be released some time the next day.

"Do you have someone at home to look after you?" the doctor asked, and Tom had welled up. He wasn't entirely sure he would ever return to his house on Coleridge Way again. It would never feel like home now that Laura had gone, and there were far too many memories. He couldn't live with her absence.

Besides, he would be a sitting duck, far too easy for Laura to find if he returned to his house. "I'll go and stay with my daughter," he answered, thinking of Heidi. "If she'll have me."

"Jolly good. I think that's the best thing," said the doctor and went on his way.

Tom tried to settle down for the night, but the general hustle and bustle on the ward kept him on edge. Finally, after his nearest neighbour's visitors departed, Tom hoped for a little shut eye, however the man turned his television on. Tom was uncomfortable, his mind racing, and more than a little scared.

Eventually the lights were dimmed in the ward, the televisions were turned off, and the gentleman in the neighbouring bed fell asleep. Tom dozed for a few hours himself, tossing fitfully, waking easily. The pressure of his bladder some time in the early hours woke him. Rather than bother a nurse, he slipped out of bed and made his own way to the nearest toilet. It was engaged. He headed out into the corridor, passing the nurses' station, currently unoccupied, and pattered in his bare feet to the next available toilet. He entered the small room, but when he closed the door, he realised the lighting was not automatic and the little room remained in pitch darkness. He opened the door a crack in order to look around to find the light switch. He located two cords. One, with a red cord, was the emergency alarm for anyone taken ill, and the other with a white cord was the light pull. You didn't want to get the two confused. He was about to tug the white cord when he noticed a familiar figure pass by the door.

Tom did a double take. Could that be Laura in the corridor? The figure was wearing Laura's familiar dark pink fleece. He stared in horror at her back as she walked purposefully towards the nurse's station, her head swivelling as she went. She paused at the nurses' station, and he realised she was reading the patient information board, looking for his name no doubt. She cast a glance down the corridor, back towards him as though aware of being watched, and he shrunk away behind the door, glad that the room remained in darkness. With any luck she hadn't caught sight of him. Hardly daring to breathe, Tom braved peering out through the tiny gap once more. Laura appeared to be scanning the doors, looking at bed numbers. She disappeared into his ward. Now it was only a matter of time before she discovered that his bed was empty. Empty but only recently vacated.

Tom dithered. He wasn't sure what to do. Should he make a run for it? Where would he go? What if she saw him fleeing and followed him? Tom had no idea how anyone could enter a hospital at night without being questioned. Where were security? Why hadn't they stopped her?

The thought pulled him up short. How could he alert security to the fact that there was an intruder on the premises? Perhaps if he could get to the nurses' station and ring them they would arrive before Laura found him and tore him limb from limb. He squinted through the gap again. No sign of her. He considered making a run for the station when he remembered the second cord on the wall of the cubicle. The red cord. The one you pulled if you were taken ill.

Without thinking twice, he pulled the cord. Immediately an alarm began going off at the nurses' station and he heard running footsteps.

"Where is it?" a male voice asked.

"Patient bathroom three," said a woman and the steps

headed his way.

He walked into the corridor to meet the two nurses head on. "I'm sorry," he said in a loud voice, too loud, "I pulled the wrong cord. I just wanted to use the toilet but I couldn't see. Silly me. I'm so sorry." An older female nurse arrived at the nurses' station and switched the alarm off just as Laura was drawn out of the side ward by the commotion. She spotted Tom and smiled. It was a smile that turned Tom's bowels to ice.

She moved towards him, drawing the attention of the nurse at the station. "Excuse me, madam? How did you get in here?"

Laura, setting her sights on Tom, ignored her.

"Madam?" When there was still no response, the nurse said, "I'll have to phone security."

Laura took a few paces towards Tom but must have heard the nurse speaking into the phone. She turned sharply about, rounded the nurses' station in three easy strides, and knocked the nurse to the floor. The male nurse who had answered Tom's alarm rushed to his colleague's aid, the other pushed Tom back into the bathroom.

"Lock the door," she said. "Security are on their way."

Tom locked the door behind the nurse and leant against the door listening. He could hear shouting and a nurse screaming. Some patients began to call out in alarm. Bells were sounding, buzzers going off. The clump of heavy boots passed close by in the corridor outside as security personnel arrived. Tom held his breath. An angry howl. Swearing. The sound of something—someone—being dragged came closer to where he was hiding. As it drew level with him, a terrific thump against the door made him rear back in fear.

"I know you're in there, you dumb fuck!" screamed Laura's voice. "You're a dead man! A dead man, Tom! Do you hear me?"

"Come on, you," said a deeper voice, presumably a security guard. "Get away from there. Joe? Can you give me a hand here? It's going to take three of us. She's absurdly strong..." and the voices disappeared down the corridor.

***

An hour later, Tom was exhausted. He had spent some time answering questions from security about the strange woman. What could he tell them except that she was his wife and wanted for murder? It was easier than telling them the truth, but even so the news caused some alarm. In light of Tom's information about Laura's warrant, security had contacted police, and she had been escorted to the police station in the city centre. Tom was notified the police would return in the morning to speak to him if he was well enough.

"I will be," said Tom, understandably weary, but pleased that Laura had been locked up. He could never feel safe while she remained on the loose.

Tom declined a sedative from a nurse. His gut told him he needed to keep his faculties intact. Eventually left alone, the ward restored to quiet once more, he peered out of the window into the darkness beyond. The car park lay in front of him, virtually empty at this hour of the morning, the shiny tarmac lit by halogen lamps.

Tom wasn't surprised at all to see Abelia silhouetted under one of the lights, her horrendous head angled in such a way that she could only have been staring up at the window and the frightened man who looked out at her in dread.

CHAPTER TWENTY-TWO

Heidi arranged a freshly unwrapped Battenberg cake on the coffee table alongside a steaming pot of tea. "Would anybody like a piece of cake?" she asked, cutting herself a small piece and picking delicately at the marzipan.

Her forced cheeriness couldn't lift the morose mood in the room. Adam was standing next to the window staring out at the park beyond. Tom, his face ashen with pain, huddled on the sofa, wrapped in a blanket. He had called Heidi this morning to ask whether she would put him up once he had been released from hospital. She had agreed without hesitation, but as she didn't drive she had cheekily called Adam to ask whether he could collect Tom from hospital.

Tom had been released from the hospital in Exeter in mid-afternoon, and now here they were, three lost souls, trying to figure out what to do next.

Something was bothering Adam, big time, and Heidi had made an attempt to discover what that could be, but the detective remained introverted and distant, tension apparent through the set of his jaw and the way his head hunched and disappeared into his shoulders at times. Heidi often caught him looking into the distance, lost in his own thoughts, unusually reticent to join in any banter. Not that there was much of it today.

Tom shook his head, but finally Adam left the window to bend over the coffee table. He cut two large square slices from the end of the rectangular cake and stuffed the first one in his mouth. In a couple of hard chews, it was gone. The second followed quickly after.

"I haven't had Battenberg for years," he said, noticing Heidi's astonishment.

"When was the last time you ate?" she asked, and Adam shrugged.

"I can make you some dinner, if you like?" said Heidi. She never had much of an appetite herself these days. She wasn't the world's greatest cook at the best of times, but she could manage pasta in an emergency and there were always sandwiches.

Adam was about to refuse, but he realized with a sudden pang how hungry he actually felt. He didn't want to put her to any trouble though. "Don't worry," he said, "I can always ring for a pizza."

"With ham and pineapple?" asked Tom, his eyes hopeful. He hadn't eaten much in the past forty-eight hours either, and certainly nothing with any flavour.

"Nobody needs fruit on a pizza, Tom," said Adam, horrified at the notion.

"It's part of your five a day," Heidi chimed in, and Adam shook his head in mock disgust. "Do you think you could eat pizza, Tom?" asked Heidi, relieved that her offer to cook had been so quickly rebutted and happy that the men had shown an interest in something.

"I could probably manage a slice," Tom responded, "but I'll need an early night soon afterwards, I reckon."

"That's not a problem," said Heidi, "I have the bed made up. But I don't have any pyjamas that will fit you, or a spare toothbrush or anything."

Adam observed the look of worry that passed over Tom's face. "Don't fret, Tom. Why don't I take your keys and go over to your house and collect some things for you?"

Heidi smiled appreciatively. "That would be great, Adam, thanks."

"Are you sure you don't want me to come with you?" asked Tom, looking almost sick at the thought.

"No, definitely not. You stay here and keep warm."

Adam loitered by the window once more, peering out, scanning the road outside as well as the park beyond.

"Heidi," Adam called, and she joined him at the window. He lowered his voice so that Tom couldn't hear them. "If there's the slightest hint of trouble or Abelia shows up, I want you to call me straight away. You've got my number, right?"

"Yes," she said.

"Put it on speed dial, and make sure your phone is fully charged, okay?"

"Will do."

Adam raised his voice. "Where's your keys, Tom? I'll pick up some pizzas on my way back. But believe me, mate, none of them will have any fruit on them whatsoever."

***

Adam let himself into the Goodwin's house. He stood at the front door for a while, acclimatising his senses and listening out for anything amiss. The house was cold and still. Almost forlorn. He'd popped into the neighbour's house to introduce himself and to inform them that Tom was safe and well. They were good people, worried about Tom. He put their mind at rest without telling them where Tom was staying. He knew it wouldn't take much for them to find out, but in the meantime it seemed safest all round.

Satisfied that everything was quiet and as it should be, Adam stepped into the hall and firmly closed the front door behind him. He ducked his head into the kitchen. Clean and tidy, apart from a few newspapers on the kitchen table. Adam opened the fridge door to discover it almost empty, with the exception of a third of a pint of milk, some bacon, a loosely wrapped block of cheese, half a soggy lettuce, and a jar of raspberry jam. No beer or wine. He closed the fridge door again, his eye scanning the magnets stuck to the front: Lyme Regis, Bournemouth, Shanklin, Ffestiniog railway, Caernarvon Castle. There were a number of receipts and a shopping list beneath the magnets.

His colleagues had been in the house and performed their usual thorough job, the finger print dust all over the living room made that obvious. The remains of the vase were scattered across the floor although the coffee table had been righted. Spots of blood on the carpet had clearly been

185

swabbed. Adam checked the patio doors. They had been locked and the key dangled from the lock. He took the key out of the door and pocketed it. Better to be safe than sorry.

He stared out into the garden. There was just enough daylight outside to show how neglected the once magnificent and well-loved garden had become. This had been Laura's pride and joy, but now the grass could have done with one more trim before winter, weeds poked their heads between paving slabs, and the rose bushes badly needed trimming.

Satisfied the back of the house had been properly secured, Adam made his way upstairs. The first door he opened at the top of the landing was a bathroom. Adam hazarded a guess that the blue toothbrush was Tom's. He found a wash bag and added Tom's shaving kit, soap, flannel, and deodorant. He located the airing cupboard and pulled out a clean towel to add to the stash.

The master bedroom was neat and tidy as though Tom had recently cleaned and hoovered, although the bed clothes had been thrown back. Adam searched the top of the wardrobe and found a small case. He packed Tom's toiletries in there and searched through a chest of drawers to locate underwear and pyjamas, t-shirts, a jumper, and socks. He added a dressing gown and some trousers and decided that would probably keep him going for a while. Adam could always come back if Tom needed more.

Job done.

He paused at the remaining door on the landing, then turned the handle and pushed it open. This was the spare room; the room Laura had been occupying since coming home from the hospital after her stroke. It was the polar opposite of the rest of the tidy house, smelling faintly stale and littered with detritus. There was a TV with a DVD player attachment and DVDs were scattered all around the floor. Adam shuffled through some of them. Laura must have had varied tastes. Fast and Furious. Saw. The latest Star Wars movie. James Bond. A couple of Sandra Bullock movies. Many of them looked like charity shop purchases. There was nowhere else in Durscombe to buy DVDs. Adam assumed the Goodwins didn't have a subscription movie service.

A pile of magazines had spilled under the bed. Film mainly, an astrology magazine, interior design, and a pristine copy of a Woman's Weekly, looking somewhat sedate and out of place among the rest of magazines.

Adam dropped the magazines and quickly shifted amongst Laura's other belongings on the floor. Among the underwear and a few t-shirts, there were sweet wrappers, crisp packets, and a couple of empty fizzy drink bottles, some empty sandwich cartons, and even a plastic noodle pot.

Adam stood, perplexed by what he was seeing. If anything, the stink was worse on the floor. The rest of the house had been pristine on each of the occasions it had been visited by the police. Perhaps Tom was the house-proud partner. Adam made a mental note to ask him, then left the room abruptly, switching off the light and closing the door tightly behind him. He retraced his steps, the master bedroom, the bathroom, and downstairs.

Dusk had fallen outside, and the kitchen was gloomy. Adam switched the lights on, and as they blinked above his head, his eyes returned to the fridge door.

Not the magnets, or the receipts that they restrained, but the shopping list. He plucked it off the fridge, sending the Shanklin magnet flying. It smacked into a cabinet, slipped to the floor and bounced into a corner.

Adam placed the list on one of the work surfaces and smoothed it out, caressing the page gently, examining the scruffy writing, obviously written in a rush.

AA batteries for remote

Honey Nut Cornflakes

Pepsi Max (not Diet Pepsi)

Bananas

Pasta

Something in Adam's mind nagged at him, but he couldn't think what it was. He would ask Tom about it, but it was probably something and nothing. As his phone began its insistent ring, he folded the list up and tucked it in his jacket pocket, swapping it for his mobile.

Polly. "Hi," he said.

"Where are you?" she asked.

"Out and about." She would hate the vagueness of this, he knew, but she wouldn't pry. "What's up?"

"I've got a bit of bad news for you."

"Go on."

"Laura Goodwin? CPS aren't pressing charges. Exeter have to let her go."

"You've got to be kidding me. They've got witnesses at the hospital to an assault. Credible witnesses. Nurses for Pete's sake. What else do they need?"

"She's been cautioned, because as far as CPS are concerned, it's a first offence. They can't hold her any longer."

"Polly! What about Nicola's murder? She's wanted for questioning for that."

"Calm down Adam, don't shout at me. You know how this shit works as well as I do!"

Adam flipped the kitchen lights off and grabbed Tom's bag. "She needs to be held, one way or the other. I'm going to head over and make sure Petty understands that!"

"There's no point." But Adam ended the call and was out of the front door and into his car before Polly could tell him it was too late. The deed had been done. Laura was on the loose once more.

CHAPTER TWENTY-THREE

Alone in her little dwelling under the cemetery, Cassia added another log to her fire. She had a feeling that no matter how high she banked the fuel, she was never going to warm the house or herself today. Shivering, she rubbed her hands together and held them out to the flames. How could a fire burn so impossibly cold?

She knew the answer.

She stood wearily and plucked a throw from the back of the sofa. One of her mother's favourites. Folding it in half on the diagonal so that it resembled a shawl, she draped it around her shoulders and slumped into her accustomed seat. From here she could look out through the port holes or stare at the fire, whichever took her fancy. What she couldn't see, because she had her back to it and had angled the chair away, was the empty mirror frame on the wall behind her.

She didn't want to see it, but she knew it was there. The frame called to her and had done every second of every minute that Cassia spent in the dwelling ever since the séance. Or rather something or someone beyond the frame called to her, and she found herself oddly unnerved by this. She was used to spirits, but this was different. If she listened closely she could discern a chorus of sinister voices, all with something less than complimentary to say about her and her world. She tried to close her mind to the content, but she couldn't close her ears to their voices so easily. Now she understood why Amelia Fliss had chosen to kill herself the way she had, for if what her mother had told her was true, Cassia now understood the intrusive nature of spirits who refused to be silenced.

In addition to the voices, the freezing draft flowing through the house leeched the warmth from her bones. It emanated from the frame and spread through every room of the house. Condensation clung to the portholes and glass and brass

189

objects, tiny beads of moisture glittering in the light from the ever-burning fire, a million open eyes that watched her every move.

In a vain attempt to halt the encroaching freeze, Cassia had nailed branches and pieces of driftwood she had rescued from the beach across the frame, but to no avail. She understood that there was nothing practical she could do on a human level; any long-term solution would have to come from the spirit world.

She had a sense that something in the shadows was secretly watching her. Some tiny dark matter, something skittish, clinging to the dark places, jumpy when she looked its way. She feared that this was the beginning of an avalanche of souls seeping out of the frame on the wall, searching for some way to become physical, perhaps looking for a host they could commandeer. She had no idea whether they were good souls or bad souls. It didn't bear thinking about, so she tried not to.

Cassia was finding it difficult to sleep and impossible to relax. She was exhausted and scared and she didn't know who to turn to. She longed for her mother. She at least would have known what to do.

The fire sputtered unhealthily. Cassia threw back her makeshift shawl in frustration and freed her arms. She reached for the poker to attack it once more. After a few minutes of poking and prodding, and attempting to draw the heat through the chimney, she knew it was pointless. The fire gave off no heat and struggled to keep going while at the same time a gale was blowing against the back of her neck and shoulders. She was destined to freeze if she didn't take action soon.

She wished for somewhere else to go. Anywhere with a soft bed and peace and quiet. She wondered about Gloria. Cassia was sure Gloria wouldn't turn her away if she needed someplace to stay temporarily, but of course, she had her own kids, lots of them, mainly teenagers, and that usually indicated a houseful of people and a huge amount of noise. She dismissed the thought as untenable and opted to run a bath instead. The hot water would warm her through and then she could clamber into bed and stay warm under the duvet while drowning out the voices by covering her ears with pillows.

She filled the bath with the hottest water she could bear mingled with distilled lavender oil and sank gratefully into the water. After lighting a dozen candles or so, she closed the door firmly, wedging a rolled up towel to act as a draught-cum-noise excluder. The scratching, whispery voices could still be heard, drifting from the direction of the living room, but the sound seemed far away and was almost bearable if she tried to think about something else.

She lifted a foot from the water and examined the chipped black nail varnish on her toes. She had let herself go a little over the past week, but now she wasn't sure she really cared.

It had suddenly struck her just how much of her witchy persona had been for effect. She had grown up believing her mother's stories of her inherent abilities, and she had assumed she had great powers–just like her grandmothers. She had relished being different at school, enjoyed emphasising her otherness, particularly at secondary school where her gothic looks and fortune-telling abilities had won her notoriety, if few friends. But now, for the first time, she recognised how much of this had been a façade. She had not been an adept student in any subject, including, it transpired, witchcraft.

She had played with magick because it suited her to do so. She had utilised it for her own ends. Now she came to realise that there were powers far greater than hers in the world and outside the world. She was little more than a transparent shrimp in one of Durscombe's rock pools. She would be eaten alive by much bigger fish.

***

She walked slowly alongside her mother. The pair of them ambling through the cemetery. The trees were heavy with early summer foliage and the paths were lined with gloriously bright flower beds. At every point where the pathways intersected, an iron post stood guard, a sentinel from a bygone age, each hung with a pair of hanging baskets. The bees were busy, motoring between blooms, their buzzing making the air feel oddly heavy.

Cassia gazed at her mother through a filter of longing. She appeared well. Her cheeks rosy, her hair greying at the temples but still the rich dark brown Cassia remembered. Her eyes were clear, no sign of the jaundice that had plagued her in those final weeks.

"I'm dreaming, aren't I?" said Cassia, and her voice was thick with disappointment.

Her mother stopped walking and faced her only child. "Oh my little love. Always you diminish the most magickal of gifts. I was hoping you would have seen that by now. Have the past few weeks taught you so little?"

"Not a dream, then?" asked Cassia, reaching out. Her mother caught her hand and tucked it under her arm, pulling her daughter on. Cassia was overwhelmed to once more have a sense of the physical being her mother had been.

Her mother squeezed her fingers. "I'm somewhere between the land of the living and the dead."

Cassia's heart warmed through. "I miss you, Mum. I had hoped it would be you I connected to at the séance. I did everything wrong."

"It's certainly true that you've opened a Pandora's box of sorts," her mother answered carefully. Cassia couldn't register any disapproval, and she knew her mother was not one to judge, but she would recognise how dangerous the situation was. "It was an error. You must strive to fix it."

"I'm not sure I can."

"You give up far too easily, Cassia. Your friend was right."

"My friend?"

"The one who has the mark of death upon her," her mother said. Cassia remembered how Tansy had caressed the scars on Heidi's scalp. "Only you can fix this. You have all the skills you need."

"How do I do that? How do I persuade Abelia to go back to where she came from? And the other spirits? How do I close the void?"

"Abelia will go back when she has custody of the soul she is chasing. The sooner she has what she wants the better. In the meantime, she will destroy anyone who tries to create a portal from this world to the next. Every time a portal is created and a spirit is invited through to this world, the veil thins. It is not desirable on any level to let loose spirits arbitrarily. No-one knows what tensions that will cause. If you cannot close the void that you opened at the séance, Abelia will come after you and your friends. She has every right to do so. Abelia is a soldier. Impeccably trained. Rational to the nth degree. She lacks compassion and empathy. She is perfectly capable of destroying all of you without so much as a second thought." Cassia balked. "It is her job to prevent people leaving the land beyond the veil. You created the gateway, and therefore you must close it."

"I don't know how to do that. How do I do it? What would you do?"

"Everything you need in order to undo the harm you and your friends have caused lies within you. Trust in yourself."

"Oh Mum," said Cassia, half-cross, half-frustrated, "you were always so vague. Nothing's changed." Her mother laughed, and Cassia, wanting to relish her amusement and her shining face once more, turned to look at her, but the face that she knew best in the whole world was starting to fade from her view. She could see the gravestones beyond, coming into focus as though someone had switched her lens. "Oh no, Mum, stay!"

"I'm always with you, my little love."

And she was gone.

***

Cassia sat up in the bath in a rush, sending a tidal wave of water over the side, knocking a few tea lights from the side of the bath. Something shifted in the shadows to her left, and Cassia, half-expecting it to be her mother, turned to look that way. Nothing concrete, but as she scrutinized the shadows, she thought she could make out a shape or form. It was not her mother.

"Be gone!" she said loudly and with as much disdain as she could. Her mother had always taught her that intent was everything to a witch. The shadow skittered sideways, then slid to the floor and slipped beneath two cracks in the floorboards.

"Intent." Cassia repeated to herself. "Intent and resolve." She hauled herself out of the bath, her skin glowing in what little light remained. It was a useful reminder of how young and strong she was. Her mother had told her she could overcome this, and she was determined to try. She grabbed a dry towel hanging from a hook on the door and wrapped herself in it. In the steam of the mirror that hung above the basin she wrote three words.

Intent. Resolve. Clarity.

Her tenet going forwards. She was ready to take action.

CHAPTER TWENTY-FOUR

When no pizzas appeared to be forthcoming, Tom turned in for the night earlier than usual. His encounter at the hospital had left him feeling bruised and more shaken than he cared to admit. The previous twenty-four hours had been stressful beyond belief, and he wanted to forget, at least for a short time. How could his beautiful wife, whom he had loved so much for so long, metamorphosed into that aggressive entity he had witnessed at the hospital? Remembering her as she had been just months ago, compared to the banshee who had been dragged kicking and screaming down the hospital corridor yesterday evening, made his heart hurt.

Tom abandoned Heidi to her solitary reading in the living room. She wanted to stay up and await Adam's return, but when Tom had indicated his desire to turn in, Heidi had kindly pointed the way to the spare room. Located at the top of the house, it was clean and unfussy, equipped with a double bed, a small chest of drawers, a wardrobe, and little else. The bay window faced front, looking out onto the street and the park beyond, with a good view of the river from this height, although of course, Tom couldn't see much in the darkness.

Adam's continued absence was a mystery to them both. Tom had expected Adam to return within the hour. Heidi had attempted to contact him a few times, but his phone went straight to voicemail, and he hadn't called her back. Without pyjamas or toiletries, Tom had come to bed in his shirt and brushed his teeth using his finger. He didn't mind, he only hoped Adam was all right and wondered what it was that was keeping him. Hopefully he hadn't run into trouble at Coleridge Way.

He slept well at first and didn't hear Heidi come to bed, but some time after one he woke up and recognised an all too familiar urge to pee. He was warm and comfortable and could quite happily have remained in bed, but he knew he wouldn't get back to sleep, so he pushed himself up and groggily went in search of the bathroom.

Mission accomplished, he stiffly made his way back to bed, feeling the aches and pains taking residence in his limbs but grateful not to be repeating the adventures of the previous night. A sound from outside drew his attention. He thought he heard a car drawing up. Figuring that Adam had finally arrived with Tom's necessaries, he pulled the curtain to one side and peered out. There were plenty of cars parked up, but none had their lights on or looked as though they had recently pulled in. There was no sign of Adam.

Budleigh Place was a quiet street. The lighting was subdued overnight, and Tom could make out the drizzle falling softly where moisture cut into the light from the street lamps. Under normal circumstances he loved this kind of weather, proper seaside weather. He and Laura had loved to walk along the promenade during the winter, relishing the rain on their faces. It made them feel fresh and alive.

A small movement beyond the parked cars drew Tom's attention. A fox. He smiled to see it. It walked calmly, crossing the park and edging into a circle of light, its own theatrical space. It came to a halt, dead centre, and lifted its head, staring up at Tom's window. Tom wiggled his fingers and smiled, as though he thought the fox would see him and somehow acknowledge his presence. It was conceit, he supposed, to think the animal would have any interest in him.

The fox raised its head towards the sky and barked. Tom, deciding on a whim that the fox was female, figured she was attempting to communicate with another of her kind, so he scanned the park for a mate. There were no other animals to see at all. That wasn't surprising, he supposed. It was a dreary night. What creature would want to be out in the cold and damp?

The fox dropped its head and stared at Tom's window once more. Tom shivered. The light glinted on the fox's eyes. They glowed brightly, somehow unearthly, boring into Tom's own, so much so that he shut his eyes against the glare and suddenly he didn't feel so enamoured of the little mammal. He shuddered and dared to peep back at the fox. With one cursory glare, as if sensing Tom's sudden disdain for her, she turned tail and trotted to her right, angling back towards the river and away from the direction of town.

Tom watched the fox go. It disappeared into the darkness. He waited to see if she would stray into the circle of light under the next lamp. She didn't do so.

Tom's arm ached. He needed to lie down. He was about to drop the curtain and cosy up under the covers once more when he spotted the one thing guaranteed to freeze his blood. Walking towards him, from the direction the fox had headed, came the veiled woman, Abelia. A number of large black birds flew around her as she made her way under the street light to take the fox's place, standing in the same spot the fox had temporarily inhabited, angled slightly sideways. She too tilted her head back to gaze at the sky. Tom hardly dared to breathe. He waited for her to mimic the fox's yips. She didn't oblige. As Tom continued to stare at her, she leisurely dropped her head and turned instead to face him.

Tom remembered his encounter with her at his home, the hardness of her flesh and the iciness of her voice. He shivered, the room freezing cold, his thin shirt inadequate in this room without any heating. Attempting to drag his gaze away from Abelia he found himself helpless to do so. His head and shoulders, suddenly made of lead, refused to respond to his urge. Abelia faced the house directly, tipped her head to look up, and he understood that she, in the same way as the fox, could see him framed in the window.

The birds circled and danced around her, cawing and calling. One of them broke off and flew towards the window, intent, it appeared, on flying headlong into the glass. Tom grimaced and cried out, but at the last second the bird pulled up, fluttered a few times, then settled on the windowsill. It cocked its head and peered in at Tom, its eyes glittering with a hard intelligence. Tom shuddered, and the bird pecked at the glass. A thin sound, tap tapping. Tom stepped forwards and slapped the flat of his hand hard against the window. The bird squawked and took flight, flew in a circle, ogling Tom before dropping towards Abelia, joining the throng of ravens and crows around her and flying amongst them, before landing at her feet.

Throughout the whole episode, Abelia hadn't broken her gaze on the window. Now, as Tom's focus was drawn reluctantly back to her, she slowly began to lift her veil. Tom whimpered. She had never done this before. Nobody had ever seen her face, or not remarked on it in his hearing. His instincts were telling him that he didn't want to cast his gaze upon her flesh. "Please don't," he begged, "please don't."

Abelia didn't hear him and wouldn't have cared if she had. She continued to lift the lace, and the progress was measured and relentless.

Tom's whole body trembled, and he struggled to catch his breath. "If I see this, if I see this, if I see her face, surely I'm a dead man?" he said to himself, his words loud in the small room. "A dead man." In passing he wondered whether it would matter to anyone. Without Laura what was he? She had been his life. And here he was, only sixty-one. Not old by any means. He could potentially enjoy another twenty years or more of living with good health. Time enough to rebuild the wreckage of his life alone without the woman he loved if he wanted to. If he could get through this. If he could survive. It suddenly seemed incredibly important to hang on to life. After all, it was all he had left.

Abelia however, had other ideas. She finally lifted the veil above her face, exposing the lace of her high necked dress, her mouth tilted—a bride expecting to be kissed. She allowed the veil to fall back from the centre of her head, and for the first time Tom saw the face of this angel of death, this warrior of the world beyond the veil. She wore no headdress. The thick horns curved from each side of her skull, as one with her flesh, twisting as they stretched for the stars.

In the limited light available, Abelia shone. Everything

about her seemed blanched of colour. Her face, cast solid like stone, was bleached as alabaster, and even her lips appeared devoid of pigment. Her pale hair, shimmering silver and white in the subdued light, was drawn tightly back from her face, stretching her forehead smooth. But it was her eyes, huge in the centre of her face, that froze the blood in Tom's veins. A cold light poured out of them, fixing him in their ghastly beam. He stared in morbid fascination, his stomach rolling with terror.

Fear turned to adrenaline and pumped through his veins. He shot backwards, away from the window, away from the vision of hell silhouetted in the street light below. He whipped around, meaning to call out to Heidi, to alert her to the danger. They would phone Adam and the detective would help them. Then they could put their heads together and all find somewhere safe to live while they figured out exactly how to get rid of Abelia. They had to find a way.

But he didn't get any farther. He had taken his eyes off Abelia for less than a second, but somehow in the blink of an eye, she had manifested herself in his bedroom. As he turned away from the horror at the window, he ran straight into her. Tom had no time to cry out, he barely had time to notice what was happening to him.

Abelia lifted her forearm, catching Tom in her strong fist beneath his chin, then drove him backwards against the wall next to the window. She was absurdly strong. She carried her momentum forwards, pushing her weight against him, popping ligaments, tearing muscle, crushing his windpipe and the vertebrae around his spinal cord. He was dead before he could acknowledge her presence.

She relaxed her arm, and Tom dropped to the ground, floppy but heavy. The cast on his arm clunked against the wooden floor as he fell. Abelia pulled her veil over her face once more.

CHAPTER TWENTY-FIVE

Adam's heart sank as he stared down at Tom's body, lying prone at the foot of the bed. The older man's eyes were half closed, his mouth slack. He was wearing nothing except his pants and a shirt and in his death throes had soiled himself. Adam desperately wanted to cover his modesty, but he knew his colleagues would be following him here shortly, and he didn't want to disturb the scene. Having established that Tom was beyond help, he backed out of the room and made his way downstairs.

Heidi perched on the edge of the sofa, her arms wrapped across her chest, her eyes shining with unshed tears. Adam sat next to her and drew her into his arms. The floodgates opened, and she sobbed into his jacket for a few minutes.

She pulled away and fished around in the turned up sleeve of her dressing gown to find a tissue. She blew her nose loudly.

"I can't believe he's gone," she said, finally trusting her voice, and Adam nodded.

"He was a lovely man," Adam agreed.

"I wish I'd heard something earlier, maybe disturbed…" Heidi looked around fearfully, then whispered, "whomever it was."

"I should have been here too," said Adam, but his words seemed hollow even to himself when he thought about the shopping list and the frantic trip home to search for examples of Dan's handwriting. He shook the memory off for now. Time to return to that and torture himself some more, a little later.

"You didn't hear or see anything?" he asked, his professional persona taking over.

"No, nothing. But something did wake me up, I just don't know what. I lay there a little while and then I heard a bang from the bedroom. I went up to his room and found him on the floor. I checked for a pulse, but he was obviously dead. I mean... his head?" Heidi swallowed. "His neck is broken, isn't it?"

Adam nodded, and Heidi started to cry again.

"The window was open?" Adam asked. Nobody could have climbed up to the second floor from the outside and let themselves in, but all avenues have to be investigated in a murder investigation. They might have climbed down from the roof he supposed. It seemed unlikely.

"Well... I opened it. It was closed when I went in there."

"Why did you open it? My colleagues will want to know. You need to be straight about what you're going to say."

Heidi hesitated. "I felt compelled to. That sounds stupid, doesn't it? Don't they say something about letting the spirit out of a room, though? I've heard that somewhere before. That was my intention. But while I was at the window I found these." Heidi slipped her hand inside her dressing gown pocket and drew out half a dozen black feathers.

Adam held his hand out, and Heidi dropped them onto the palm of his hand. Crow or raven, Adam couldn't tell.

"It was her. Abelia."

Adam nodded, his throat dry.

A rumble from the road outside told them that a car had arrived. There would be no space for the police to park on the crowded road, so no doubt they would set up a cordon and close the road off entirely. That way they could double park. That would set tongues wagging among the neighbours and no doubt trigger a variety of complaints.

"How are we going to explain how someone else got into the house?" Heidi whispered urgently. "I'd locked up. They're not going to believe it was Abelia, are they?"

There was a swift tap at the front door, and Adam hauled himself to his feet, intending to let his colleagues in. He stopped. "No, I suppose they're not," he said.

***

"The front door was open when you arrived here, was it sir?" asked Gibbs politely, his head bent to his notebook as he scribbled Adam's responses.

"It wasn't open, Gibbs, as in ajar. It was merely unlocked."

Gibbs met Adam's eyes. He looked shattered. Adam wondered how long his current shift had been and felt sorry for ribbing the younger officer.

"Yes, it was unlocked," Adam responded more kindly. "Ms Huddlestone had rung me on my mobile, and I came over here."

"Why didn't she call the police straight away?"

"As far as Ms Huddlestone is concerned, I am the police, Gibbs. And I live a damn site closer than you do. She knew I could respond more quickly."

"No signs of forced entry when you got here, sir?" Gibbs asked, ignoring the barb.

"None." Adam sighed. "But Ms Huddlestone had been in her bedroom and anyone could have gained entrance through the unlocked front door, I'm sure you'll agree."

"Ms Huddlestone—"

"Could not have done that to Tom Goodwin's neck. You need to look elsewhere." Adam fixed the younger DC with a hard stare. Gibbs closed his pocketbook with a snap. Adam began to turn away, but Gibbs stopped him.

"Sir," he said softly, turning himself to direct his voice at Adam only, away from the other officers and investigators hanging around. "I'm not blind. There's more to this than you're letting on. What's your involvement? Why are you so certain Heidi's not involved?" When Adam didn't answer, Gibbs, frowned. "Can you at least tell me what I should be looking for here?"

Adam shook his head. How could he make a rational response? "Just look for the intruder, Gibbs. Then you'll find who did this," he said and walked away.

That much held true at least.

***

Adam waited in the park, leaning against the railings well out of the way while his colleagues attended to Tom and Heidi and processed the scene. He knew he would have to answer more questions. The dawn arrived, and the early morning dew soaked into his clothes. He felt miserable and alone, mourning Tom's passing, the guilt gnawing away at his insides like acid. He should have been here last night instead of fruitlessly driving into Exeter and arguing with Petty. He'd tried to track down Laura's movements after she had been released from the station, but she had disappeared without a trace.

A commotion at the end of the street dragged his attention from the depths of self-recrimination. Another black and white car, this one with blues flashing had turned up outside the cordon. Adam recognised Polly's blonde hair. She spoke to the constable minding access to the road, and he lifted the tape to allow her to pass. Someone pointed in Adam's direction.

Polly glanced over, ducked her head, then jogged in his direction. When she was close enough to speak to him she stopped and regarded him, her own face bleak.

"Plymouth CID have been on the phone, Adam. You need to come with me."

CHAPTER TWENTY-SIX

In spite of the warmth of the car, Adam's face was numb. His stomach, knotted with heaviness, turned over with every new thought that flitted through his mind. He sat in the passenger seat of Polly's car, looking out of the window as she flew down the one-way system and along the seafront, before she could head back inland towards Adam's home on the outskirts of Durscombe. Fortunately, thanks to the time of day and year, the town was free of confused pensioners rambling around and stepping randomly off pavements, and the roads were relatively clear and free flowing, the seasonal traffic a dimming memory.

The journey seemed to take an age in any case. Adam forced himself to focus on the trees dotted along the roadside. He noticed how they were changing colour. The tree tops changed first, fading to gold, then brown, with the rest of the tree slowly following suit, until an autumn breeze shook the leaves free. Eventually the first storm of the winter would denude the entire tree, and it would stand stark against the dead sky. There would be no place to hide among the foliage.

Apparently, this was how Dan had finally been located. The blackberries were long gone, and the hedgerows had begun to die back. A passing motorist, stopping off for a pee on the side of the road, had spotted Dan's bicycle and investigated. He'd found more than he bargained for.

It transpired his son had been lying in the hedgerow for months. Since May.

And Adam hadn't known. Hadn't guessed.

What kind of a father was he?

Adam swallowed the terror building inside him. It wouldn't do to start questioning himself now. He had to hold it together. Do his best for Dan. Make the final arrangements. Answer questions. And ask them. He had to find out what had happened to Dan.

Occasionally Polly spoke to him, and he would slip out of his reverie to answer her as if from a distance. Was he warm enough? Did he want the radio on? He didn't know what the answer to those questions were. Everything seemed incredibly complicated.

They arrived at his house, and Polly parked up. Adam pulled himself out of the car with difficulty, and waited for her to collect what she needed. He wanted to tell her she didn't have to stay, but in a way he was glad of the company. She was a reassuring presence. Calm, efficient, adult. She led the way to his front door, and he fumbled around in his pocket for his door keys. Adam had heard of ketamine addicts existing in a bubble, and he wondered if that sensation was akin to this disassociated feeling he was experiencing. Polly met his eyes and took the keys from his hand. Her hands were warm, and his were freezing. She opened the door and they stepped through, just as a silver SUV drew up outside.

"That's them," said Polly. "You go through. I'll show them in."

'Them' consisted of DCI Adrian Yeardley and a family liaison officer named Moira Wilkins. Adam shook hands with them both and showed them through to his living room. He was absurdly aware of the coffee rings on the tables, the smudges on his windows, and the dust accumulating on pretty much everything else.

"I'm very sorry to be here under these circumstances," DCI Yeardley said, and Adam nodded. He understood from experience this was one of the most difficult parts of the job. He knew the script well enough too. But he would let them get on with their jobs. He had always felt bitterly sorry for the families he had dealt with in murder and fatal accident cases. Now here he was, and the boot was on the other foot.

"Thank you, sir. Please," Adam indicated his suite and everyone found a place to sit, Yeardley in Dan's favourite armchair, at right angles to the sofa where Polly sank next to Adam.

"I regret to be the bearer of such bad news, DS Chapple. Earlier this morning a passer-by found a bicycle and on further investigation he spotted human remains. That much I believe you know."

Adam nodded again, watching the DCI's face carefully. Human remains. All that remains of a human. Dan.

"We sent in a team and recovered a body. We believe it to be the body of your son, Daniel Chapple." Yeardley cleared his throat. "It is obvious that the body has lain in situ for some time, and I'm afraid we won't be asking you to identify it. We recovered a number of the personal effects, and we have photos." Yeardley produced a file. "May I?" he asked.

Polly cleared a space on one of Adam's side tables and positioned it between him and Yeardley. Yeardley lay the first photo down. A red and black bicycle, the back wheel crushed and misshapen and the frame twisted. Adam picked the photo up and studied it carefully. Yes, the bike was the same make and model as the one Adam had bought Dan for Christmas the year before last. His last year of sixth form. There, near the handlebars, green electrical tape had been wrapped around one of the brake cables. It had been a decent make but several of Dan's fellow school mates had owned the same one, so they had distinguished Dan's bike with the green tape and a brightly-coloured cycle lock.

"That's Dan's bike," Adam confirmed and pointed out the tape to Yeardley.

Yeardley nodded. He offered the next image to Adam. A black backpack. Adam recognised it as the one he had found a receipt for. It was on the large side. Ideal for someone who wanted to travel.

"What was in it?" asked Adam.

Yeardley passed him a set of photos. A pencil case. Tottenham Hotspur. That had been Dan's team. The pencil case contained pens, pencils, a sharpener, and a couple of erasers. Nothing special.

There were two textbooks in the bag. Remarkably well preserved given they had been out in all weathers. Both library books. Adam looked up and met Yeardley's direct gaze. Of course the DCI and Plymouth CID knew these were Dan's belongings. The first thing they would have organised was a check with the University library to find out who the books were on loan to.

Yeardley nodded, sympathy in his eyes. "We have confirmed these were Daniel's books."

The final images were a photo of a navy blue hoodie with Varsity lettering decorating the back, and a set of keys. Adam recognised the keyring. A worn and filthy seagull. They had bought it together, in a gift shop downtown, when Dan had been thirteen or so. Adam had been amused at his son's insistence on purchasing it. He could have chosen from a variety of cool designs, but no, the soft and squidgy seagull was what he wanted. It seemed a lifetime ago.

A knot of pain lodged in Adam's chest. He cleared his throat. Tears pricked his eyes.

"Yes. I recognise the keyring, and that looks like our house key." Adam circled a finger around one of the keys. "You can check that easily enough." Adam's vision tunnelled. He watched his hands shake slightly as he held onto the photos. They might have been someone else's hands or he could have been viewing them from a distance. He didn't dare look back up at the other people in the room yet. He sensed, rather than saw, the looks exchanged above his head.

Moira rose and made her way to the kitchen. Cupboards were opened and a tap run. The kettle began its familiar roar. Beside Adam, Polly, in uniform, shifted her weight so that her thigh touched his. He breathed in deeply, then exhaled, a sharp breath. There would be time for his personal grief when he was alone. He wanted that moment to come soon, but there were all the formalities to see to first.

He hauled his shoulders back and looked at Yeardley again. "You'll be running a DNA check?"

"Yes, that's in hand."

"Okay." Adam glanced down, shuffled the images. Picked up the photo of the bicycle. "Tell me how he died," he said.

"We don't have all the facts in yet, I'm sure you understand."

Of course they didn't have the results from various tests, and probably wouldn't do for weeks. But this was something they always said to relatives. They couldn't ever be absolutely certain about anything. For starters, they would need to wait until the results of the post mortem were in, and that would be tomorrow or the next day at the earliest, presuming they had already recovered Dan from the scene. There was a lot they couldn't know yet, but Yeardley would know enough for now. Adam furrowed his brow. Get on with it.

"What can you tell me?" Adam asked, his voice direct and surprisingly firm.

"Initial findings at the scene, the condition of the bicycle for example, would suggest your son was struck from behind by a vehicle. We're assuming a car at this stage rather than anything bigger than that." Adam understood this probably meant Dan hadn't been crushed, but rather thrown from the road.

Adam frowned. "Do you have a scene photo?"

Yeardley picked up his phone and flicked through some images, careful to keep the screen turned away from Adam. Adam was grateful, he knew what he would see on there, and that wasn't how he wanted to remember Dan.

Yeardley handed his phone over. Adam examined the photo carefully. There was a kerb running along the road. No pavement. A border of grass ran up to the side of the road. The hedgerow lay approximately ten to twelve feet from the kerb. If Dan had been impacted from the rear, he had potentially struck the kerb and been sent flying.

"Dan was thrown into the bushes by the force of the impact?" Adam's asked, his head whirring. Had Dan been alive when he landed on the ground? Had he needed help and nobody had seen him lying there?

Adam absently flicked the image on the phone left to see what came next. This image showed a patch of brambles and bracken that had partially been cleared. A jeans-clad leg. One neon yellow trainer. Faded and filthy.

Adam swallowed and handed the phone back to Yeardley.

"We don't think so," Yeardley said carefully. "We think he was moved to where he was found. He was tucked away, parallel to the road. The bicycle was placed next to him. He wasn't tangled in it. It was all a little neat. The guy that found Dan had stopped for a slash. He saw the bike, then spotted the shoe."

"You think…?"

"We are considering the possibility that someone struck the bike from behind and stopped. Dan was unconscious, possibly already dead, and the driver decided to move him off the road and cover up what he had done."

It made sense. In Adam's experience this wouldn't be the first time such a thing had happened. The driver might have been drunk. Or afraid. It took a certain type of brigand to move a body though, in Adam's experience. It was unforgivable.

"You'll be looking at CCTV along that road?"

"We've started with locating cameras and recordings. At the moment we don't know exactly when he died, so it's like looking for a needle in a haystack. Do you have any idea of his last contact?"

"I have a text from him. I'll find the date."

"That would be helpful. We spoke to his friends at University at the time, but we'll probably re-interview them."

Except for Matthew Riley, thought Dan. He's no longer with us either.

"Good idea," said Adam. "I'll check again with his old friends around here." Yeardley nodded and made a note.

Adam swallowed. Lines of enquiry were ongoing, and in good hands from what he could see, but there were things he needed to know. "What can you tell me about Dan's injuries?" he asked.

Yeardley's voice was steady. "Waiting on the post-mortem results, but what we know for sure is that Dan suffered a skull fracture. A traumatic injury, probably fatal."

The wind whistled through Adam's constricted throat, and he hung on tentatively to this good news. With any luck Dan had been entirely unaware of what had been happening. He wouldn't have regained consciousness. He wouldn't have experienced any pain. Adam hoped his son hadn't suffered.

Moira had returned with a tray of tea things.

"Do you want tea?" Polly asked doubtfully, and Adam shook his head. Tea. His whole life as a working police officer had involved tea in one form or another. Making it, offering it, drinking it.

Polly ignored him and poured him one. "Drink it," she ordered, and he took it from her. It was a good colour. Moira was well versed in the art of family liaison. The liquid sloshed in the mug as his hands trembled.

***

Adam made his way out into the lanes beyond Durscombe, pounding against the tarmac as though the devil was behind him. He thought of nothing except of placing one foot in front of the other and avoiding the pot holes. He kept a steady rhythm, but he pushed himself harder, faster than normal. As he started the climb up the South side of Nabb's Hill, his breathing became ever more laboured and his heart beat in his chest until he thought it would burst. He refused to stop, refused to give in, until he had reached the top.

The woods began here, popular with dog walkers and family ramblers. He turned to face Durscombe, and in the dimming light he had a good view of the town. A higgledy-piggledy layout of modern houses interspersed with older ones with thatched roofs, and beyond them all, the sea, an ominous slate grey, curving away on the horizon. Behind him, a different landscape altogether, ancient woodland, managed using modern methods. The ground sloping down and then up again, ululating steeply in parts, heading for the next town inland, Abbotts Cromleigh.

This was his environment, his landscape. It was pretty

much his life, and it was certainly all Dan had ever known until he went to Plymouth. Dan hadn't ventured to a University farther afield because he hadn't felt secure enough, Adam understood this, although it was not something they had ever really discussed.

Perhaps he should have insisted Dan had seen a psychiatrist or someone who could have helped his son sort through his sense of betrayal and hurt. But in the end, it wouldn't have made a difference. Dan had been killed while cycling. Hit from behind, by a person unknown, who hadn't the decency to call the accident in.

What sort of person could live with that?

Adam doubled over with his hands on his knees, gulping in air, struggling to breathe and bring his heart rate down. He straightened up and walked into the woods. This is what he had been craving all day. Total privacy. He wasn't being watched up here. Back at home his mobile had been buzzing constantly since Yeardley and Moira left, promising to keep him apprised of all developments. Polly had remained behind until she sensed that Adam needed to be alone.

But it was the silence at home that had done for Adam in the end. He couldn't bear it. While Dan had been away at University, the silence had been a temporary thing. Now it would be a permanent fixture, and the place marker that had once been kept for his son would instead be inhabited by total absence.

Adam started at the sound of keening. He turned, expecting to see a wounded animal behind him, but then he sank to his knees, because the only wounded animal in the vicinity was Adam himself. He fell on the soft ground and dug his fingernails into the soil beneath the mulch and forest detritus, heaving and crying, and renting his soul where no-one would else would possibly hear.

CHAPTER TWENTY-SEVEN

Adam lay on the sofa, one arm over his eyes, attempting to block the light out. He had a headache—the result of too much Scotch. He'd passed out with the television on, and the adverts suddenly blaring out had woken him.

A little under forty-eight hours since he had received the news about Dan. Yesterday he had held it together as much as he could, made some preparatory calls to the local funeral director, phoned the few relatives he had who needed to know, had even let Dominic Fallon know out of courtesy, after all Maryanne Fallon was Dan's half-sister.

After that he had spent some time cleaning and tidying. People would be in and out of the house constantly over the next few weeks. He'd tidied and sorted, hoovered and washed floors. A little after seven, Polly had turned up unbidden on the doorstep clutching Chinese takeaway and a bottle of whisky. They sat together, saying little, Adam's meal largely untouched, watching a movie on Film 4. Occasionally Adam would sob, and Polly would add another inch to his whisky glass.

At eleven she had kissed his forehead and bid him goodnight. She had work; she had obligations. She was a great friend.

Adam drew himself upright slowly. He felt rough all right, but he'd live. He popped the kettle on and then dragged himself upstairs.

The shower helped. He stood underneath the spray of hot water for much longer than usual, wishing the water would slough away layers of his misery.

Feeling slightly more human, he towelled himself off then changed into his running gear. It wasn't ideal to run with a hangover by any means, but running until he vomited was one way to cure his hangover quickly. His plans were interrupted by a tentative tap at the door. Too light and hesitant to be anybody on official business.

His heart sank when he opened the door to Cassia and Heidi. Cassia, devoid of all her make-up, seemed vulnerably young. Her black hair was drawn back into a youthful pony-tail, unfussy and clean. There were holes in different parts of her face where her piercings would normally be.

Heidi hovered behind her, dark rings around her eyes. She looked as though she hadn't slept for days. A multi-coloured beanie was pulled tightly around her head, but the scars that Adam could see looked pink and angry against the paleness of her skin.

"Ladies!" Adam tried to sound jovial, intending to ask them what he could do for them and then send them on their way. He was off duty. He was in mourning. He deserved to be left in peace. However, something in Cassia's face stopped him. The last time he'd seen Cassia he'd ordered her never to darken his doorstep again. But here she was, quietly determined to speak to him regardless.

In any case, the words died in his throat as he spotted tears welling up in Heidi's eyes.

"Adam," began Cassia. "I know you said—"

"We heard about your son. Polly came to see me. She told me. I told Cassia." Tears slipped down Heidi's cheeks. She made no effort to brush them away.

Adam looked up at the sky momentarily and tightened his jaw. Every fresh thought of the loss of Dan caught him newly by surprise, as though the pain could be momentarily erased, but then brought rapidly back into sharp focus with instant realisation.

"You'd better come in," he said and stepped back. Cassia and Heidi trooped quietly into his hallway. Adam paused as though someone was missing. Tom of course. He was gone too.

Adam closed the door firmly, then scooted past Cassia to get into the kitchen. The kettle was warm from earlier but was less than a quarter full. He topped it up and switched it on. For once he welcomed the loud roar it emitted as it did its work. Nobody could speak above the noise.

He took some extra mugs out of his newly clean cupboard, plonked them on the worktop, and busied himself finding milk and sugar. "Tea or coffee?" he called to the women hovering awkwardly at the entrance to the kitchen.

"Tea for me, no milk or sugar," replied Heidi. Of course. He should have remembered.

"Coffee. Black. Strong. No sugar." Cassia appeared beside him and offered a small smile. "Let me," she said. "I think Heidi needs to sit down. She hasn't long been out of the police station."

"They held you, then?" Adam asked Heidi, and she grimaced, her face woebegone.

"Endless questions, but what could I tell them? Poor, poor Tom!"

Adam nodded and retraced his steps into the hallway. He went to take Heidi's arm then abruptly wrapped her in a hug. She welcomed it. Held him tightly.

"I'm so, so sorry," she said into his shoulder, and he felt her hot tears through his t-shirt.

They stayed that way for some time, before Adam took Heidi's arm and led her into the living room. They sat together on the sofa and Heidi asked softly, "Dan has gone?"

"I think I must have known," Adam said and shook his head. "At least, I should have guessed. I was in denial."

Cassia arrived with a tray. She handed Heidi a mug of tea and set coffee, milk, and sugar on the table before throwing herself into the armchair.

Adam addressed them both as though Cassia had heard the earlier part of the conversation. "I mean, I made an assumption, perhaps reluctantly, that Dan had simply gone travelling. Because that's what he had always wanted to do. He often told me that's what he was aiming to do, and we talked about the places he wanted to visit. And he'd spoken about doing it when I saw him at Easter. But," Adam stared at the coffee pot with intensity, "he really wasn't himself. His mental health had deteriorated. He seemed withdrawn but also absurdly angry about nothing at all. He was supposed to be home for two weeks but he only stayed one. I offered him a lift back to Plymouth, but he insisted he would take the train. So the last time I saw him, he was leaving here, in a bit of a huff."

Heidi grimaced.

"His friends have told me that he changed during that last semester. He became more introverted. I should have tried harder. The police in Plymouth had him marked as a missing person, but perhaps none of us were serious enough about looking into it. Maybe I should have made sure he saw our doctor. I thought he was just being a moody teenager, that it would pass."

"That's irrelevant, Adam. Dan didn't kill himself, did he?" Cassia asked.

"No," Adam rubbed his face. "Hit and run while he rode his bicycle by the look of it."

"I'm sorry," Heidi said again, her face a picture of misery.

"Thank you," Adam replied and tried to smile. "I'm sorry you have to be around me and hear all this. You've been through so much these past few months."

"This has kind of brought it all back," admitted Heidi. "Hopefully Dan had no awareness of what was happening to him. I know I didn't. Or certainly, I can't remember anything about it now. Just blackness."

Adam found this comforting.

"But it wasn't blackness, was it? Not in your case," Cassia said. "Far from it. We've established that."

Heidi was taken aback. She had only wanted to offer some consolation to Adam. "No, that's true," she frowned at Cassia, "but it was initially."

Cassia sat tall in her seat, her spine ramrod straight, her dark eyes challenging Adam. "And if we believe what happened to Heidi is the truth, and we do don't we? Then it follows that everyone ends up exactly where Heidi did when she died."

"So?" asked Adam, and his tone was sharp. He wasn't sure

what Cassia was getting at but she seemed to want to cross a line.

Cassia held his gaze stubbornly.

Heidi interjected. "I didn't get a sense that it was a bad place, you know, where I was going. I wanted to travel there. Look Cassia, if Dan went there, I'm sure he'll be happy."

Cassia stood abruptly and twisted away from them both, ostensibly examining a pair of framed Oasis posters on the wall. Then she breathed deeply and turned back to Adam and Heidi.

"I'm sorry about Dan too," she said, and her voice was calm, "I really am, Adam. But you have to help me. The séance we ran, it opened a can of worms, a Pandora's box. I can't stay in my house. There are spirits everywhere! Not just my foremothers. There are spirits trying to climb through the gateway we opened."

Heidi shuddered.

Cassia shook her head. "For the most part they are harmless, and nothing we particularly need to worry about. But the gateway we created that breached the veil is proving to be an issue."

Cassia hesitated, then blurted out, "Look, I know I probably shouldn't have but I contacted Tansy again last night." Adam frowned, and Cassia waved his objection away before he could say anything. "That's how I know that these … these spirits? They're not going to be any trouble." Cassia blew a few stray hairs out of her face. "It was chaos. I was attempting to converse with Tansy and yet I could hardly get a word in edgewise. Maybe half a dozen came through. They just want to contact loved ones." She shrugged, but there was something else, a new awareness of the depth of her ability, something she had suspected but never actually put into practice. A new confidence.

Heidi clapped her hands. "Well surely that's the key, isn't it? Can't Tansy talk to Abelia? Call her off?"

"Remember what we found out last time? Tansy told us that Abelia is a warrior, a soul warrior she called her. Abelia collects souls. Those stray spirits that wonder on our plane when they need to be beyond the veil. Abelia takes them back to the world beyond. Tansy is a free spirit. I don't know why she's able to communicate with me. Perhaps she hasn't crossed?" Cassia laced her fingers together. "Abelia is furious with us for what we've done, and she is incredibly dangerous."

"And what about Laura? She's still at large. Did she kill Tom?" asked Heidi.

"We can assume it was either Laura or Abelia, I suppose," said Cassia, looking to Adam for confirmation, then back at Heidi. "You said you found feathers."

"We did," agreed Heidi. "That would indicate Abelia, wouldn't it?"

"There were no signs of a break-in at Heidi's house, but the front door was locked and there was no other way in," Adam responded dully, reluctant to be drawn back into this murky case while his attention was elsewhere, "Yes, my money is still on Abelia."

"What's to stop Abelia coming after us?" Heidi asked, and the others heard the fear in her voice. "Perhaps she'll target us one by one."

"I'd say it is a certainty that she will," Cassia said. "Adam? What do you think?"

Adam mulled it over in his mind. "I think you're probably right. That doesn't help us solve the problem of Laura, does it?"

Adam's head throbbed. The shower had largely abated his headache earlier, but it was back with a vengeance. He poured himself a mug of coffee. He hesitated, his hand over the carton of milk. He normally took his coffee with milk and sugar, but today he wanted the hit. What he really needed was some food. Perhaps eating something would help him think straight.

"Give me a sec," he said, rising and heading into his kitchen. He gathered together a bowl and cereal. Opening the fridge, he found a void where the milk should be. It was already on the tray in the living room of course. He paused for a moment, staring at the meagre contents, then flicked the door closed, laying his forehead against its cool surface. Once upon a time he had stuck Dan's artwork to the fridge. He hadn't kept any of it. He found himself wishing he had. An image flashed into his mind of the shopping list on Tom's fridge, the odd requests for snacks from an older woman after a serious illness. He remembered her spidery writing.

So much like Dan's.

An avalanche of emotions sent Adam reeling across the room. The realisation took his breath away. The links between Dan and Laura. Who held a grudge against Nicola? Dan did. And what about Matthew Riley? Were the murders down to Dan?

Laura was Dan. Dan was Laura. A teenaged boy in an older woman's body. And he was killing off the people who had hurt him.

It seemed impossible, and yet, when Adam factored everything in, what alternative explanation was there? And how could he prove it?

Adam's mind raced. Given everything he knew about Heidi's experience, it was reasonable to assume that Dan had been the one who had rushed out of the doorway and collided with Laura. Somehow he had found a way to come back, but for some reason, unlike Heidi, he couldn't claim his own body and had therefore commandeered Laura's. Perhaps his injuries were too severe. Perhaps his body would never have functioned again in the event he managed to survive.

Adam cast around for his mobile. It would be on his desk in the lounge. He stumbled through to grab it, and Cassia started to talk to him. He held his hand up and speed-dialled Polly. She picked up quickly.

"Hey! How are you doing?" she asked.

"I need you to do something for me," Adam said in a rush. "Moira Wilkins is the family liaison officer on Dan's case, right? Can you get in touch with her and find out which DCs are looking into CCTV footage?"

"Sure thing… but?"

"When you've found that out, then you need to get in

touch with them. Mention that one of Dan's friends received a message from him in the early hours of 22nd May."

Heidi, listening in to the conversation from her place of the sofa, bolted upright. Adam grimaced at her. "Tell the DC they need to look at CCTV from the 22nd May. I think we'll find that's the last possible day Dan was alive."

Polly agreed and said she'd get back to him. Adam ended the call and turned to face Heidi and Cassia, wondering how to explain what he suspected.

***

"Perhaps it's a positive for us. He's your son. You can talk to him. Do you think you would be able to reason with him?" Cassia was asking.

Adam came back to the present. He had been trying to envisage having a conversation with Dan as Laura, and failing. The Dan he knew had not been a murderer, but the Dan in Laura's body had killed both his own mother and Matt, someone he'd once considered a friend.

"But then what?" asked Heidi. The afternoon sun pouring into the room was making her warm. She pulled her beanie off, and Adam noticed for the first time the fine fair hairs that were spouting all over her skull. He imagined they would never grow over the scar tissue, and she would always have a few bald spots, but she could cover them with her hair when it was longer. Amidst all the doom and gloom of the circumstances they found themselves in, it was a tiny glimmer of hope for Heidi's future.

"What do you mean?" asked Adam, but he understood what Heidi meant.

Cassia nodded, her voice grim. "Abelia wants Laura. Or the person inhabiting Laura. Dan, if that's what we now believe. Abelia will take Laura back."

Adam rolled the idea around for a moment, trying to figure out how it would feel talking to Dan under these circumstances. It all seemed unreal. He examined the scenario from different angles and found himself struggling to comprehend Dan as Laura, but until he could confront him, maybe he would never wrap his head around it. On a rational level—if indeed any of this was rational—of course they would need to hand Laura/Dan over to Abelia.

Could Adam find it in his heart to do that?

"The only way any of this is going to stop, the only way we'll ever be able to go back to our own normal lives, will be if Abelia takes Laura," said Heidi, her voice plaintive, reading his mind.

Adam sighed, more loudly than he intended, a future without his son appeared impossibly bleak. "Or what will now have to pass for normal," he said. He studied the two women in front of him. None of them could possibly escape from this situation unmarked. Heidi with her trauma, her injuries, and her scars. Cassia with one foot in the world beyond. And he himself, forever alone and now childless.

Heidi reached over and squeezed his arm. "I'm sorry," she said. It was so like her to be continually apologizing. But this wasn't her doing. None of it was her fault. Simple biology had filched Laura from her life. An arrogant and careless driver had stolen Dan's life. A terrorist had tried to claim Heidi's. They were all victims.

This thought lit a spark in Adam and anger surged through him. He had spent his whole professional life working to bring about justice for victims. He couldn't stop now.

"Don't be sorry," he said. "Let's all stop being sorry and sort this fucking mess out!"

***

"We're just going around in circles," complained Heidi, her drawn face white with strain. They were grouped around Adam's kitchen table with a drawing pad and pens, trying to talk through options.

"I really don't think another séance would work though," Cassia continued arguing. "What good would it do? Laura is this side, not spirit side."

"Ideally, we need to get Laura and Abelia together," Adam reiterated.

Heidi slumped, exhausted, her head in her hands. "But we can't think of a way to do that."

"If only we knew where Laura was hiding out, that would help," Cassia said.

That was where they were up to. Between them they had decided that locating Laura was a priority. Abelia was happy following them around, presumably because they could lead her to Laura. That seemed simple enough.

Maybe.

However, Cassia was concerned that this didn't go far enough. Somehow they had to find a way to close the rift in the veil. They needed to prevent other spirits making their way into the world.

"We opened it," she said, "we're responsible for it." Neither Adam nor Heidi could argue with that.

In addition, they were unsure whether Abelia would be appeased even if they managed to lure Laura into her general vicinity, allowing her to do whatever she needed to return Laura, or Dan, spirit side.

"If only there was a way to find out. Some kind of precedent," said Cassia. "Someone else who's been through something similar. Or who knows how it works." Cassia slapped the table in frustration. "But if Tansy can't help us, then finding someone else is going to prove impossible. I really don't know what else to suggest."

Heidi peered out through her fingers. "But there is someone else," she said quietly. "Of course there is."

Cassia shook her head, "Who?"

Heidi straightened up, thinking, her eyes suddenly shining, then she announced, "The woman in the waiting room." When the others looked puzzled, Heidi bounced on her chair. "Do you remember? I told you how I joined the queue after my accident. And we all moved forward. One by one we waited to step through the veil. There was a woman. Just one woman. I thought at the time she was counting people in." Heidi tapped the table. One-two, one-two. "She tapped on her knee. She was wearing a dress, and I could hear the scratch and the tap. It was all I could hear."

"Who was she?" Adam asked. He did remember Heidi telling him about this woman, but it may have been a detail Cassia had missed out on, as she still looked perplexed.

"I don't know."

"Had you seen her before?" Cassia asked.

"At the time I didn't think so, but you know, afterwards, I thought she reminded me of my old Sunday school teacher. Mrs Lewin she was called. As a kid she seemed impossibly old to me. She used to play the piano for us, and we would sing songs. She always wore her best clothes. I remember she had one dress in peacock colours that I used to love, but at the same time, I didn't like to get too close to her because her skin was wrinkly and she looked so old. When I died, what I saw, it could have been her, but she was even more ancient. The woman in the vision or whatever it was, she had skin like thick paper. Dried out. Almost mummy-like. But—yes—it was that dress. She was wearing the peacock dress. Don't you see? We could try and talk to her?"

Cassia frowned. "I'm really not sure another séance would work. I don't know enough about her. We can't just try and contact the world beyond and hope she shows up. It's not very specific." Cassia saw the disappointment in Heidi's eyes. "Sorry," she said, but there was an element of fear in her eyes. Cassia was frightened of trying to make contact with the spirit world, and Adam had some sympathy after what had occurred before.

Adam rocked back on his chair, the feet screeching against the ceramic tiles of his kitchen floor. There had to be a way. He stared up at the ceiling, seeking a solution there, absently noticing the preponderance of spiders' webs dotted around. October, the time of year when many spiders relocate indoors from the garden. He'd removed a number of the huge horrors the previous day. Apparently his cleaning hadn't been so

223

thorough after all. His eye was drawn to one specimen in the corner of the room. It wasn't particularly large, but it dominated the space, and once you had seen it, you couldn't un-see it. Couldn't forget it existed.

How many eyes does a spider have? he wondered. The arachnid hung lightly from the ceiling above them, watching their every move, but blissfully unaware of Adam's train of thought.

Rather like Heidi's wizened old woman.

How long had she been sitting on her wooden seat, counting the dead as they shuffled from one world to the next? Observing but never talking. Had anyone ever stopped to chat with her?

Adam slammed his chair legs back down on the floor with a clatter. Heidi and Cassia jumped in alarm. "There is a way to find out!" he exclaimed. "One of us needs to go to her."

"That's ridiculous," Cassia retorted. "In order to get to where she is, you'd need to be—"

"Dead," Heidi finished.

CHAPTER TWENTY-EIGHT

"Are you suggesting one of us needs to die?" asked Cassia, her face twisted in dismay. Heidi clasped her hands to her mouth in horror.

"I don't know. I don't know what I'm suggesting." Adam pushed his chair away from the table and stood. He paced restlessly, pausing by the sink at the window and looked out into the street beyond. Adam watched a large grey hatchback rumble past. A kid, maybe eleven or so, on a bike with no lights cycled after it, weaving left to right across the road and oblivious of other road users. God help him if anything came towards him.

The thought drew him back to reality, although it was a kind of supra-reality he supposed. He remained at the sink, his back to the women. The light outside was failing, and the street lamps were flickering on one by one. It was damp and drizzly outside. There would be a mist off the sea later. The air would feel damp and prickle the skin. Grotty weather and nevertheless a miracle. Dan wouldn't see the perfection of this. That knowledge made Adam's heart ache.

Finally, he turned to face the women. "One of us will have to die. Yes, I suppose that is what I'm suggesting." Heidi started to protest, but Adam held his hand up. "Not you two. Me. I'll do it."

"No. It's impossible," said Cassia sharply.

"It's not. We have to find a way."

"We won't let you do this, Adam," Cassia shook her head.

"Listen to me," Adam said calmly. "If everything goes according to plan, I'll be as right as rain. Heidi?" He turned to her. "You told us you were officially dead for 180-odd seconds."

"Yes. That's right. Just over three minutes. There was a nurse on the scene, and she started heart compressions and mouth to mouth. She brought me back."

"That's what you two are going to do for me."

"What? No," argued Cassia. "This is a stupid idea. Insane."

"There's no 'no' about it, Cassia," said Adam, holding her gaze, "and I'll tell you why it will be me. A, because Heidi isn't strong enough. B, because we may need you to speak to a spirit or someone from beyond. And C, because it was my bloody idea."

"Well it's a crazy idea," said Cassia, her eyes filling with tears.

"But it isn't, is it?" Adam said, his tone soothing. He walked across to Cassia and pulled her up into a tight hug. "What's the worst that can happen?"

"That we can't bring you back," Cassia whispered.

"You have to. I'm asking you to." Adam stared down at Cassia's upturned face. "And you know what, so what if you can't? I don't have anything to lose. There's nobody I'm leaving behind if it all goes wrong. You—"

"I don't have anyone either! Let me do it."

"No. I need you this side. Because if the worst does happen, then I will try to make contact with you and you with me. If there's any way it can be done, we must do it."

Heidi rose and moved around the table. "Then why not let me, Adam?"

"Because you have your dad. He's already lost you once. It wouldn't be fair on him. And besides Heidi, you've made it this far in spite of everything that happened to you. In spite of your injuries, you haven't been beaten. You deserve to go all the way. Live a full life." Adam shook his head. "No. The only logical plan is for me to be the one to die."

Cassia shook her head but said nothing else. Satisfied that he had silenced the arguments for now, but aware of the possibility of more, Adam stretched. "And I think we should do this sooner rather than later. Who's with me?"

***

"Are we all set?" asked Adam, his voice booming in the confined space of the bathroom. His heart fluttered, his stomach clenched. Nerves. Determined not to show how he felt, he rearranged the towels and got a grip of his emotions. Heidi meanwhile was struggling to breathe, so great was her terror. "Heidi?" Adam asked. "I need you to focus. You've got the timer, right?"

Heidi glanced down at the phone in her hands. She was all thumbs, struggling to make the damn thing work. The screen kept flipping back to the home screen. "Yes," she said, but she didn't sound confident.

"You need to start bringing me back when you think I've been gone for three and a half minutes. Try and be accurate about that." Adam laughed nervously. "I have no idea what the science is, but if it's generally accepted you have four minutes, let's keep within that time frame, okay?"

Heidi nodded, "Definitely."

"Cassia?" Adam turned to look at her. "I'm counting on you in so many ways. I'll try not to struggle, but I guess that may be natural. Do what you can to keep me down there."

Cassia's eyes were bleak. "I will. But—"

"Then I'm counting on you to bring me back. You're confident you can do it?"

"Adam, you know I've never had to do first aid. Ever. Even at school. I know in theory how to do it. Stayin' Alive and all that."

"That will do. And it's all I can ask." Adam stripped his t-shirt off. "I've left a letter on the table downstairs, exonerating you of all blame should the worst happen and people start asking difficult questions. Which they should do, if they know how to do their jobs properly."

He hugged first Heidi and then Cassia. Kissed each on the forehead. Then abruptly he turned away from them and stepped into the bath. It was a large old-fashioned style tub. Nicola had chosen the style many years ago. Apart from a lick of paint, the bathroom hadn't been altered in nearly two decades. It could probably do with a facelift. Perhaps he should resolve to see to it, if he made it out of this misadventure alive. If he deemed it important enough.

"Cuff me," he instructed, turning to allow Cassia to do so. She slid the cuffs over his wrists and tightened them as he had shown her. In all his years in the police force, he had never imagined he would put his equipment to this use.

He'd chosen to run the bathwater cold, although he didn't know if that would make a difference. Now he shivered as he sat in the freezing water. He smiled reassuringly at the two women hovering anxiously above him. "Here goes," he said. "See you on the other side."

***

The women watched helplessly as Adam immersed himself under the water, and, as instructed, Cassia lay a plank of wood on top of him, eight inches wide by about four feet. It covered him from his forehead to the middle of his thighs. She hoped it would be enough. Adam had found the wood in his shed and had decided it might help them to overpower him if he started to panic. She gently lay a hand on the plank, waiting for the moment when she needed to get serious.

Heidi kept a nervous eye on the mobile, panicking that it would turn itself off and she would mess up the timing.

"It's going to be fine," Cassia intoned, "everything will go according to plan."

The first thirty seconds stretched by interminably, then Cassia noticed an almost imperceptible twitch. Adam was beginning to fight his need to breathe. She pressed down a little harder. Another fifteen slow seconds and Adam bucked under her hand. Cassia put her weight through the plank. One hand on his face, the other on his chest. Ten more seconds and Adam was trying to fight her.

"I need your help, Heidi!" Cassia urged, and Heidi placed the phone on top of the toilet lid and rushed to help. She placed a hand between Cassias' and one above Adam's groin. Beneath their combined weight, Adam's hips bucked once, twice. Water sloshed over the top of the bath, and for a moment Cassia thought Adam would throw them off, and then suddenly he was still beneath them.

As she'd promised him, once he stopped moving, Cassia needed to try to locate a pulse without letting him up. As soon as she was sure he was gone, Heidi had to start the timer.

Cassia leaned forwards into the bath and took her weight away from the plank. She gently felt along Adam's neckline, becoming anxious that she was searching for a pulse at the wrong point. She lifted her other hand to her own neck, to locate the beat under her own skin. Yes, there. She replicated the position on Adam's neck. Felt around. Dug her fingers in more deeply.

Nothing.

"He's gone! Start the clock."

CHAPTER TWENTY-NINE

His worst nightmare, suffocation.

Adam's heart raced. His shoulders strained against the wrist restraints. The pain in his chest expanded like a balloon, filling the cavity until he couldn't take it anymore. His brain screamed at him, until at last he was compelled to suck oxygen in. Instead, the water filled his lungs. With no air to breathe in and none to breathe out, blackness descended rapidly and his panic faded away, until the agony was a distant memory. He could no longer feel the water around his body. In fact, all sensation faded away.

For a while there was nothing at all, just an awareness of self, until he sensed his body drifting, cocooned in the pull of something with a stronger will than his own. He went with it because he had no choice.

He coasted peacefully in the dark for what seemed an age in itself, until gradually his awareness of what he had left behind came back to him. There was a reason he was in this place. He had a mission to accomplish. The knowledge made him marginally anxious. The pull was strong, and the urge to remain here and bask in this newfound peaceful existence was attractive. Never to worry about anything ever again.

Responsibility. Duty.

He forced himself to conjure the faces of Heidi and Cassia, to remember what he had agreed to do. Surely he was already running out of time? Why hadn't they called him back? He had been here, in this deep pitch black, for an eternity.

Did he still have enough time to find the Gate Keeper?

He sensed a conclusion to his journey, as though his ship had sailed into port. The blackness changed colour, became somehow less black if that was possible, as though a single candle illuminated a vast cathedral. He moved forward, without physically doing so, and decided he was upright although he had no physical sense of self. He followed the light.

There were others on his journey. This was as Heidi had described. They didn't hinder him. He urged himself to move forward more quickly but could not do so. He found himself on a metaphysical conveyor belt that moved in one direction only, and at one speed: slow and steady.

The available lighting gradually increased until the space around him developed a dull yellow glow, and the people moving with him acquired characteristics, not faces and hair particularly, but certainly a sense of being, or perhaps, having been.

He stared forwards, imagined he could see walls ahead, the colour of old newspaper, or a tea stain. And yes. There! A door, covered in a thick layer of buttermilk lace, the exact colour and texture of Abelia's coverings. He observed as the person at the head of the queue approached the door. The veil was lifted from the other side, and they stepped through. It was a simple, clean process, surprisingly rapid. The queue carried on. There was no disagreement from those waiting, no dissent, no revolt.

To the left side of the door a woman sat alone on a plain wooden chair. She stared forwards, hardly noticing the throng of people queuing for the door, but every time someone moved through, she scratched the silk fabric of her dress against her knee. One, two. One, two.

This had to be the Gate Keeper, the woman Adam required an audience with, but she was not as Heidi had described her—a Sunday school teacher with a peacock-patterned dress. This woman appeared oriental. Japanese. Her hair was elaborately coiled around her head, and her face had been painted a startling white, with the exception of black eye paint and a rosebud mouth. She wore a long kimono in delicate pink and a vibrant grass green, tied with a black obi. She seemed oddly familiar to Adam, but he couldn't immediately place her.

Adam was unsure he would have the strength to break free of the multitude around him, heading for the door. He half-imagined that stepping away from the queue, walking diagonally to the woman, might result in instant repercussions from a force or entity that he couldn't see, and briefly, the sheer effort required to leave the safety and sanctity of the gathered throng was more than he could bear. Yet simply by adjusting his thinking, it was surprisingly easy to side-step the people and head towards her.

At first he didn't think she had noticed him. She kept her eyes forwards, staring into space, and her fingers marked the passing of the souls in the queue as they moved through the veil, but Adam saw a slight shift in her gaze as he came.

He wondered if there was some sort of etiquette about speaking to her—who would take her place and count if she wasn't able to do it—but she stood and moved to greet him, bowing as he approached her.

Heidi had described the woman she had encountered as old, and in this she was correct. At this proximity, Adam could see the deep wrinkles that lined her leathery, careworn face below the carefully applied paint. She smiled up at him with a closed mouth. Her upturned lips lifted her cheeks and crinkled the skin further around her bright black eyes. Adam was surprised how tiny she was. She must have stood at just over four feet. In his physical body, Adam towered above her.

"Welcome Adam," she said. "That is your given name."

"Yes," Adam replied.

"Adam, born of Louise, who was born of Elizabeth, who was born of Anne. You come from a long line of good women Adam. Their strength and the strength of your forefathers is with you."

"That's good to know," Adam replied. She knew who he was, but he knew nothing of her.

"You are curious. That's natural. But who I am and where I originate from is irrelevant. All you need to know is that I am the Gate Keeper, and I monitor everyone who arrives here."

"You must see millions of people," Adam said.

"I see nothing." She waved a spindly hand, replete with age spots in front of her eyes, perhaps indicating blindness, Adam couldn't be sure. "And yet, I see all. Everything that needs to be seen." She laughed, a gentle tinkling giggle, perhaps sensing his confusion. "You have travelled here by your own volition?"

"Yes."

"Life is a gift. You chose to forsake it. That is a strange choice."

"I need some information."

The woman nodded sagely, "Indeed."

"Several months ago, May 22nd, a friend of mine was waiting here, to step through the veil. But someone else came out before Heidi could go though. Do you remember that?"

"Time holds no sway here. It can be bent and ignored at will. It has no meaning." Adam tried to break in, and the woman held a warning finger up. "However, I do recall the moment of which you speak. It is rare indeed for someone to travel in the opposite direction. We call them recreants. It caused a little consternation."

"You sent someone after this recreant?"

"We always dispatch a soul warrior to reclaim the lost soul. There can be no going back, no returning to a previous life. We can only move forwards."

"The soul warrior in this case, is called Abelia?"

"In the time and place where you reside, yes."

"Can Abelia be called off?" asked Adam.

"All souls belong beyond the veil, there is no going back. If they leave us, they must be reclaimed. This is the way of things."

"But that's not all Abelia does, is it?"

The woman was quiet, staring vacantly into the distance. She might have been looking into the past, or the future, Adam couldn't tell. He pressed on. Time was of the essence. "You know Abelia takes lives as well as hunting down the recreants, do you?"

When the woman didn't respond, Adam prompted her. "That's all right, is it?" She remained silent, much to Adam's exasperation. "Listen, I don't know what kind of a set-up you have here, what kind of an afterlife you are offering, or even if there is something beyond that damn veil, but back there, what Abelia has been doing, is murder. Five kids in a caravan, burned to death. Laura's husband Tom, who became a friend of mine. He was killed for no real reason, except he was trying to find out what happened to his wife. I've left two women back there, who are scared for their lives. To be honest, I'm a tad worried myself."

"Abelia has her reasons for doing what she does," the woman said, but she spoke so quietly that Adam struggled to hear her.

"What reasons?" Adam demanded. "What reasons could there possibly be for taking more lives? For cutting kids off in their prime? For murdering an old man?"

The woman's tone changed. "In Abelia's mind, you and your friends are guilty of creating a fissure between your world and this. Can you imagine what it would be like if your world was overrun with the dead? How would you cope? What could you, as mere mortals, do? Many of the inhabitants of our world are harmless, but some of them are not. We choose not to distinguish between the entrants to our world. We do not pick and choose. We take everybody who comes here. But it is imperative that no-one returns to you. By tampering with the boundaries in place between your world and ours, by thinning the veil that acts as a doorway between us, do you not see how irresponsible this is? You and your friends are accountable for the most serious breach that has occurred here in many, many years."

Her response, while understandable was nonetheless galling. "But still. Murder?"

"Death is the sentence that Abelia chooses to impose on those who make her mission difficult. And remember, she is not simply dealing with one breach. Yours is the worst by far, but every time someone succeeds in calling a spirit from the world beyond, the veil becomes thinner. In Abelia's mind, death is not the end, just the beginning, and by cutting lives short in your world, she successfully erases the threat to our world and beyond."

Adam was getting nowhere. Aware of the time ebbing away, he cut to the chase. "If Abelia finds Laura, she will kill her?"

"Laura, daughter of Sarah, wife of Tom, is already dead. Her soul has been claimed. She successfully crossed over. Tom, son of Valerie, also."

Adam glanced back at the door and the people waiting to enter. Tom had stepped through there. What was beyond? How could he not be curious? The thick veil hid Abelia's world from his sight, but he found himself oddly compelled to head towards it and peer through. Whatever existed there, it exerted some kind of magnetic hold on him, on all of those lining up to cross over. They waited patiently, without the least sense of rancour.

His thoughts returned to Dan. If he was right, Dan had not crossed over.

"And my son, Dan?"

"Daniel, son of Nicola, is already dead. He has not crossed over. Abelia will reclaim his soul." No flicker of emotion.

Adam listened to her words and played them over in his head. He felt no pain as his mind repeated what she had said. He couldn't process pain here. It was not the time or place. There would be pain enough when he returned to the land of the living. "So, nothing can prevent Abelia from doing this?"

The tiny woman in front of him looked solemn. "Abelia will not allow Daniel to remain in your world. That is a certainty, for it is her duty."

"Once Abelia has Dan, she will leave?"

"The rift between worlds must be closed, or Abelia will choose to stay to guard it herself."

Adam's eyes flicked uneasily back to the door. The lure of the veil called to him. He felt himself being physically drawn towards it. He had nothing to lose. He could cross over.

But no. He had to resist the temptation.

Quickly he asked, "And how do we close this rift?"

"The same way you opened it. Abelia will continue to clean up the recreants that pass through it, and she will punish those who open a passage between the worlds."

"Cassia doesn't know how to close the passage."

"She will find a way. She must. If she doesn't, Abelia will claim all the souls she desires, and the job will be done for you."

Adam noticed that his world was greying at the edges. What little light there had been appeared to be dimming. He experienced the sensation of floating once more.

"What's happening?" he asked.

"You are at the transition point. If you stay for much longer, the veil will claim you."

Adam considered this. The door with the veil glowed now, red-gold around the edges. When he glanced back at the woman, she had faded into the shadows. He couldn't make out the figures in the queue. The warmth emanating from the doorway was rapidly becoming a most attractive proposition, but all the same, logically he knew this was not his time. It could not be his time.

"I have one more question," he called, on the verge of panic when he couldn't see her. "Will Dan be all right? Will he be at peace?" There was a buzzing in his ears and suddenly the temperature dropped. It was freezing, and he was colder than he had ever been in life. He called out once more, "Can you tell him I love him?"

Afterwards he could never be sure whether he heard a response from the woman or not, but the words "Tell him yourself" echoed through his mind.

***

"What time do you have?" Cassia demanded. She had never experienced time passing as slowly as this before. She had asked Heidi at least a dozen times.

Heidi, standing beside her, shivering uncontrollably, holding the mobile in her blanched fingers, watched each second turn over, her eyes wide in concentration.

"Two fifty-four, fifty-five, fifty-six ..."

"Fuck it!" Cassia spat and leaned forwards into the bath. She grabbed Adam by the arm and tried to lift him. He was a dead weight, and his head rolled back into the water. Heidi dropped the phone on the floor and reached to help. Cassia lifted his head above the water. His eyes were open.

"Heidi pull the plug!" Cassia urged, and Heidi did so. Cassia tried to grip Adam under each armpit, but the water had made him slippery. Water slopped over the side of the bath, drenching the women. "Come on, come on, come on!" she beseeched, more to herself than Heidi. The water began to drain away, but too slowly for Cassia's liking. Beside her, Heidi was crying in fear.

Downstairs, the front door closed and Polly's voice sang out, "Hello? Adam?"

"Up here!" cried Heidi, and raced out onto the landing. "Polly! Polly! Quickly! Help us?"

"What's happening?" Polly called, and Cassia could hear her thumping quickly up the stairs.

"In the bathroom!" Cassia called out.

"What the hell's going on here?" Polly roared, and her voice was at once full of fear and anger. She leapt into action straight away, possessing a strength that Cassia could only dream of. She batted Cassia out of the way and then with one swift move, scooped Adam out of the bath. He slipped like a wet fish onto the floor.

Polly flipped him on to his back then quickly turned his head to the side. Water drained from his mouth and nose. "Jesus," Polly muttered and removed her phone from her jacket pocket and handed it to Cassia. "999 and ask for an ambulance. Tell them the patient is non-responsive. How long was he under the water?" She turned Adam's head back to the centre and lifted it slightly, slipping her fingers into his mouth to check for obstructions, then pinched his nose and began mouth-to-mouth resuscitation.

"Three minutes," Heidi said from the doorway. Her arms wrapped around herself, aware this was not strictly true. It had been three minutes since Cassia had felt a pulse.

Cassia spoke to the emergency operator while Polly put her ear to Adam's mouth, watching his chest.

"Come on Adam," Polly said.

"Yes," Cassia was saying. "We have a police officer here. Yes." Then to Polly she said, "There's an ambulance on the way."

Polly nodded. "Tell them to hurry!" She checked Adam's pulse. When she couldn't feel anything, she placed her hands on Adam's chest and began compressions.

CHAPTER THIRTY

"Seriously Adam, are you going to tell me what you were playing at?" Polly glared at Cassia and Heidi, huddled together outside the doorway. Adam sat on the edge of his bed, wrapped in towels and a blanket. The paramedic who had attended him busily wrote some notes while his colleague returned to the ambulance. They were insisting that Adam went to the hospital with them, and Polly was intending to accompany him. She was clucking over him like a mother-hen, and for once he didn't mind. Truth to tell, he felt a little ropey.

"It was a prank that went wrong, Polly," Adam said firmly. He'd been trying to tell her this for the past fifteen minutes, but surprisingly enough, she wasn't convinced.

"You're forty-four years old, Adam. I seriously doubt it was a prank that went wrong." She examined his face closely, and her voice softened. "You weren't trying to end it all, were you Adam? I know you're upset about Dan. You're bound to be. Honestly, it's hard. I know it is. We've seen it time and again—"

"Stop worrying, Polly. I wasn't intentionally trying to kill myself."

Polly blew her cheeks out. "That's something I suppose." She looked again at Heidi and Cassia. "Did you expect them to be able to save you?"

"Polly," Adam started.

"I know, I know," she held her hands up. "It was a prank that went wrong."

The paramedic looked up. "We're ready to take you now, Adam."

"Is it really necessary?" Adam asked half-heartedly. On the one hand, he would have loved nothing better than to lie down and have a sleep, but on the other? He wanted to get moving. Locate Laura. Time was growing short, and he hadn't had a chance to fill Cassia and Heidi in on what had happened while he'd been out. They needed to make a plan, and he couldn't do that from a hospital bed.

"He already told you they need to check you out properly," Polly growled and pointed at the door.

"It's just—"

"Things to do and people to see?" Polly put her hands on her hips, annoyed with him.

"Exactly."

"The hospital will check you over thoroughly," the paramedic said cheerfully, "and they'll probably release you within a few hours. Given the lack of beds at this time of night. You know how it is."

Adam groaned. He certainly did know. He was liable to spend the whole night in a corridor or a cubicle somewhere, waiting for an overworked doctor to give him the once over. Plus, given the circumstances, if someone somewhere decided he needed a psych evaluation, on the grounds there was a suspicion he had tried to kill himself, he was likely to be in for a lot longer.

"Come with me," he said to Polly. If anyone could get things moving and rescue him from a tiresome situation overnight, it would be her.

Polly rolled her eyes. "Would that be okay?" she asked the paramedic and he nodded. "All right then," she said to Adam and reached down to help him stand. He tried to shake her off, but the paramedic took his other arm and between them they began to help him out of the bedroom. "What about the rest of your harem?" Polly asked, and Adam was pleased to hear something approaching normal humour in her tone.

Adam smiled wanly at the waiting women. Heidi had a hand clasped to her mouth, her eyes huge. Cassia on the other hand was hopping from foot to foot. He knew she wanted the lowdown on what had happened. He attempted a wink her way. "Why don't you two stay here?" he said, and when Heidi started to protest he cut her off. "It will be safer. Heidi take my bed. Cassia, there are spare blankets and pillows in the cupboard next to the bathroom. I'll get back here as soon as I can."

"Are you sure?" Cassia asked.

"Yes, I am," said Adam, as Polly pulled him away. "We'll talk soon."

"We'll be here," Cassia replied.

Adam nodded, and his glance strayed away to a picture on the wall behind her. It was a print his mother had kept in her house her whole life. It depicted a Japanese woman wearing a delicate pink and green kimono, tied with a black obi, her hair elaborately styled, and her face painted white. Adam had passed this picture a million times, both as a child in his mother's hallway and latterly as he passed it on his own landing, but now he realised he had never really seen it before. The slight woman appeared to gaze down at him, through eyes that saw nothing … and everything.

***

Adam's worst fears were confirmed. The hospital was busy, although he had seen it worse. The staff moved around, quiet and efficient as always, and appeared to have everything under control. There were no troublesome patients and none of the chaos he had witnessed on some of the evenings he had attended incidents here. He was triaged quickly enough. Then it was a matter of sitting and waiting for a few tests to be arranged.

Polly returned from a meander down the corridor, clutching a cup of tea.

"Is that for me?" Adam asked, reaching for the cup, but Polly batted his hand away.

"No, it's for me. You heard the nurse. You're not allowed anything until they've run their tests."

"That's so unfair. I'm gagging!"

"Well, you shouldn't have tried to kill yourself," Polly said tartly. "Then we could have been sitting at your place, watching some shite on TV, crying into our beer." Her voice faltered, and she looked away.

Adam's heart sank. Polly, usually his reliable and capable

friend, was desperately upset and trying not to show it. He'd hurt her, completely unintentionally of course, but he understood perfectly how his actions had consequences.

"Pol," Adam reached his hand out and gripped hers. She shrugged away, and he settled for stroking her arm instead. "I'm sorry."

"Why did you do it?" she asked, her voice thick with emotion, still not looking at him.

Adam started to say something dismissive but stopped himself. She deserved more than some cock-and-bull story about a game gone wrong. She had seen the plank of wood in the bathroom, found Cassia and Heidi there too. She was a good police officer, aiming for CID herself. If something stunk to high heaven, then Polly wasn't stupid enough to believe it was a bouquet of fresh roses.

He sat silently for a while, contemplating exactly what to tell her. Polly sniffed and wiped her eyes. Eventually he found his voice.

"I'm not sure what to tell you. I don't know what you might believe."

"Tell me the truth," Polly said and this time she did look at him, and her eyes shone with the challenge. When Adam didn't immediately respond, she tutted. "How about you tell me why you befriended Heidi, for example?"

"She needs friends. She's had a really rough time this year."

"She's a suspect in a murder case."

"You know as well as I do that someone else is in the frame for that."

"But Heidi has not been completely exonerated, and as far as Exeter CID are concerned–your colleagues, remember—she remains a person of interest. Gibbs told me so."

"Well if we're splitting hairs, I'm still a suspect too. It was my ex-wife after all."

Polly sighed in exasperation. "And what about the goth girl?"

"Cassia."

"She is very odd company for you to keep."

244

Adam shook his head. "Now that I can't deny."

"What's the link between them and Tom Goodwin?"

"All along Heidi said that the person who killed Nicola was Laura Goodwin."

"I suppose what I don't understand is why Tom would suddenly become super-friendly with Heidi then? She accused Laura of murder, identified her through the e-fit and CCTV, and yet Tom is happy to fraternise with her." When Adam opened his mouth, Polly waved a finger at him. "And. And! In addition to that, Tom is then found dead at Heidi's home, and from what I hear, there is no evidence of a break-in, and there she is claiming that the front door was left open by mistake when she went to bed. Fancy that!"

"If that's what she said, then I'm sure that's the case."

"That's bullshit, Adam. I'm not Gibbs. I'm not buying it."

"Polly," Adam said, worried about the stridency in her tone. "Do you think I had anything to do with these murders?"

"You're at the centre of everything that's been happening in Durscombe lately. Can you explain that?" Polly asked, her eyes narrow with suspicion.

Adam rolled back onto the bed, feeling suddenly exhausted.

"So, let me ask you once more," Polly said, more gently this time. "What is going on?"

Adam threw an arm over his eyes, blocking out Polly's scrutiny as much as the invasive light. He remained that way, thinking for some time.

Polly was quiet. Adam hoped she had left him alone.

He peeked. She hadn't.

He rolled onto his side and took her hand. "You're going to think I'm completely crazy," he said.

"From what I can see, you tried to kill yourself tonight. I'd say you're pretty bloody certifiable already."

Adam scowled in frustration. Polly wasn't going to stop pressing him. He talked her through a synopsis of the events since the discovery of the murder of his ex-wife, faltering over some of the less believable aspects of what he had seen and heard, and leaving out the fact that he now assumed Dan was inhabiting Laura's body. Polly listened without comment. The silence continued until a nurse came to take his blood pressure and listen to his chest. He appeared to notice some tension in the room and tried to dispel it as he hooked Adam up to an ECG and monitored his pulse. Polly studiously avoided looking at Adam, instead swapping small talk with the nurse. Finally, when he and Polly were on their own again, Adam cleared his throat and made her look at him.

"Is your throat sore?" Polly asked.

"No. I feel fine. Tired. Just tired." Adam tried to stretch his hand out to her, but now that he was hooked up to the machines he couldn't reach. "I should never have told you," he said. "I didn't think you would believe me. You don't, do you?"

Polly made a small sound, that might have been a laugh. Adam wasn't sure whether it was a snort of disdain or of merriment.

"It's difficult to believe. You do understand that, right? I mean, it's not often that a rational man starts talking about ghosts and séances and people coming back from the dead, is it?"

"No, I suppose not," Adam said miserably, and they lapsed into silence once more, Polly's head down while she considered the impossibility of all that Adam had told her.

***

Polly and Adam arrived in front of his house just as the dawn was beginning to poke its head above the horizon. The mist had been rising off the moor, floating on the cool air as they were carried out of Exeter and through the countryside. As Adam exited the taxi, sparrows twittered in his neighbour's well-kept hedges.

Polly, who had been quiet throughout the whole journey, paid for the taxi before pulling her own car keys out of her jacket pocket. "You owe me for that," she nodded her head as the taxi departed.

"I owe you for everything," Adam soothed, and Polly offered a small smile. It wasn't much but it was something. Adam felt relief at the gesture.

"You look knackered," she said.

"I am. So do you!"

"Yeah, and I have to be at work in less than three hours."

"Sorry." Adam genuinely was.

"At least I can get my head down in my own bed for a few hours. It's a shame you won't be able to."

Adam looked up at his bedroom window. The curtains had been pulled. Of course, he had offered his bed to Heidi, and Cassia would have the sofa.

He shrugged. "There's always Dan's bed," he said, and his voice was hollow.

Polly sighed and came around the back of her car to where Adam was standing. In lieu of a jacket, he had thrown his blanket around his shoulders. She pulled it tighter and closed it up at his throat, resting her hands on his chest.

"Listen," she said quietly, not wanting to be overheard by Adam's neighbours. "After everything you've told me, I don't know what to believe, but I know two things. One, I trust you didn't try to kill yourself on purpose, and two, you believe everything you've told me." Adam opened his mouth and Polly lay a finger on his lips. "That has to be good enough for me." She patted his mouth gently then lightly gripped his lips. "So to that end, I'll help you if I can. But if I ever find out you've been stringing me a line, I will sew your mouth shut, then I'll cut your balls off, blend them in a food liquidizer, and feed them to you through a tube in your nose. Are we clear?"

Adam tried to respond, but Polly held on to his lips for a moment more. Then she winked, let go, and walked around to the driver's side of her car. "Try and get some rest," she said, sliding into the car and slamming the door. Adam watched her roll her head around on tired shoulders before she started the engine up and drove away, waving once.

Adam stepped into the familiarity of his own home. Quietly he tiptoed to the living room and glanced in. The curtains were open in here, and he could clearly see Heidi asleep on the sofa. Cassia slumped in an armchair, covered in a blanket. Her eyelids flickered open, and she smiled when she saw him. She stood quickly and dropped the blanket to cover the distance between them in two quick bounds. She pulled the living room door softly closed behind herself then threw her arms around him in a spontaneous hug.

"I'm so glad you're all right. We were both so worried about you." She whispered, dragging him into the kitchen and closed that door too, before filling the kettle and switching it on. "We decided it would be best if we left your bed for you in case you came home in the night. You look like you could do with some sleep."

"I could," Adam replied and immediately yawned. He could feel the tension in his body giving way to exhaustion.

"Listen," I want to know all about what happened while you were gone, but it can wait. Go on upstairs and lie down. I'll bring some tea and then you can get your head down. We don't need to chat 'til the morning when you've had a few hours' sleep."

Adam, feeling rather like a child being sent to bed when he wasn't well, did as he was told. He brushed his teeth and washed his face, blearily, before creeping under his quilt.

CHAPTER THIRTY-ONE

Adam's fingers scrabbled at the covering against his head, fighting against the sensation of drowning all over again—the pressure in his chest, the encroachment of the water, the sense of claustrophobia. He called out in fear and lurched forwards to find himself sitting up in bed, the room shadowy although it was light outside.

He gasped for breath, his heart racing, and with trembling hands reached for the phone on his bedside table. It wasn't there, instead he found a cold mug of tea. Of course his phone wasn't in its accustomed position. He had loaned it to Heidi the night before.

The night before. The memories flooded back. What foolishness. What had they been thinking?

And yet, it had all been real. He knew it had.

A movement in the room. Adam cried out, startled, a dreadful image of Abelia filling his mind.

"It's okay. You're home safe. How are you feeling?" Heidi's soft voice drifted towards him from the chair in the corner of the bedroom, the one where he tended to dump his clothes.

Disoriented, Adam swallowed, trying to order the thoughts tumbling around his head and combatting the sudden pain in the pit of his stomach. Dan was dead. And yet not dead. Adam had drowned himself just so he could go to the world beyond the veil and talk to a strange woman who had given him no direct answers. What had the woman said? Dan was dead but had not crossed over. Abelia would reclaim his soul. He didn't feel he was any further forward. To add to his misery, he'd been at the hospital till dawn and Polly was mad at him.

Shit. What a mess.

"What time is it?" he asked, his voice sounding groggy.

"About quarter past twelve," Heidi replied. She stood and drifted quietly out of the shadows. She looked like she hadn't slept much either. "You were having a bad dream."

"Not surprising really." Adam cleared his throat and swung his legs out of bed, then realising he was naked, he paused. "Ah—"

"I'll go and get started on breakfast," Heidi said diplomatically and limped from the room.

Adam waited until the door had closed behind her and then struggled wearily upright. He walked to the window and pulled the curtains back. Outside, the trees were bending in a blustery wind, leaves blowing down the street. The sky glowered with the promise of rain. It would be a miserable afternoon. It suited Adam's mood perfectly.

A knock on his door.

"Just a minute," he called and grabbed his robe from the hook behind the door, flinging it on, and opening the door to Cassia.

"Sorry," she said, holding his phone up. "Heidi said you were awake, and I thought you might want this. It's been ringing a lot this morning. We charged it for you, and there doesn't appear to be any water damage." Cassia smiled. "See you downstairs. I'm itching to find out what happened."

Adam took the phone from her and flicked back through his missed calls. They were all from Polly. He wasn't sure whether that was a good thing or a bad thing, but decided that if she was trying to reach him he had better respond. He had her on speed dial.

"Hey," he said, when she picked up.

"Where've you been?" she asked, sounding annoyed.

"Sleeping."

Polly grunted, and Adam felt a pang of guilt. She'd been up most of the night, thanks to him, after all. "I suppose you needed it," she said grudgingly.

"Sorry."

"Listen I have a little intelligence for you." Polly's voice turned confidential. "Wait a minute," she said, and he heard her moving around and then a door closing. He wondered where she was. He could imagine her trying to find somewhere quiet down at the station. "Okay. I've been out and about this morning, asking questions at the Lighthouse, and around the bus depot."

The Lighthouse was the local homeless charity. Where possible they helped the dispossessed who ended up on Durscombe's streets.

"Okay," said Adam.

"I figured that if Laura was hanging around anywhere, someone on the streets might know something. I mean it's hard to miss an older woman living rough, right? Especially around here."

"True."

"I think I might have a lead, anyway. One guy tells me that someone has been staying at Wick Lodge in the grounds of Hawkerne Hall."

Hawkerne Hall was a large stately home on the edge of Durscombe, now boarded up and decaying. It had been empty for at least a decade, and damp seeped in the windows and through the roof, and although it was looked after by a security firm based in Exeter while the current owner tried to find a buyer for the house and grounds, it was a contentious area for many locals who felt the council should do more to keep the once glorious building in the local domain. The hall had been badly damaged in a fire in the 1860s but lovingly restored after that and lived in for many years, until it had been utilised as a convalescent home during the Second World War, and a sanatorium after that.

A number of lodges had been built on the grounds, and these were still habitable and usually rented out over the summer. Now that the summer was long gone, the lodges should have been closed up.

Definitely worth checking out.

As though Polly could hear Adam's brain ticking over, she said, "You're not going out there. I'll go."

"I—"

"No. It's worth checking out, but it could be something and nothing, and you're not at work, remember."

"If it's Laura…"

"If it's Laura, she'll need to be arrested, Adam."

There was a drawn out silence. Adam could feel the beginning of a headache. He massaged his eyes.

"Let me go and have a look and I'll get back to you. That's the best I can do. All right?"

"Yes. Thanks," Adam replied, and Polly ended the call.

Adam sighed. He supposed he could get dressed and dash across to Hawkerne Hall himself, but if Polly found him there this would piss her off no end, and he could do with her on his side. Far better for him to have something to eat and set himself up for the day.

He was in dire need of a new plan.

***

Cassia had been out to the local shop and now Heidi was busy frying sausages for a late brunch while Cassia poured juice into tumblers and set the table for breakfast.

"You two have certainly made yourselves at home," Adam remarked, smiling wryly.

"You don't mind, do you?" Heidi asked, her anxiety and fears constantly bubbling at the surface.

"No, no, of course not." He made himself comfortable at the table and fiddled with the salt cellar. "It's really kind of you to be looking after me like this. All these years I've had no woman to look after me, and now I have two!"

"Don't get used to it," Cassia said, as Heidi placed bacon, sausage, egg, and beans in front of him, and slid into her place directly across from him. Heidi had a fried egg and a slice of toast. She joined them once she had located some pepper in the cupboard.

Cassia picked up her knife and fork and then paused. "It's no use. I can't wait any longer. You have to tell us what happened."

"Did you go through the veil?" Heidi asked.

Adam nodded with his mouth full, famished. "I did," he

said, chewing rapidly and swallowing. He washed down the mouthful of sausage with juice, then began to fill them in on the details.

"So it was just as you described Heidi, pretty much," Adam finished, "but unless either of you have any bright ideas, I'm not sure how we put this whole thing to bed?" Adam fixed Cassia with a beady eye and then scooped up a mouthful of his neglected fried egg.

"You mean you went through all of that, and we still can't repair the veil?" Heidi asked, full of woe.

"That's about the size of it." Adam scraped the remnants of his breakfast onto his fork and finished eating. "Does anyone want any more toast?"

Cassia shook her head and gathered up the plates, "Let me do it," she said. She walked over to the sink. In Adam's house, the kitchen window opened out onto the drive, and the street beyond. She could imagine seeing Abelia out there, but instead, she watched as two children, brothers perhaps, in fancy dress, skipped down the street, obviously on their way to a children's party somewhere.

"Do you know what today is?" Cassia asked, her gaze fallowing the children as they rushed up the drive to a front door adorned in orange and black balloons.

"Saturday?" Heidi said helpfully.

"It's Halloween," Cassia shook her head and turned and looked at Heidi and Adam at the table.

"So?" Adam said.

"The veil is thinnest on Halloween. We could be in serious trouble."

Cassia returned to the table with more toast and a pot of tea. "How can it have slipped my mind? Samhain is a huge part of our tradition. It's known as a time to commune with the spirit world. My mother and my grandmother set great store by this night."

"What happens?" asked Heidi.

"The best way to describe it, is as a kind of new year. It marks the boundary between seasons. On one hand we have the harvest after the summer's growing, and the long days of light, but on the other we are moving into the dark season. Tonight we are on the cusp, and the veil between the world of the living, the physical plane, and the world of spirit, will be at its thinnest. It is known as a night when the dead can walk between worlds. It's a time when we, all of us, can get in touch with the spirits that have passed. It's a night for reflecting on what has been, and divining what will be."

Adam nodded. "I've heard of this. I figured it was all mumbo-jumbo before."

"Now we know it isn't," said Heidi.

"In the past, people would set a place at the table to welcome their deceased loved ones back to their home and share a supper with them."

"Presumably they all went home again afterwards?" Adam asked, only half in jest.

"Yes," Cassia said and then seeing what he meant, "Oh. You mean how?"

"Exactly."

"I don't get it?" Heidi glanced from one to the other.

"He means they pass through the veil to us, and then they return through the veil to the spirit world. They don't stay here and then they don't come back, not until the following Halloween." Cassia shook her head. "But I still don't know how that happens, or how to make it happen."

Adam picked at a tooth, "Maybe we're overthinking things. If it's natural occurrence… why are we trying to force the issue? Cassia, maybe you should try and make contact with Tansy again. Or your mother?"

Cassia sighed. "I suppose so. I can try at least. I'll have to go home."

Adam nodded. "Take Heidi with you. I don't want either of you to be alone. There's strength in numbers."

"What are you going to do?" Heidi wanted to know.

"I'm going to track down Polly and see if she's found anything out about Laura."

***

Adam dropped Heidi and Cassia off at the gates of the Victoria Gardens Cemetery after checking they had a means to contact him. He remained in the car, watching them walk away along the neat path. He could see one of the council workers, clad in a fluorescent jacket, picking up litter. Good. There were people around, the women would be safe enough for now.

He had seen no sign of Abelia. What was she up to? He imagined that Halloween was a busy night for soul warriors generally.

He started the car up just as his mobile rang. Polly.

"Hi," he greeted her. "Do you have news?"

"I'm just on my way back to the station now. There's definitely someone living in Wick Lodge, but when I checked with the letting agency, it turns out the property isn't officially being let at the moment. I walked all around the perimeter, and it looks like the back door has been forced some time recently, then fixed up. It's a botch job though." Polly's voice broke up and then came back. Adam heard the ticking of her indicators. She was driving. "I spoke to one of the neighbours there, and he hasn't seen anyone. If it is Laura, she's keeping a low profile."

"He might just be saying that because he should have reported it and he hasn't."

"That's true."

"Did you go in?"

Polly hesitated. "Without a warrant?"

Adam waited.

"There was a sleeping bag in the living room and lots of empty food wrappers lying around. Not much else. Except..."

"Except?"

"There were a couple of items of soiled clothing. A lemon-coloured jumper, and a dark pink fleece jacket in a size that would fit Laura. They match the description of the clothes Laura was a last seen wearing after the attack on Tom in the hospital."

Adam nodded into the phone. Bingo. "There was no sign of her on the premises though?"

"Not while I was there. However," Polly hesitated. "I did get the sense I was being watched. The lodges back onto the woods there as you know, so while I couldn't see anyone, it would be worth getting a search party out there."

Adam trusted Polly's instincts. She was a good copper. If she thought there were eyes on her, he would take her word for it, but he didn't want anyone else out there, scaring Laura off. "Not yet," said Adam.

"Come on Adam, she's a suspect at large. She's potentially incredibly dangerous. I need to get the forensic crew out to examine the clothing in the house."

"Give me an hour."

"Adam!"

"Just till it gets dark, please. What difference will it make?"

CHAPTER THIRTY-TWO

Cassia surveyed her little dwelling with a critical eye.

"Are there any spirits in here?" Heidi asked, shivering.

"Not that I can see. Perhaps they've all wandered off." Cassia lied smoothly. She smiled and winked at Heidi. "I'm going to lay a fire. You'll soon get warm."

Heidi looked relieved. "Can I help?"

Cassia pointed to the back of the house at the door between the port holes. "If you go out of that door, you'll find the log store a little way up the side on the right. Don't turn left, you're liable to end up in the drink."

Heidi did as she was asked. As she opened the door the wind caught her by surprise. The cliff edge was less than fifteen feet from Cassia's dwelling. She glanced left and saw how the path narrowed, following the line inland. As instructed Heidi turned right. The log store was tucked into a natural alcove and covered with a heavy duty wooden roof and tarpaulin that had been weighted down by rocks. Heidi reached inside to extract some logs. They were well seasoned and perfectly dry. Hugging the wall to her left, she quickly found her way back into the dwelling before vertigo got the better of her.

Cassia had her head bent to the grate, deftly cleaning the remnants of the previous fire. When Heidi returned, she was already scrunching newspaper into balls and laying it ready.

"I didn't realise you were so close to the cliff out there," said Heidi. "It took my breath away."

"Yes, it's pretty spectacular, isn't it? Fortunately, there's not much erosion in this part of Durscombe. I think the cemetery is largely built on rock. On the other side of the bay, it's all sandstone and clay, and it's constantly crumbling onto the beach beneath."

Cassia added some firelighters to the pile of paper and

sticks in front of her and struck a match. The fire caught quickly, and Cassia nursed it for a few minutes, murmuring to it, adding more sticks to build the flames. It was magical to watch.

"You're an expert at this. It takes me ages to get a fire going."

"Practice makes perfect," Cassia smiled, but Heidi was right, she had the knack.

Cassia stood and moved to the place on the wall where the mirror had been. The frame was still in place. Heidi watched her.

"What are you going to do?"

"I'm not sure what's best," Cassia answered and indicated the fire. "My grandmother was fond of reading the flames, but my mother preferred scrying. I haven't had enough practice either way."

"Didn't Adam say, the Gate Keeper said the answer lies within you?" Heidi asked. "And earlier on, what did you say? This is the night for divination, but also for reflection on what has been? I'm no expert Cassia, but perhaps reflection is the key? Maybe you need to start with yourself?"

Cassia nodded. Heidi had a point. She pulled the heavy drapes over the porthole windows, then asked Heidi to sit on an armchair close to the fire and its circle of warmth, but at a distance to where she herself intended to work.

Cassia set herself up on the dining table, covered now with an old velvet cloth the colour of red wine. She placed herself opposite the frame in the wall, in the seat that Adam had taken before. Instead of the enormous mirror on the wall, she had a small circular shaving mirror. She placed candles strategically around the table and lit them with a single match before sitting quietly and grounding herself by concentrating on her breathing, paying attention to what she could feel happening to her body and around her environment.

Cassia closed her eyes, and Heidi faded from her mind, along with the sound of the fire, gently crackling in its grate. Instead she concentrated on feeling the floor beneath her feet, the table beneath her lower arms and hands, and the chair against her lower back and thighs. She could smell the faint scent of sulphur from the matches and burning wood. There was a tinge of incense in the air.

She breathed in and out, in and out. Then opened her eyes and stared into the mirror. Her own young face gazed back at her.

"I call upon my ancestors, upon those whose blood runs in my veins, whose memories are imprinted on my soul. I call upon my foremothers, upon the women who walked here upon this Earth, and in this place, long before I, and who are now dust in the wind. I call upon you, sympathetic to my needs, to hear me now. To join me this afternoon. To commune with me at this time when the veil is thinnest, in this place where the land meets the sea, and the physical meets the spiritual. And I ask for the gift of sight and prophecy. And I humbly request that you will watch over me and all I do. I ask for your protection and guidance."

Cassia paused. Her own face stared back at her from the mirror, her lips drawn into a line. Her eyes naked. She peered deep inside herself. Sought a well of deep honesty, a place of introspection and truth.

"I have been a poor witch," Cassia intoned. "Youth and arrogance and my own disdain of the powers that lie within me and those around me are the faults I see I bear. I was a poor student while my mother was alive, and now I recognise that I have squandered my potential. All I should have learned from her, I wish to learn now, if it is not too late."

The energy in the room changed, and Cassia became aware of it. The physical binding between the physical world and the world beyond crumbled around her. The room filled with shapes. Shadows occupied every corner. They flitted in and out of the rooms, floated towards the stairs, disappeared up the chimney.

Cassia tilted her head and listened to the whispers. What were they trying to tell her? Her reflection stared back at her, and Cassia became aware that while her own head dipped towards her left shoulder, the head in the mirror tilted in the opposite direction, towards her right shoulder. They were mirror twins, but not the same person. They made the same actions but somehow did them differently. They stared at each other, and Cassia's heart beat out of time to see a sentient being that was like her but not her. She was somehow in this room of her own house, sitting at her dining table, and yet somewhere else entirely. She was here and not here, and yet she was at one with…

"All That There Is," Cassia whispered. "I see that now. See the illusion of separation. The ethereal curtain, the veil between worlds. It is a construct. Something we put together. It is nothing but perception. It is a way that we protect ourselves. Yet, by limiting our consciousness, surely we harm ourselves?"

The realisation was a bolt from the blue. Her mother was here; her grandmother was here. All the women who formed her matriarchal heritage bustled around her in warmth and love. Cassia thought her heart would overflow. "Greetings, my teachers. You are most welcome here."

CHAPTER THIRTY-THREE

Finding a parking space on a rainy, blustery day was never going to be an issue in Durscombe, especially out of season, surely, but Adam had circled the car park three times before a space became vacant. The elderly driver in the tiny Fiat struggled to reverse out of the space and turn, but eventually he managed the manoeuvre, and Adam zoomed in. He jabbed some coins into the parking metre and grabbed his ticket. He could hear the sea roaring in the bay behind him; a storm was brewing.

He flipped the collar of his jacket up as he hurried back to the car to display the ticket in the window, concerned that time was running out.

He cut down the passageway behind The Blue Bell Inn, crossed the road, and ran through the iron gates that opened out onto the Edwardian arcade. Most of the shops were deserted, one or two had closed early, but a warm light glowing in Gloria's shop reassured him that someone was home. Adam burst through the door, and a coterie of gothic teenagers gathered around the till, replete with dark eye make-up and piercings, spun around in shock. To Adam's relief, Craig was one of them.

Craig smiled when he recognised the visitor.

"DS Chapple," he said, and the other teenagers eyed Adam suspiciously. "Are you here to see Mum again?"

"Not this time, Craig. I need to ask you a favour."

"Anything."

"Can you get away? Can you come with me?"

"You mean now?" Craig asked, looking towards the side door. No doubt Gloria was ensconced inside, busy giving a reading. "I don't know."

"Is he under arrest?" one of Craig's friends demanded.

"Don't be daft," Craig said.

"Yes now. I really need your help, Craig. I wouldn't ask if it wasn't important. Can you get cover for the shop?"

"Hey, I'll run the shop for you, Craig," a young woman with bright blue hair exclaimed, sequins where her eyebrows should have been.

"Cool! Then we're set. I'm all yours, detective."

***

Twenty minutes later Adam and Craig stepped out of the car and surveyed their surroundings. They were higher than the town centre here, and the roar of the wind in the trees was deafening. Leaves blew around them. They walked down the hill a little way, trying to avoid the worst of the mud and puddles from the latest downpour. A couple of hundred metres brought them to the stone wall and the locked gates of Hawkerne Hall. The hall dominated the skyline here with its tall chimneys and imposing vanilla stone façade. The gardens, once immaculately sculpted and well kept, were mainly given over to lawn these days, and the windows and doors were boarded up. Polite signs warned of active surveillance and the potential for prosecution.

They turned left, skirting the hall's boundary walls to their right, walking along the rough road that led to the three lodges. They were sheltered from the wind and rain a little and could at least hear each other speak.

"Are you clear on what we're doing?" Adam asked, his voice purposely as low as he could make it.

"Yes," Craig confirmed.

"And you know that there is a risk attached to this. If you and I become separated, you should call 999 at once, and get to a place of safety."

"Yes," Craig answered, his voice patient. Adam had explained what he wanted from Craig several times, although without really saying why.

"And don't accept lifts or sweets or anything from women over the age of forty."

"Got it," Craig said, resisting the urge to giggle.

"Here we are," Adam paused outside the front door of Wick Lodge. There were no lights on inside. Nothing appeared to be moving. Adam surreptitiously scanned the area, looking for the faintest sign of movement. Nothing he could see. The faintest tingle of a wind chime came to them from somewhere close by, perhaps the neighbour's house.

"This is what you wanted me to see?" Adam asked, his voice louder now, to be heard above the dull roar of the wind in the trees behind the lodges.

"Hey man, look, I was told this was going to be the site for a wild party tonight." Craig answered, his volume matching Adam's.

"Well there's no-one here now," Adam turned round and round, scanning the horizon, peering into the shadows.

"It's early yet."

"If there was going to be a rave, they'd be here setting up the sound equipment by now. I know how these things work."

"Back in your day you probably needed a truck to move the equipment." Craig sounded genuinely amused. "Now you can run a party using only your handheld. Trust me."

"Even so," Adam replied. They walked around the corner of the lodge into the back garden. They looked out into the woods behind.

"Nah," said Adam. "I think you've got it all wrong, Craig. There's no-one here. There's not going to be any kind of party."

"I'm telling you straight, mate," started Craig.

"Detective Sergeant to you," Adam spat. "You've turned into a real timewaster. I used to rate you when you were a kid. You seemed brighter than the average idiot that Dan hung around with."

"Oh, whatever."

"What happened there, Craig? Did Dan see through you?"

"See through me?" Craig raised his voice. "See through me? What was there to see? It was your son that used to freak everyone out, with his little episodes."

"What episodes?" Adam asked. They had talked through the script they would use, but it still stung for Adam to hear the words coming out of Craig's mouth, especially with this level of vitriol.

"You know, one minute he was fine, the next he was having a meltdown. He'd be all quiet and introspective and then flip."

"He had issues," said Adam.

"He was a fucking head case, your son. Complete loony toons." Craig did a passable imitation of Porky Pig and tapped his head. "Th-th-th-th-that's all, folks."

"He thought you were his friend, all throughout primary school."

"He was easy to string along. We all used to laugh at him behind his back. He was weak and pathetic."

"He was upset about his mother leaving home," Adam defended his son.

"Hey, we've all had problems with our folks. I never even knew my father. I seem to have held it together pretty well, I'd say. Dan needed to man up and get over it!"

Adam sensed movement in the woods behind them. His heart lurched.

Craig must have heard something too because he looked vaguely worried for a moment, and Adam gave an imperceptible nod of encouragement.

"Dan was pathetic," Craig said. "A complete waste of oxygen. A mummy's boy without a fucking mummy."

Adam turned on his heel as though he had had enough of the conversation and stalked away. Craig warily took a look back over his shoulder and hurried after him.

"You're a toad, and your information is bad, Craig," snapped Adam. "I'll have a patrol come out here this evening and check the place out, but you're full of shit." He stomped away.

"Hey, Detective Sargent," Craig called after him. "Any chance of a lift back into town?"

"I'm not going into town," Adam replied, "I'm heading for

the cemetery, and to be fair, pimple face, I ought to let you fucking walk."

***

It started pouring again. Adam stalked back to his car, ducking his head against the stinging rain, but all the while checking that Craig was following and not too far behind. He had purposefully parked a little way from the lodges. The road headed up over a hill, then dipped around the headland towards Durscombe, joining the main road from the moor, and Exeter beyond. The Victoria Gardens Cemetery would be on the right as they approached Durscombe.

Craig joined him in the car, looking studiously ahead. Adam could sense his tension, and it wasn't just acting. Adam started the car and drove slowly up the track, windscreen wipers batting to and fro noisily. He kept one eye on the rear-view mirror. He couldn't be absolutely sure, but he was fairly certain there was someone in the trees, pale clothing moving slowly.

They travelled quietly until the car turned onto the main road, out of sight of the hall and the lodges, and anyone hanging about in the general area.

"Well done," Adam said and glanced quickly at Craig.

Craig blew out shaky breath and laughed nervously. "That was crazy," he said. "I didn't expect to feel..."

"Nervous?" Adam asked.

"No. Well that too."

"What else did you feel then?" Adam asked, his curiosity piqued. The young man seemed to have been affected quite markedly by the experience.

"There was darkness there," Craig said. "Real darkness. Couldn't you feel it?"

Adam shook his head, but not dismissing or diminishing what Craig was telling him for one moment. His recent experiences had taught him there was a world beyond the one he knew, and plenty he would never be able to understand. His life had been turned upside down over the past few weeks, and he wasn't quite sure which way was up any more.

"Around the lodge?" he asked. "Or the general vicinity of the hall? The hall has something of a reputation for ghosts."

"Yeah, that hall is definitely haunted. When I was a kid we used to ride our bikes up there and hang around at night. Not vandalising it or anything," he added quickly when Adam glanced his way again.

"I should hope not."

"But no, I meant around the Lodge. There's a bad energy. It's fresh but faint, like something's lurking there."

Adam examined Craig's expression. He seemed deadly earnest. He and Cassia would make a good team. "You sure you're okay with all this? I'm hoping that whatever was there is following us now."

"I reckon it will be," Craig turned his head and looked behind him, as though he would be able to spot the darkness encroaching on them like a black raincloud, but of course there was nothing to see except for a few other cars on the wet road and the windblown and rain soaked scenery they had passed.

"I'd drop you at home, Craig, but I'd like to make sure you're going to be all right first. We're in a bit of a pickle, and unfortunately you're the bait."

Craig nodded. "It's fine."

"I really hope it is," replied Adam pulling into the cemetery car park.

***

It was approaching five o'clock. Fortunately, the caretaker wasn't around and didn't see them entering through the main gates or he would probably have chased them out again. It was too close to closing time, and he wouldn't want to encourage too many waifs and strays into the cemetery on Halloween. The evening was closing in rapidly. It would be easy for kids to hide here so they could hang out for the night, and experience the thrill of a few scares. They wouldn't let the stormy weather put them off.

Adam skirted the cemetery, trying to avoid puddles and

hogging the overgrown hedges and the shadows, heading for the older area. He could find his way easily now. Craig followed swiftly behind him, instinctively recognising the need for stealth.

The mulchy smell of earth was stronger in the old cemetery, and the paths more slippery. Adam trod carefully, picking his way through the dimly lit corner until the Fliss tomb came into view. A light burned inside, candles lit and sheltered behind the iron gates. Cassia and Heidi were at home then. Adam was relieved.

He opened the gate and allowed Craig to step through, the young man's face a picture. While Craig had been aware that Cassia lived here, he had no idea what the dwelling was like inside. Adam moved farther in, and Craig reverently touched the coffins lining the walls.

"You need to mind your head here, and at the bottom," Adam said and pulled the door open to allow Craig to step through first.

***

The four of them had gathered at the foot of the stairs. Adam, Cassia, Heidi, and Craig.

"How long do you think we have?" asked Cassia, and Adam shrugged.

"How long's a piece of string? We know that if Laura is going to follow us she'll do it on foot. We haven't broken the land speed record to get here, but there's no doubt that we're way ahead of her."

"I'm kind of hoping that Abelia will find her before we do, and this whole thing will go away," said Heidi.

Adam sympathised with that desire but couldn't leave anything to chance. "I'm going to head back out. We're trying to lure Laura/Dan here using Craig, but ideally I don't want the mouse to come into contact with the cheese. No offence, Craig."

Craig laughed. "None taken. But are you sure you don't

want me in plain sight?"

"No. The thing is, neither Laura nor Dan know about this place, strictly speaking, so I don't want to run the risk she'll give up looking. Plus, if Abelia does show up, we need to make sure we get them together."

"I still think—" Craig began, but Adam stopped him.

"Too dangerous." Craig nodded and backed off, looking crestfallen. "Stay here, stay quiet, and dry off."

Adam turned to Cassia. "Did you find anything out? Do you know how to close the rift?"

"It's complicated, but I don't think we need to."

"What?" Adam looked aghast. This went against everything he had assumed they were trying to do.

"Trust me. When the time comes, just follow my lead."

Adam rolled his eyes. Spontaneity was something he particularly disliked, but they were running out of both time and options, and he was feeling anxious. "You come up top with me, Cassia. Heidi, you and Craig stay down here where it's safe."

"Do I need my coat?" asked Cassia.

"Are you kidding? Look at the state of me. I'm drenched."

***

Except the rain had stopped and the wind had quietened down a little. Rainclouds skidded across the bright pock-marked surface of a large moon, now waning in the dark sky. Periods of relative light, were followed by darkness. To the east a faint glow from the town lit up the horizon. Adam stilled his breath, the better to listen to every sound: drops of water dripping from the leaves in the trees above; a slight rustling in a nearby hedge. A bird perhaps, or a fox.

Adam tapped Cassia's arm. "Come this way," he whispered. "I want to make sure the caretaker has finished for the day."

They crept away from the Fliss tomb, once again keeping to the shadows where possible, and on high alert for the slightest movement or noise that might potentially give away the presence of another.

Adam could hear the sound of cars on the main road, heading out of, or into, Durscombe. It was a low rumbling noise, slightly louder than usual because the road was wet. He strained his eyes, scrutinizing every shrub and bush, every gravestone and memorial, and more than once whirled around to find absolutely nothing behind him.

The decorative iron lamps around the fountain glowed reassuringly. Cassia and Adam were halfway to the cemetery entrance and nothing seemed untoward. Progress was slower now, they were taking more care on the off-chance that any council workers were working later. The last thing they needed now was to be spotted and sent packing.

A small single-storey building was located to the right of the entrance. It housed an office in one half while the other was used to store tools. One small light burned under the eaves, lighting the ground in the immediate doorway, but other than that the place was closed up and in darkness.

Adam felt reassured by this.

"There is only the main entrance and the hole in the fence, isn't that right?" he whispered to Cassia.

"Yes," she hissed back at him. "We can check that the gate is locked up, and then we'll just need to keep an eye on the unofficial entrance."

They crept cautiously to the main entrance. A tall streetlamp near the bus stop threw the world into stark relief here, and they would be seen from both the main road and the car park if anybody cared to look this way.

The caretaker had locked and securely chained the gate. Adam rattled the chain for effect and then grunted in satisfaction. Everything appeared to be falling into place.

He glanced beyond the gate into the car park. When he and Craig had arrived, his car had been alone. He hadn't thought about the possibility this might alert the caretaker to his presence, but it obviously had not. However, his car had now been joined by another. In the dark it was difficult to see the true colour, but the shape suggested an older Citroen C3.

A small bell rang in a compartment in his brain. He couldn't see the number plate from this distance, and he couldn't think who had a Citroen. It was probably something and nothing. Maybe he was wrong. Maybe the car had been there when he'd arrived and he hadn't noticed in his rush to get out of the rain and get Craig to safety.

He put his doubt aside and followed Cassia. She headed for the east side of the cemetery, for the fence panel close to the bus stop. She pushed through the bushes. Adam coming directly after her was showered with water. It didn't really matter; he couldn't get much wetter. Suddenly Cassia stopped, and Adam ran into the back of her.

"Shit."

"What's up?" Adam asked, although he had a good idea. He stepped around her. The light was bright enough here for him to see that the fence had been fixed. Recently. The wood was a lighter colour than its neighbours.

"Damn it," Adam exclaimed angrily. "When did they fix that?"

"I don't know," Cassia said defensively. "I haven't noticed. I rarely use it."

That stopped Adam in his tracks. The single alarm bell that had been ringing had now turned into a crescendo. "What do you mean you rarely use it? What do you use?"

"Oh," Cassia's face crumpled.

"Cassia?"

"I use my back door, of course. The one that opens out onto the cliff. But it will be fine, right? Not many people know about it."

"We need to get back to the house now!" Adam shot through the bushes, slipping on the wet earth, and falling forwards, jarring his wrists. He cursed loudly. There was no point in being quiet any more. The damage was done.

"Laura couldn't have made it here this quickly, surely?" Cassia said, helping him to his feet.

"No," Adam replied but the little ringing bell in his head was getting louder by the second. "Wait," he said, and racked his memory for what was bugging him. "There's a car in the car park. I think it's a Citroen C3. If I remember correctly that's Tom's car. I'm betting that Laura stole the keys, or had access to a spare set."

"Laura didn't drive, did she?"

"No, but Dan had taken lessons. And its Dan in Laura's body. He'll have arrived here much sooner than we supposed."

Cassia started to reply when a scream ripped through the slumbering solitude of the night, originating from the older part of the cemetery.

"She's found them!" Adam shook Cassia off and ran as though the hounds of hell were after him.

CHAPTER THIRTY-FOUR

Adam pelted directly across the cemetery on the grass, dodging headstones, his shoes finding it difficult to make purchase on the wet ground. Somewhere behind him he heard Cassia call his name, but the memory of that scream—it could only have been Heidi—drove him forwards. He approached the fountain and skidded to a halt.

Abelia stood in a circle of lamplight, shimmering with a deadly energy. She was fully veiled, but Adam knew from the tilt of her head she was looking straight at him. He halted, breathing hard, wondering what she intended to do, speculating whether he could outrun her.

Cassia thudded into the back of him and grabbed his arm.

"We've got company," Adam said.

"So I see."

"I've got to get to Heidi. I'm going to make a run for it. If it all goes tits up, call the police."

"Adam, wait!" Cassia said and pulled him back.

"There's no time!" Adam wrenched his arm away and took a few steps to the left so that he could position himself to run to the left of the fountain and towards the older part of the cemetery. Abelia moved incrementally to her right, blocking his route.

Checkmate.

Cassia stepped ahead of him and walked slowly towards Abelia, her hands palms upward. "You'll get what you came for, Abelia," she said, her voice soothing, "but you need to let us get to our friend."

The adrenaline coursing through Adam's body made him tremble. He swallowed. "Cassia," he warned.

"It's fine, Adam. Just go," Cassia replied without taking her eyes away from Abelia's face. "Abelia's not going anywhere, so we have all the time we need." She side-stepped around Abelia, effectively blocking her. Adam took the opportunity this afforded and dashed past them. Abelia lashed out as he whipped by, and Cassia was sent flying. Adam couldn't pause to think; he had wasted enough time.

He sprinted towards the Fliss tomb, his feet pounding on the old path. Beneath the trees here, it was drier and he made swift headway. In his peripheral vision he saw movement, shapes that rose out of the ground like a damp, heavy mist. Spirits that turned to watch his progress and followed at a distance, hollow-eyed and wide-mouthed.

Far behind him now, he heard Cassia calling out, but he couldn't make out what she was saying. He faltered, unsure whether to turn around or go forwards. He had to make a snap decision, and he felt he owed it to Heidi, who had already suffered so much, to go to her rescue.

The Fliss tomb was up ahead, the glow from the candles inside was unmistakeable in this darkest corner of the cemetery. He hurled himself against the iron gates, afraid they would suddenly be locked, but they opened easily. Dashing through the tomb, he threw the door open with such force it rebounded and he smacked his head. He took the stairs two at a time and landed on the floor at the bottom, wrenching his ankle painfully.

"Heidi?" he shouted and ran into the living area where the fire was still burning brightly, casting warm shadows on the wall.

"Adam!" Heidi called, drawing his attention to where she was squatting in a dark corner of the room, Craig by her feet.

As Adam started to move to where they were, a sudden movement at the back door caught his attention. It was a woman, late fifties, her hair dishevelled, a mix of caramel and blonde streaks but with a great deal of grey at the temples. She had been attractive once, but now her skin was sallow and her eyes were wild, glowing red, reflecting the embers of the fire, or her own personal hell.

"Laura," Adam said and held his arms wide in a gesture of reconciliation. "You have to stop running." He took a step forward, his ankle griping immediately.

Laura moved an equal distance backwards.

"I'm not going to hurt you," Adam said. A silence stretched out between them. Something unspoken. Then, "Dan."

That single word broke the spell. The woman drew herself up, roared with a terrible ferocity, and ran from the room, out of the back door, turning left.

Adam limped over to Heidi and knelt down. Craig was out cold. Adam felt for a pulse in the younger man's neck and found a strong one.

"She came in through the back. We weren't expecting that. She hit him with a log from the wood pile," Heidi explained, her hands smoothing Craig's hair from his forehead.

"Call 999, ask for an ambulance and the police, and tell them exactly where we all are. And call Polly. I'm going after my son."

***

Adam hobbled through the back door and looked around. To the right lay the wood pile housed in a wooden shelter and a path that ran along the side of the cemetery wall, eventually leading onto the new housing estate behind. If Dan had headed that way, Adam would have struggled to find him, but he hadn't, he had turned left.

Adam followed the rough path to the left. It too ran along the cemetery boundary but there wasn't as much room between the wall and the cliff edge, less than eight feet in some places. Adam trod warily. The cliff fell sharply away with a steep incline in places, a sheer drop in others. Below, there were the jagged rocks that stretched out part way across the bay where, 150 years ago, several ships had run astray ashore and dozens of lives had been lost.

Adam paused. The light was poor in places, better when the clouds moved away from the moon. Below the cliffs, the sea sounded angry, waves hissing as they dashed themselves against the rocks and the cliffs. Adam knew from experience that in a really bad storm the waves could spray thirty feet or more into the air. At such times, anybody on this ledge would find themselves in danger of being washed into the sea below.

A noise up ahead spurred Adam on. The path opened out into a small clearing, almost circular. There was a bench here and some sort of homemade memorial stone, with flowers only a few days old, in an old vase, tucked away out of the wind. The path came to an abrupt end. The boundary for the cemetery continued, but the wall and the old iron railings almost came up to the cliff edge. It would be dangerous to go any farther. Laura had run out of room to run. She was positioned in the corner, close to the edge, her eyes darting around in fear.

"Dan?" Adam asked, his voice thick with emotion.

"How did you know? How could you tell?" asked the woman, in a woman's voice.

"I've been beyond the veil. I know you have too. And I know what happened. I know you didn't want to stay there. My friend Heidi was there too, and when you came out she saw you." Adam said, keeping his voice calm. "You had an accident. Do you remember that."

"No," Laura frowned. "I was on my bike. I was going to the library. Then it went dark."

"What happened after that?" asked Adam. He was curious. His son had actually stepped through the door and knew what came after.

"It became lighter, brighter, warmer. There was… joy there. Calm. Peace."

"But you didn't want to stay?"

"No. I didn't feel peaceful. I felt angry. I needed to come back. I wanted to finish things. It was my mum." Laura's face contorted in emotional agony. "You know, Dad? She hated me, she did. My whole life I was trying to figure out what I did to her to make her hate me. I tried to meet her, to ask her. Maybe to become the son she wanted. I just wanted to talk to her. But she refused. And I was so angry."

"I know, son."

"I found out that I have a half-sister. Did you know about her? Why wouldn't Mum have told me about that? I wanted to meet Maryanne, but Mum wouldn't let me. She texted me and told me to stay away. What did she think I would do? I'm her son. She was supposed to love me. Why couldn't she love me?"

"I'm sorry Dan." Adam thought his heart would break all over again. "I tried to be there for you, but I wasn't enough, I appreciate that. You needed your mother."

Laura danced in fury at the edge of the cliff. "I did need her. But she didn't want me. She was just a cold-hearted bitch!"

"So what did you do?"

"I came back from beyond. I broke out. I needed to get to my mother. I wanted to show her. I just snapped." Laura's eyes shone with bitter hatred. "I've done terrible things."

"Yes. You have." Adam couldn't deny that, but when Laura cried out in anguish, Adam took a tiny step towards her, reaching for her. "It's okay. What you did, it can't be undone now. But what's done is done. Isn't that what we always used to say when we made a mistake? When you were little? What's done is done, Dan. Do you remember? Your mother was not a nice woman, and that was not your fault." Adam took another small step forwards, angling himself so that in order to move away, Dan would have to start edging inland.

"But I killed her. And I was glad to do it. Do you see?" Laura moved away from the cliff edge, body taut with anger, moving towards the bench. "When I came back from wherever I'd been and realised I was in somebody else's body, I kind of flipped. At first it scared the crap out of me, but then, I realised I could do even more stuff as an old woman than I could as a kid."

"Tom?"

"Bloody Tom, such a nag!"

"Tom was a good man," Adam said, and Laura frowned and shook her head.

"He was a douche. Once I'd killed Mum, there was nothing else to stop me. I could do what I liked, when I liked. I thought everything would be okay, but I still had to exist, didn't I? And I just couldn't do it. No money. Nowhere to sleep—till I remembered the lodge." Laura finally made it to the bench. She slumped onto it and bowed her head, thoroughly exhausted.

"You know you can't go on like this, Dan?" Adam said, his voice kind. He moved to within several feet of where Laura was sitting.

"Who's going to stop me?" Laura asked sharply, glaring up at Adam. "You?"

"If I have to, yes."

The scurrying sound of footsteps along the path caused them both to glance up at the same time. Cassia. She shouted a warning and pointed next to them. Abelia apparated in the clearing next to them.

Laura's reaction was instant. She shrieked and cowered into the corner of the bench, moaning in terror. "Go away! Get her away from me!"

"Dan, Dan," placated Adam.

"She wants to take me back. I don't want to leave! Don't let her take me!"

Adam put his arms on Laura's shoulders. "Listen to me, my wonderful boy. Daniel, listen." He stroked Laura's shoulders, not the bony shoulders of his athletic son. "I don't want you to go either. I wanted you to grow up and find happiness. I imagined you would be such a success, have a career, find love and have your own family. I thought you would provide me with half a dozen grandkids who all looked just like you. Most of all I wanted you to really experience the meaning of love. Your mother was my mistake, and her not loving you enough, that was her mistake. But you–you were my life Dan. You were no mistake. You were my reason to get up in the morning, to go to work, to earn money… and my reason to come home and cook dinner. And do the whole thing again, day after day."

Laura whimpered in fear, and Adam's voice broke. "You have been everything to me, and you always will be. But there's no going back. I can't save you now. It's too late. You can't stay here. You belong with Abelia, beyond the veil."

Laura sobbed aloud, her upper body shaking with fear, wracked with sorrow. Adam pulled her to her feet and wrapped her tightly in a bear hug. Tears coursed down his cheeks, running in rivulets along with the rain. "I didn't get to say goodbye before. I didn't even know for sure you'd been taken from me. But my boy, my Daniel. I will always remember you as magnificent, and you will be my shining star forever."

Adam kissed Laura's forehead. "I love you Dan."

Laura drew back and stared into Adam's eyes, the disbelief there finally replaced by acceptance. She squeezed Adam tightly, then broke free. Abelia stepped forwards, and Adam held a hand out towards her. "Don't hurt him!" Adam shouted. "Don't hurt my son! Please don't let it hurt him."

Abelia's head swivelled from Adam to observe Laura as she lunged for the cliff edge. Cassia cried out in alarm, her hands to her face, unable to watch any more. Laura paused, poised on the very edge, just inches between her and the drop, gravel cascading over the edge, falling into the sea below. She spun to face Adam.

"I love you too, Dad," Laura said and when she smiled, Adam could see his son in her face for the briefest of moments, then Laura released the tension in her body and tumbled backwards. Adam shot forward to make a grab for her but slipped on the wet earth and fell to his knees as his twisted ankle gave way, watching his son disappear from his view.

Dan was gone. He would not be saved.

Abelia was beside Adam in an instant, and for one moment, Adam thought the game was over for him too. In that space and at that time, he wished it could be so with all his heart. Instead, Abelia gazed down at him through her veil, her hidden eyes scouring his face. Then, her decision seemingly made, she slowly, slowly raised her hands and gathered her veil, pulling it gently over her head, allowing it to fall back from her face, a face that was as sculpted and beautiful as any number of the Victorian memorial statues in the cemetery behind them.

Her horns, twisted and dark, that had once appeared to Adam to belong only to the bleakest of nightmares, now seemed majestic. Her head tipped back as she lifted her face to the moon. Her alabaster skin, bathed by the light, shone bright white as though radiating some inner heat. Her whole person shimmered, growing hotter and brighter, and Adam knelt before her, staring up until his vision blurred and for one final moment he saw Dan, smiling and at peace, complete and whole and in his own form, wrapped tightly in Abelia's nurturing embrace. A mother with her son. Then, with a soft sigh, Abelia exploded, dissipating into a trillion stars, each of which took to the skies, floating gently, ever upwards, intent only on reaching the sanctity of the heavens above.

CHAPTER THIRTY-FIVE

"He's not gone, you know." Cassia had taken Adam's arm as he limped towards the cemetery gates. He paused, the reflection from flashing blue lights illuminating the headstones around them. He looked down at her, his eyes red rimmed, his expression hollow. "The veil is a construct we've created to separate our physical reality from the spiritual plane."

"You're saying there's no separation, then?" Adam asked, and his tired mind struggled to turn this information over. He could see Polly by the gates, interrogating Heidi, while a number of his other police colleagues stood around speaking into phones and an ambulance crew attended to Craig. He wondered what Polly would have to say about all this and whether she would ever truly believe him when he explained what had happened.

"None at all. The veil is a metaphor. I didn't have to repair the fissure in the veil because neither the veil nor the fissure exist unless we believe they do. It's all about perception, and the way we construct what we believe—our so-called truths. Those in spirit are always with us, and we all have the capacity to connect with them if we want to. You simply have to reach out—outside your ordinary consciousness, let the blinkers fall away, look beyond what you consider to be reasonable, and you will see them. They're all around us. Always."

"That sounds… impossible, Cassia. Impossible. Improbable. Implausible."

"Forgive me for stating the obvious, but up until a few weeks ago, you didn't even believe in ghosts."

Adam smiled, and then laughed. He pulled Cassia into a one-armed hug and they stood together staring up at the moon. The wind had blown the clouds away, and now a bright array of stars speckled the dark night sky, twinkling down on them.

"You'll see Dan again," Cassia said, and Adam, with tears in his eyes once more, welcomed the sincerity in her voice.

Please consider leaving a review?

If you have enjoyed reading *Beyond the Veil*, please consider leaving me a review.

Reviews help to spread the word about my writing, which builds an income for me, and helps me take a step closer to my dream of writing full time.

You can review on Amazon or on Goodreads or both!

If you are kind enough to leave a review, please also consider joining my Author Street Team on Facebook – Jeannie Wycherley's Fiendish Street Team.

You can find my fiendish team at www.facebook.com/groups/JeannieWycherleysFiends/

You'll have the chance to Beta read and get your hands on advanced review eBook copies from time to time if you wish, and input when I need some help with covers, blurbs etc.

Or sign up for my newsletter http://eepurl.com/cN3Q6L to keep up to date with what I'm doing next!

Coming Autumn 2018

The Municipality of Lost Souls by Jeannie Wycherley

Described as a cross between Daphne Du Maurier's *Jamaica Inn*, and TV's *The Walking Dead*, but with ghosts instead of zombies, *The Municipality of Lost Souls* tells the story of Cassia Veysie's great great great great grandmother, Amelia Fliss and her cousin Agatha Wick.

In the otherwise quiet municipality of Durscombe, the inhabitants of the small seaside town harbour a deadly secret. Amelia Fliss, wife of a wealthy merchant, is the lone voice who speaks out against the deadly practice of the wrecking and plundering of ships on the rocks in Lyme bay, but no-one appears to be listening to her. As evil and malcontent spread like cholera throughout the community, and the locals point fingers and vow to take vengeance against outsiders, the dead take it upon themselves to end a barbaric tradition the living seem to lack the will to stop.

Set in Devon in the UK during the 1860s, *The Municipality of Lost Souls* is a Victorian Gothic ghost story, with characters who will leave their mark on you.

If you enjoyed *Beyond the Veil*, you really don't want to miss this novel. Sign up for my newsletter or join my Facebook group   today.

Coming August 2018

The Wonkiest Witch: Wonky Inn Book One

On the day her mother dies, Alfhild inherits an inn.

Unfortunately, she also inherits a dead body.

Having been estranged from her mother, and committed to very little in her thirty years, including her witchy heritage, Alf surprises herself when she decides to start a new life. She heads deep into the English countryside intent on making a success of the once popular inn.

Discovering the murder throws her a curve ball, and she suspects black magick. In addition, she gets a less than warm welcome from several of the locals too, and realises that a variety of folk – of both the mortal and magickal persuasions – have it in for her.

The dilapidated inn presents a huge challenge for a woman alone, and uncertain who to trust, Alf considers calling time on the venture.

Should she pack her bags and head back to London?

Don't be daft.

Alf's magickal powers may be as wonky as the inn, but once a witch always a witch, and this one is fighting back.

Sign up for my newsletter or join my Facebook group for updates about the Wonky Inn series!

Also by Jeannie Wycherley

Crone (2017)
A Concerto for the Dead and Dying (short story, 2018)
Deadly Encounters: A collection of short stories (2017)
Keepers of the Flame: A love story (Novella, 2018)

Writing as Betty Gabriel

The Fly Man (2017)
Autoerotic (2015)

Non Fiction

Losing my best Friend: Thoughtful support for those
affected by dog bereavement or pet loss (2017)

Follow Jeannie Wycherley

Find out more at on the website
https://www.jeanniewycherley.co.uk/
You can tweet Jeannie https://twitter.com/Thecushionlady
Or visit her on Facebook for her fiction
https://www.facebook.com/jeanniewycherley/

Sign up for Jeannie's newsletter http://eepurl.com/cN3Q6L

Acknowledgements

Beyond the Veil was never supposed to be my second novel. It was just an idea I ran with after seeing a wonderful image of a horned and veiled woman on Pinterest. Abelia was easy enough to give birth to, and Heidi too – but Cassia and Adam came as a complete surprise to me. In the way that characters do, they had their own stories to tell, and so even though *The Municipality of Lost Souls* was already completely drafted, *Beyond the Veil* took over my life once I'd started writing it.

What I had initially figured would be a long novella or a short novel became something much bigger, and I hope you enjoy it reading it as much as I enjoyed exploring the world of my characters.

Huge thanks are due to Jeannie Wycherley's Fiendish Author Street Team, especially Debbie Jefferson Zhao, Heaven Riendeau, Holly Hill Mangin, Ruth Nahmiash Nix, Danielle Apple and Tabitha Hill. Thanks to Amie McCracken for the wonderful editing as always!

For saving my bacon and producing the most wonderful cover when I was let down by my original cover designer (who kept my money), extreme gratitude and heartfelt thanks to Francessca Wingfield of Francessca's PR & Designs.

Thanks also to my friends and family who have kept me going when at times I felt bleak – Julie Archer, Joy Yehle to mention just two (go and read their stuff!) and my wonderful husband John, without whom any writing would be impossible.

My eternal gratitude to the two experts who shared their police knowledge with me, DS Inderjit Basra, and Richard Sharp, my 'baby' brother, the running detective on whom

Adam Chapple is modelled.

Given the content of this novel, it seems oddly fitting that I used to play at being a witch as a little girl, just to scare my brother, but he grew up to be a pillar of the police community. Like all his colleagues he does amazing work, makes the UK a safer place to live, and I am prouder than words can say.

This book is lovingly dedicated to you, Snitchie, and all of your colleagues.

Jeannie Wycherley
12th July 2018

ABOUT THE AUTHOR

Jeannie Wycherley is the author of the award winning novel Crone (2017) which won an Indie B.R.A.G Award, and a Chill with a Book Award. She is a contributor of many short stories and articles in publications across the globe.

Jeannie lives somewhere between the forest and the sea in East Devon in the UK, collects dogs, hugs trees, and cooks her evening meals in a cauldron.

Printed in Great Britain
by Amazon

16959157R00169